AN ERRANT
WITCH

WITCH KIN CHRONICLES, BOOK 3

E M GRAHAM

AN ERRANT WITCH

1

This was how condemned men must feel in the moments before sentencing; each second slowly ticking towards the death of hope, and right now hope was all I had left to cling to.

How could it still be pitch black outside? This night was never ending; as dark outside now as it had been since my flight landed in Scotland and I'd been whisked off to this hilltop castle. Still the same night, then, but surely dawn would come soon.

Unless the Kin had magicked time itself.

We were in a huge room in the bowels of Inverness Castle, the fortress in the middle of town, high on a hill overlooking the entire river valley. Cold stone walls surrounded us, softened only by the burning sconces set at regular intervals whose light did not reach up to the mullioned windows far above our heads. The only furnishings were rows of hard oak benches like pews, empty now save for me, and Hugh across the aisle. At the front of the room and above us, the row of Witch Kin elders perched like a line of crows on a telephone wire, casting their beady eyes all over me to check that they hadn't left any morsels to pick out of my tender flesh. I couldn't meet their eyes now, didn't want to see the judgement there, needing to hold on to my magic even for a few minutes longer.

Johanna, the chief elder, stood to deliver and finally I had to lift my face. I couldn't decipher her expression as she looked in my direction; sorrowful, or perhaps that was regret in her eyes? This was not good.

'Dara Martin,' she began, then paused.

Hugh had explained the two possible outcomes of this Inquiry. The worst decision for me? I would be declaimed as an errant witch and the elders would bind my power, making me forget everything magical. A painful process for all involved, but afterwards I would head back home and resume a Normal life as if nothing had happened.

The best decision for me would see them forgiving my trespasses against the Kin, recognizing my immense natural power despite being a half-blood, and allowing me to study under Hugh and become a productive member of their society. But that didn't look like a possibility from where I was sitting, right at this minute.

Everything they had asked about, I'd told them in painstaking detail. About Willem the sorcerer and how he'd used my power to do his awful deeds; and how Brin the elf had escaped Alt because of me, and even how I'd misrepresented myself to the Dwarf Council and offered the bribe of fairie gold to them. Surely they could see that not everything was my fault?

The one thing they didn't ask about was the medallion which spoke my mother's name. They didn't ask because they didn't know about it, and I didn't mention it because that was mine and mine alone. In hindsight, yes, maybe I should have, and it might have saved a bunch of hassle, but that's what hindsight is all about.

She gathered her robes about her and pointed her sharp nose in my direction. This witch was petite in stature yet everyone in the room deferred to her. She continued on in Gaelic of which I understood not a word; most of the trial had been conducted in this ancient language except for my direct questioning.

I looked over at Hugh, my protector, my friend, the only person who believed in me. He too wore a black robe, and stood straight and tall and calm with his natural Kin self-assurance; only his whitened knuckles showed his stress.

The Kin ruled all things magic; it would have done me no good to attempt to run from them because with their worldwide networks, they'd have found me where ever I hid. By submitting gracefully to their Inquiry, I at least had a fighting chance to represent myself. The alternative was too horrible to think about, so I forced my face toward them and bit my lip to stop the quiver.

My dream was to study and become a magic worker - no, not like them up there. These Witch Kin used their power for their own ends and to rule the world banks and politics, although no one ever talked about it. I wanted to be a witch who policed the magic world, working on the side of the good guys, whoever they might be. A half-blood could aim that high, I knew, because Hugh was a half-blood just like me. I swallowed hard, unable to shift the lump in my throat as the elders stared down at me from the Bench in silence. Those five black robes on the dais held my future in their collective hands, and they would claim it was for the good of all the Witch Kin, and for me.

Whatever she pronounced electrified all those present. The four other elders gasped as one, looks of horror and outrage on their faces, and the tall cadaverous one with the Beatles' haircut immediately began to argue with her.

Johanna listened to each of the other four men and women in turn, meeting their vehement Gaelic protests with calmness, nodding her head but not replying. When they finally ran out of steam, she sharply knocked the gavel on the wooden table before her. She spoke crisply and without hesitation, the authority in her bearing broking no further argument.

She looked me directly in the eye with no emotion on her face as she said it, then gave a decisive nod. Her cohorts shot me black looks and one still shook his head in disagreement, but they rose together as a body and exited the chamber. The clerk spent another moment writing long-hand in his huge leather-bound book, then snapped it shut and he too left the room.

I waited. No armed guards came over to grab me, and that must be a good sign. I looked over again at Hugh who stood with his head bowed.

He looked up and gave a small smile as he made his way over, letting out a deep exhale as if he realized he'd been forgetting to breathe.

'Not the end of the world then, Dara,' he said as he shook off his robe, but he avoided my eye. 'In fact, better than I could ever have hoped for.'

'Does this mean they're not going to bind my magic?' I asked. The relief was tremendous, but I had to be absolutely clear.

Now he looked directly at me and shook his head. 'No, you get to keep your power.'

'Yes!' With these words, I felt as light as an elastic band released to fly across the room, a huge cloud of doom lifted off my shoulders. My future was secured. I would live, I would practice magic, I would...

He placed his hand on my arm to bring me back to earth.

'Conditionally,' he continued. He took a breath as if to say more, but then he shut his mouth and held his words.

Of course there would be conditions, there always were with the Kin, and I understood it wasn't going to be easy.

'What's the matter, can't you be happy for me, Hugh? And when do we start?'

'That's the condition,' he said, shaking his head. 'I admit, I'm surprised by this. You'll still be going to the Outer Hebrides, but to a... special place. A very special island.'

'We won't be staying with your family then?' That made me pause. I knew nobody else in this country or even this continent, and I'd been counting on having the familiarity of him by my side. Part of Scotland's lure in the beginning, before the events that had led to the Inquiry, had been the knowledge that I would be closely working with Hugh as my tutor. 'So, what is this place?'

Hugh walked me back to a large cloakroom where he handed me my winter jacket and shrugged on his own elegant black wool coat.

'Scarp,' he mused aloud as he took the ends of his long red scarf in hand. 'The island of Scarp, that's where you're going. It's the center for higher learning, the Holy Island of the Kin. Many request to continue their studies there, but only the best and the brightest are accepted.'

I stopped still with my coat half on; it took a second for his words to sink in. 'Me? They think I'm... among the brightest?'

'I know,' he agreed as he turned to look at me. He was usually so cool and collected; I'd never seen him so discombobulated. 'This turn of events has surprised me too.'

'Thanks,' I said in as dry a tone as I could, but he didn't notice. I put my other arm in my coat.

Hugh shook his head again as if to clear it. 'Scarp, of all places,' he said, an unhappy tone creeping into his voice. 'I attended Scarp. Your father was there in his time, too. But you? I don't know what to think about this.'

'Perhaps you could be happy for me?' I didn't bother trying to hide the sarcasm. That was the Kin for you. Even Hugh, who claimed to be a half-blood like me, even he couldn't escape the elitism of the way the Kin thought. 'What, the place is good enough for you and Dad but not for me?'

He continued on as if I hadn't spoken, but in such a low voice he might have been thinking aloud. 'It's a set-up for failure, as far as I'm concerned. There's no way you could possibly compete, not without years of study. You haven't been equipped to handle this kind of stress. Yet, I know Johanna, she wouldn't do such a thing...'

As he listed all the reasons I could fail, I stopped paying attention for my mind was still stuck on *the best and the brightest*. I straightened my back and allowed a ray of light into my future for the first time in ages. Finally, recognition of my power, the power I'd been coerced into hiding for most of my life. At last, someone believed in me and I could be free to become the best I could be and no longer carry the burden of other people's low expectations.

Dara (de Teilhard) Martin was among the best and brightest of the Witch Kin. I savoured the unfamiliar taste of those words on my tongue. There was a future waiting for me, and I was going to give it everything I had.

'It's just that...' Hugh raised his voice and cut across my dreams, determined to keep me firmly anchored to the ground. 'I believe they must want to keep an eye on you, after Willem. I hope you're prepared enough to handle this.'

'What does that sorcerer have to do with anything? He's long gone on a boat out of Alt. He's history, and wouldn't dare show his face around the Kin again.'

'It's not that.' Hugh shook his head. 'Willem... you said he burned himself into you, deep within your mind.'

I nodded slowly, hating the memory of it. Creepy, nasty Willem. 'That was horrible. Never again.'

He lowered his voice again and spoke quickly. 'Yes, I have no doubt you feel this way, but the damage is done. You need to heal from that, and it will take time. A lot of time. Your mind and body need to mend from the inside out, and Johanna... has decided that Scarp is the safest place for you.'

He looked at me, as if I should understand his concerns, then walked toward the door we came in all those hours ago, where he paused and turned back to me.

'You know, you'll always carry that scar,' he continued, his voice somber and his words slow. 'And there may be other effects during the healing process. Hallucinations, delusions... Willem could even, if he knows where you are, get back inside your head.'

2

Hugh was wrong. 'Not if I don't let Willem in! I can control if he comes into my mind, and while I'm learning to use magic, then I'll just get stronger.'

I was totally confident of my ability to withstand further onslaught from the sorcerer, especially now that I was counted amongst *the best and the brightest*.

Hugh sighed loudly. 'What I'm trying to say is, until you're fully healed, Willem can hurt you again, and cause worse damage this time. I wish it were as easy a matter as your strength of mind,' he said. 'I know your intentions are good, but we need to look towards the future.'

He surprised me then by draping an arm around my shoulder and giving me an affectionate hug. Never mind his words, this was icing on the cake of the judgement. I took a moment to bask in his warmth before he dropped his arm again, yet his hand lingered on my shoulder, and we turned to face each other.

In all the months I'd known him, we'd never had physical contact before, not even this casually. I searched his face for the meaning of it and found that his professional distance dropped as he gazed back at me.

My heart thudded in my ears and I couldn't tear myself away even if I wanted to. This, this was the Hugh I'd met all those months ago by the harbor of my home town, the carefree half-blood denim and leather clad Hugh with the mussed-up James Dean hair. The one I'd half-fallen in love with but dismissed it as a crush, because I knew Hugh Sabiston was far beyond my reach.

But everything was different now, for I was among *the best and the brightest*.

We might even be equals. Eventually.

'You know, some day...' he began with a whisper and a soft-ness on his face as if echoing my own thoughts. But suddenly the door creaked behind us and he jumped back from me as if scalded, as if reminded where he was and who he was and who I was, and he brought his hand up to his hair to smooth his unruly waves.

The clerk of the court poked his head in to the cloakroom. 'Ye'll be wanting the dossier, then?' His eyes rested on me with suspicion, and I was reminded again that most everyone in the courtroom had disagreed with Johanna's decision.

'Yes, please,' Hugh said, all professional and cold again.

When the door had closed again I placed my hand on Hugh's arm.

'Someday... what?'

He started at the touch. 'What?'

'You said someday... what were you about to say before we were interrupted?'

He drew himself up to his full height and looked over my head, ignoring my question.

'The thing is, if you don't properly recover from the damage inflicted, that burn will always be a vulnerable point, your Achilles heel. And if you're heading where I think you have your sights, then you'll need to be in top notch form.'

'You mean, to work with you? Eventually?' We'd reached the outer door, and I could see a lightening of the clouds outside the window.

'Perhaps. The world is full of possibilities and potentialities. Just, do yourself a favour, will you?'

'Yeah, I know,' I said with a touch of impatience, then gave my best parody of Hugh's Scottish accent. 'Drop the arrogance, Dara.'

'This is serious stuff,' he said. His eyes narrowed as he looked down at me. 'I've gone out on a limb to plead your case. Your father's name is also at stake.'

'You're afraid I'm going to embarrass you and Dad?'

'Apart from that aspect,' he said as he brushed it aside with his gloved hand, then he sighed and turned to me. 'The expectations are going to be high and, let's face it, you have no background in magic.'

I could only stare at him, lost for words, but that didn't last long.

'You've taught me lots, and I spent all Christmas reading those books of yours,' I shot back at him to hide the deep cut he'd made. 'Remember how quickly I picked up on things?' I had my hands on my hips and I was ready for battle. I wouldn't allow him to take this away from me.

'Yes, you're a fast learner,' he said. 'But you'll need more than that. I'm afraid...'

'Afraid for me?' I flicked my hair away as I stood toe to toe with him and stared up at him. I was exhausted from the travel and the tension of the Inquiry and now the sudden rebirth of my dreams, and I had little control at my command. I'd finally grabbed hold of the brass ring, and nothing, not even Hugh, was going to make me let go.

'Yes, afraid for you!' He was almost shouting, but caught himself and looked hurriedly all around the empty cloakroom before resuming in a harsh whisper. 'Not everyone is on your side, you may have noticed. You saw the reaction of the other elders. This could be used as a set up for your failure, for some people don't believe that half-bloods have any place in the Kin. You'll need to step very carefully...'

'You think because someone finally recognized my worth, my potential, that it all has to be a lie?' I wasn't even listening to what he was saying, I was just ready to latch onto him like a terrier to flay his ankles.

'Calm down,' he commanded, holding his hand up, his face taking on a dark expression.

'No, you calm down! You're admitting that your precious Witch Kin aren't so wonderful after all? Is that it? That they cheat and play with people's lives all for their own ends? Well, congratulations, Hugh, for finally opening your eyes. Welcome to my world.'

I didn't bother keeping my voice down as I challenged him, staring him straight in the eye.

He gazed back down at me, his lids heavy. His mouth parted and he drew closer as if to speak, but it felt more like an invitation. Unable to take my eyes from his, I leaned in to him, close enough to catch the subtle undertones of smoky sandal-wood and spicy bergamot that were unmistakably Hugh. This close, I could see the gold that shot through his green eyes and sparkled like magic itself.

But right then the little door from the hall opened again and stopped him. The clerk stuck his head in, looked at us from under his bushy unibrow and silently handed out a file folder. Hugh quickly stepped away from me, leaving a rush of cool air in his wake as he accepted the envelope. The door closed as the clerk withdrew.

'You were going to say? Whatever it is, bring it on.' I was willing to carry on the fight or the kiss or whatever had been about to happen, but the heat of the moment had dissipated with the interruption, and he must have felt it too.

Turning back to face me, his face was blank as if that moment between us had never been. 'I just want you to be watchful, that's all. Scarp is... it's all about competition, and there are high stakes involved. You just don't know what you're getting in to.'

He sighed and looked away. 'I need you to promise to contact me if there's anything awry. If anything happens that's... outside your scope.'

Like if I allowed fairies to make off with Jane's baby, for example, or brought a wayward elf out of Alt. My ears started a slow burn. Would he never let my past mistakes die down?

He carried on as if that he didn't even realize what he'd implied. Flicking through the folder, he nodded. 'As I thought,' he said. 'Come on, no time to waste. The car is waiting for us.'

I had no energy left for fighting him, anyway, I told myself. No matter what he said, I was heading into my future, and the unfinished business between us could wait for another day. I breathed in deeply as we stepped outside into the wet, still dark morning, then couldn't help myself as a convulsive yawn took over.

'It's still so dark out, the clouds are barely light. What time is it?'

'Afraid there's no time to nap,' he said, watching me sneak another yawn. 'And you can eat on the ferry to the island. Your transportation will be leaving shortly.'

We slipped out the back door we'd entered, the lights of the small city of Inverness still on and spread out before me in the gloom of the northern morning. Headlamps of cars were moving through the wet streets now as the town came slowly to life in the gloom of the new day.

The same black vehicle with the silver figure on its hood waited for us, the one which had whisked me from the small airport where Hugh had met me. My suitcase was still inside the trunk, or 'boot' as Hugh had called it. Safely out of sight and protected by the car's solid steel body, he hadn't yet picked up on the supernatural contraband it held.

How long had I been travelling? My mind was muzzy and confused, for I'd left home yesterday afternoon, travelling west to Toronto to meet the international flight to Edinburgh, where I was whisked through Customs to catch the smaller Inverness flight. For someone who'd never left her own island before, this was a lot of moving.

I settled back into the plush cushioned seat and watched out the window at the river as we sped silently along the narrow roads. Ah, this was the life, I could easily get used to this luxury.

The best and the brightest. My future danced before my eyes like the lights on the rainy pavement. No matter what Hugh said, I knew I was heading for the big time now. But I was just getting comfortable when the car pulled up to a brightly lit yard full of buses.

'Here we are.' Hugh was out of the seat almost before we stopped, opening the door and stepping out into the diesel laden air.

'Hugh...' I stared out the door at the ragged group of soggy folk who huddled together in the covered shelter. Seriously? He'd never struck me as the kind of person who used public transportation. 'This is a bus station.'

'And that's your bus there,' he said with a nod over to the aisle with a big '3' sign. 'Here's the tickets you'll need. The bus will drop you right off at the ferry terminal at Ullapool, and another driver will meet you at the other end.'

He looked at me as he handed the file over together with a paper bag and a thermos. 'There'll be no excuse for getting lost.'

'Hold on a second!' I said, digging my heels in as he herded me over to the waiting bus. 'Aren't you coming with me?'

'No,' he said, then sighed as he turned back to look at me. We were standing so close I had to look up. 'Look, I might be wrong, but this is so... so unexpected. Scarp...' He fell silent.

He didn't believe in me, and didn't think I was worthy of this opportunity. He was no different from all the other Kin I knew. Dad, my half-sister Sasha, Dad's wife Cate. My heart hardened. I would show them all.

'I will be fine. I will be a success. Do you really think they'd offer me this chance if they thought I wasn't up for it?'

He tilted his head and considered. 'Oh, I know you're fully capable,' he said softly, his face unreadable in the orange glow of the streetlights. 'Of that, there is no doubt in my mind. But this is so sudden. And no, I don't think you're ready. I just wish I knew why Johanna made this decision. There are other places you could heal, places less politically charged...'

If I'd had my wits about me, I would have called him on that, I would have made him explain, never mind missing the bus for there would always be another one. But I was worn out from the past twenty-four hours, and his words were unsettling me.

'Take good care, Dara,' he said quietly, then he folded me into his arms in an unexpected hug. 'Keep your wits about you, and contact me if there's anything amiss.'

And then he leaned in for a kiss.

He had been aiming for my cheek but, unaware, I turned my head toward him to give him further hell, and his lips landed on mine, and there was magic, the kind that makes you forget your harsh words and hurt feelings and takes you into another place altogether. He didn't pull away immediately, but his lips lingered on mine. Our eyes met a second later and it was only then we broke apart; I don't know who was more surprised.

The bus gave a snort and an impatient whoosh as if it was pawing the ground, eager to leave. His hands stayed on my arms and he opened his mouth, but no words came out. My body wanted to nestle into that hold forever.

But Hugh set his mouth in a firm line and turned away to heft first my large knapsack into the luggage bay, and then the flowery carry-on. I held my breath, for the medallion with the tainted magic was inside that one. He sniffed suspiciously as if he caught a whiff of something, but the driver hurried him on, and once the bay was safely closed and locked I could relax again.

Not that I intended to begin my new life with deception, no. Lies and misapprehensions had gotten me into too much trouble already. But the coin – well, it was the only clue I had to my mother's disappearance all those years ago, and acquiring it had cost me dearly. There was no way I was going to give it up to the Witch Kin.

'When will I see you again?' I called out of the open bus door as I passed the bus ticket to the driver. 'How am I going to know where to go?'

I had no idea how I was to navigate in this strange country; exhausted, hungry and on the brink of being totally alone, the future was a terrifying blank to me.

'It's all in the folder,' he said. He laid his gloved hand on mine, and seemed to find it difficult to look at me, but when he did, his face was all cool and professional again. 'One more thing – I need you to keep your head down when you get to Scarp.'

'Keep my head down,' I repeated dully. 'Stay out of trouble. Don't mess it up.'

He sighed with annoyance. 'Sending you to Scarp is a very politically divisive decision on Johanna's part. You're going to meet with a lot of resistance from others. But... I'll be in touch.'

The rain was starting again as the doors closed between us and I could see the droplets already lacing his dark hair in the light from the advertising signs in the shelter. Then he was gone, pushing his way through the huddle of people back to the waiting car.

I could feel the warmth of his lips still on mine, even after we'd parted in the cool winter morning.

3

The bus driver coughed lightly.

'You'll have to take a seat then,' he reminded me, his hand on the gear stick. I could barely understand his words, his accent was so thick, yet his tone was kind enough.

Once settled in to the long-distance bus seat I allowed myself the luxury of looking forward to my future. I, Dara Martin, half-blood witch, had been chosen to study at this illustrious Scarp, wherever that was, in spite of everything I'd done and had done to me in the past few months. No, actually it was because of these very things, for the Kin elders would never have known I existed except for the mess I'd caused back home.

Back home. It would be early still, way too soon to call anyone to tell them the fantastic news. Aunt Edna couldn't speak to anyone before she had her coffee, while Alice wouldn't be out of bed and Brin the elf didn't have a phone yet, still being a non-person in the eyes of the law.

Jack, my sort-of boyfriend, he wouldn't understand the enormity of what had happened in the court room, for he was the most unmagic person I knew. He didn't even see the supernatural side of life, otherwise known as Alt, when it was smack up in his face. I'd told him I was going to Scotland for an interview about a college and that I may or may not be back within a week, depending on the results. He knew nothing about all the stuff that had gone on in December even though he'd been right in the middle of it. If I had returned home without my magic he would have been none the wiser, and me too I guess, for they would have taken any magic memory from me with the binding.

I would let him sleep in before telling him the news that I wouldn't be coming home for a while. Musicians kept late hours.

Besides, Hugh and I had kissed. Even if it had been a mere slip of those luscious fine lips, the sparks between us had been unmistakable. Jack was a great guy, something more than a friend, but Hugh... was a man.

There was no one close to me that I could call right there and then, yet I was desperate for a familiar voice, someone who would understand the wonderful thing that had happened, someone who had at least heard of Scarp.

That left only Sasha, my half-sister, the legitimate daughter of my father. She'd been my sworn enemy since last year, but at least she would connect the dots and I could get the satisfaction of rubbing her nose in it. She had never been asked to go to higher Kin education.

Dad, too, should hear the news and perhaps start to appreciate his bastard child, the one he dropped as soon as her mother disappeared out of his life. I pressed the button for Dad's home phone.

'Hello.'

'Sasha? It's me!'

There was an icy pause. 'This is Cate.'

Cate. His wife, that horrible witch. There was no love lost between the two of us, and I had long suspected she had something to do with my mother's disappearance.

'I heard of the judgement.'

'Yeah, that's good news, isn't it?' I tried to muster some positivity. Tried to keep the conversation civil.

'Well, that depends. I think they're making a mistake. Half-bloods can't be trusted with power. And Scarp? It's unheard of.'

Bitch.

'Still, Johanna is a good friend of mine, and I'm sure she had her reasons,' she continued, her voice as acidic and crisp as if she was standing right next to me. 'I just hope you won't embarrass your father there.'

Bitch bitch bitch. I had to bite my tongue. Johanna, the petite scary blonde, the head elder and now I found out she was a close friend of Cate's. Good thing I hadn't known of the relationship between them before the Inquiry, for sure I would have been even more nervous and had a total melt-down on the stand. My father's wife scared me.

'I guess they see something in me that you never will.' I tried, but failed to match the coolness of her tone.

'They don't know you well enough yet,' she replied. I heard the hissing of steam as she worked her espresso machine. 'Give it time. Still, apart from binding your so-called magic forever, perhaps this is the next best thing. You'll be kept under lock and key until they figure out what to do with you.'

'You never got asked to go to Scarp, did you Cate?' It was a long shot, but I just wanted to lash back at the woman with any means at my disposal.

'God, no,' she replied. 'Not that I wanted to. It'll be interesting to watch how you make out. That's if you survive it, of course.'

I really didn't like that small laugh in her voice as she said those last words and I couldn't help but ask. 'What do you mean, survive?'

'Why am I not surprised they neglected to tell you this aspect of it?' She sighed, then I heard as she sipped her coffee. 'It was a bloodbath last year, apparently. The Competition, I mean. Though perhaps you're to play the role of the sacrificial lamb, the little expendable half-blood.'

That woman knew how to work me just like her fancy coffee machine, she knew exactly which buttons to press. As a half-blood, neither full Witch nor full Normal, I was hated and feared by both worlds. Too weird and witchy for the Normals to accept me, while the Kin looked down their noses at my diluted blood. I closed my eyes against her vindictive spite.

'I'm going to a place of higher learning, Cate,' I whispered, clutching Hugh's words close against the dread that was forming at the very pit of my stomach. 'Only the best and the brightest go there. They believe in me, they know I have a lot of potential.'

She barked with laughter. 'Is that the line Hugh fed you in order to get your cooperation?'

I took a deep, calming breath as I disconnected the call, trying to shake out the crap she left behind in my head. She was not a part of my life, never had been. Hers and Dad's was a traditionally arranged marriage between Kin so it was pretty open, but when she realized he was spending more time with his mistress and her child than with his legitimate kids she put her foot down, and that's when all the trouble with Mom had started.

Had Hugh lied to me? Damn Cate for planting that seed of doubt. I thought my life was taking a turn for the better, finally; yet now, as I wondered just what lay ahead, my exhilaration of the morning slowly leaked out of me like the rain dripping down the window by my face.

And what the hell was the Competition? I was alone and abandoned in this strange country, exhausted and totally not in control of my life's direction as the bus headed north into the dreary dark morning toward a destination which might be the death of me.

....

The wheezing brakes woke me as the bus drew to a stop. Looking out the window at the rain streaming down the glass, the day was still barely lit, dawn had come and gone but the heavy clouds remained. I checked my cell phone on Scotland time - it was nine thirty in the morning. What dark and dreary place had I landed in?

After I'd boarded the ferry waiting at the combined dockside and bus terminal, and stored my luggage in the open racks, I began to uncover the true nature of this strange new land. It was a country of pastry and cakes; the Scots had perfected the magic of wrapping everything in layers of butter and flour to make it crispy and fresh. I sat in the open room area of fixed tables and chairs as I soaked up the calories and the heat from my coffee.

Refreshed from my nap on the bus and from the caffeine, I could look at my future with more light. Never mind what anyone said, I was going to a place of higher education, probably some sort of mix between university and the magical finishing school my half-sister Sasha went to in Switzerland, as all four of my father's legitimate kids would do in time. It was finally my turn to shine.

So enthusiastic was I by now, or perhaps so high on my double espresso and sugar, that I opted to brave the elements outside on the back deck. Sheltering in a corner so I wouldn't be carried away by the high winds or drowned by the torrential rain, I relished the new-found joy rising through my being and breathed in deeply of the fresh salty air.

As I watched the small town of Ullapool drift away in the gloomy half-light of the stormy day, a small smile still on my face, I slowly became aware of another's eyes on me. Turning, I saw the bold stare of a woman much the same age as me, brassy red curls framing her face while her short body was stuffed into a long lilac puffy coat one size too small. She held a burning cigarette protected in her left hand, which she lifted now to take a quick draw into her lungs.

'A'right, then?'

It appeared to be a question.

I nodded in return. 'All right.'

'Th' waither is awfy the day, eh?'

Her Scots accent was heavy and thick, so different from the careful and precise enunciation of Hugh's educated Kin voice.

'It's pretty stormy out.'

'You're no' from here, then?'

'Canada.'

She took another quick puff then flicked the butt over the side of the boat.

'Whit ye doin' here?'

Gawd, she was awfully nosy, but small places were like that. Back home you could expect to be grilled by total strangers about your family history in order to figure out any connections you might have with them. In fact, you might be offended if someone didn't care enough to ask.

However, at the moment I wasn't home. I was on my way to a prestigious academy of magical learning (never mind Cate's poisonous insinuations) and I was getting ready to take my place among the Kin; I was pretty sure my new companion and I would not find any common ground or familial connections. Her accent, the way she dressed – no, there was no whiff of the Kin about her. I drew myself up and looked down my nose as I attempted to channel my arrogant full-blood witch sister Sasha.

'Visiting,' I said, and left it at that. I turned my back on her to go inside to search for more coffee.

'You're no' as fine a witch as ye think ye are,' she called behind me, then muttered, 'ye stuck-up cow.'

I turned back to look at her, awe-struck, not minding the well-earned insult. How did she know? Her plump face was screwed up in a jeer, yet even as I watched her whole demeanour changed. It was imperceptible yet it was as if a glamour grew from within her, and she morphed before my very eyes, no longer a cheap overblown tart wearing too much make-up for the time of day. Suddenly her cheekbones were sharper and her hair settled into a bronzed halo around her flawless face, and I swear even her sausage coat changed shape to that of a voluptuous, well-fed Barbie doll.

'How'd you do that?' I breathed.

I blinked and in a flash she returned to her original self, threw her head back and cackled at me.

'I'll no' waste my energy on the likes of you,' she said. 'But I think I made my point clear.'

She lit up another cigarette, the flame of her lighter steady even in the whipping wind, and blew a stream of smoke in my direction, staring at me the whole while. 'It takes one to know one, eh?' she added.

I nodded, suddenly humbled.

'So what's your business here, then?' she asked again. 'Why are you coming to Stornoway?'

I drew myself up again in a belated attempt to regain my dignity. Witch she might be, but I was going to a place of higher learning, a special place only for Kin. The effect was spoiled by a gust of rain spattering down the back of my neck as the ferry changed direction, finally heading out to the open sea.

'Eh, let's go in out of this,' she called, making her way to the doorway. I didn't see what she did with her cigarette butt this time.

She told me her name was Fergie as she led me down a set of stairs and into a lounge at the front of the ferry, whose entire wall was glass with a view of the heavy seas we were crossing. She sat at the end of a row of comfy seats and glared at the young boy in the next chair till he rose with a sigh and moved further on down the row. Happier, she patted the now empty seat.

'Get yourself settled in, then,' she said. 'We might as well be friendly, for we've another hour to go before we reach the island. If you're getting a coffee, I'll have one as well. I take it black, and make it a large.'

My mind was buzzing again, and not just from sugar, for I didn't know what to make of her. This young woman was a witch like no other I'd met; she was common, with none of the attitude possessed by every Witch Kin kid I grew up with. She spoke her mind and cut to the quick, and I thought that once I got past the prickles and barbed wire I might like her.

By the time I came back with fresh coffees, my new companion was deep into an animated conversation on her phone. As the ferry cut through the storm on its way to the Outer Hebrides, I sized her up from the corner of my eye. She was the first witch I'd ever met who wasn't an obvious member of the aristocratic Kin, besides myself of course. She could put on the glitz, yes, but that's all it was, just a coating of shimmer that was only surface deep. It didn't give her the innate bearing, the inborn haughtiness, the absolute conviction of superiority that was the legacy of the aristocratic Kin. Her accent remained gutter Scots; her enunciation was reminiscent of the hapless heroes in the movie *Train Spotting*.

'What? No!' I saw her slide her eyes over to me as she gave me a quick once over, then she turned away and began to whisper into her phone with her other hand over it. The conversation lasted a long time and I had the uncomfortable feeling that I was the topic of her hushed discussion, though I told myself that was ridiculous.

By the time she finished the call, our next destination was in sight.

'Come on, let's get ready to get off,' she said with a nod towards the luggage racks. As we stood in line to disembark, she asked me outright for a third time what my plans were, coming to the Island of Lewis and Harris, way up north to the Outer Hebrides. I didn't like the challenging glint in her eye.

'I'm going to... a special place,' I told her, not bringing up the name for she'd probably never heard of the institution. I knew the Kin were brilliant at keeping things under wrap. 'It's a select school, I guess you'd call it.'

'A select school, is it? And where might this be?' I knew she was outright mocking me now.

I shifted my weight uncomfortably and hoisted the knapsack more securely onto my back. She'd practically ignored me once I'd bought her a coffee and now this treatment. I felt the need to put her in her place.

'A place called Scarp,' I said airily.

She cackled and threw her head back again.

'Scarp, is it? That's your special school?' There was scorn and bitterness in her voice. She looked at me, her arms crossed in front of her and a scowl on her face. 'Ye must think you're rather grand, then, going to *Scarp*.'

'I'm pretty lucky, believe me.' It sure beat out the alternative.

'Funny, ye don't seem like one of the Kin.'

'I'm not,' I replied quickly, on the defensive. 'I am so definitely not one of them.'

'Then why would *you* be going to Scarp?' She eyed me carefully as she let that dart sink in, then she barked with laughter. 'Don't worry, I know who you are! You're that half-blood errant witch that's got everyone all atwitter! This is going to be a fun term, I'm sure.'

26

I could only stare at her in shock. Among the last words Hugh had said to me were to keep a low profile, and it looked like I'd already failed him there.

How could word had spread so fast? It seemed like days ago, but the Inquiry had only finished its business four hours prior. Yet, here on this ferry slowly backing into the dock on a small island in the northern reaches of the country, it was already common knowledge.

Fergie saw the light dawning in my eyes as I tried to take in her words, and a smile slowly spread across her freckled cheeks. A more evil grin I'd never seen.

'You might as well get off your high horse, for you're no better than me. In fact, from what I hear, you haven't even got basic training in magic. Correct me if I'm wrong.'

I tried to ignore her as I stood in line behind her while we waited to disembark; that cheap tart still cackled every time she caught my eye, so I furiously stared at the iron stairs below my feet.

Ever since last December I'd had such high hopes of leaving my past behind me; yes, even through all my dread of the Inquiry's outcome, hope had always burned that this could finally be my chance to be something other than the despised bastard half-blood witch.

Fate had a funny way of granting wishes sometimes. Here I was just as I had dreamed, about to land on Hugh's home island, yet still I was carrying around my reputation like a steamer trunk on my back. And the only person I knew here was Fergie, this low-class gutter witch, and it looked like we were going to the same place.

She paused before we entered the ferry terminal proper, and turned to me. I was surprised to see her mocking smile had warmed to almost kindness, almost as if she knew what thoughts were weighing me down, and she spoke in a low voice so as not to be overheard.

'You're going to have a tough time on Scarp,' she said, her level gray eyes meeting mine in frankness. 'There's no doubt about it. I don't for the life of me know why they're sending you there when you're so unprepared, and the competition is going to be something fierce.

'It's every witch for herself there, on Scarp, because the stakes are high. We'll be pitted against the cream of the Kin kids. You know, the ones who went to private schools and have had everything handed to them on a silver platter their whole lives, and who don't think the likes of us have any right to be there. The only advice I can give you is, try not to get yourself killed.'

4

Like the small town we'd left behind on the mainland, the buildings in Stornoway were again mostly cold stone and brick, all painted white, so different to the friendlier colorful wooden houses of my home. But we didn't linger there long.

A battered black Land Rover waited outside the ferry terminal, the driver leaning against it with a sign which merely said 'Scarp'. Fergie claimed the passenger seat in the front, leaving me to hunker down in the back, and she carried on with the man as if they were old friends, lapsing into another language, probably Gaelic, and leaving me with little to do as I bounced around on my hard bench except stare out the window at the relentless mist which coated this new island, and ponder her last words to me.

Try not to get yourself killed.

Always good advice by any estimation, but the words sent a chill through me that the Land Rover's ancient heating system would never warm. When Hugh had appeared disconcerted at the news I was to be sent to Scarp, I'd misread his concern for snobbery, yet he too had also mentioned a competition. I'd been too wrapped up in the whole 'best and brightest' thing at the time to really pay attention. Cate's words I could dismiss as just another attempt to scare me and keep me in my place, but now that Fergie had brought it up, I couldn't ignore it anymore, and was seriously wondering what the elder Johanna had really sentenced me to.

The passing scenery told me nothing. We'd left behind the orderly rows of streets in the town and were headed into the heart of the countryside, with barrens and big hills and small bodies of water. Through the blanket of fog I caught occasional glimpses of a castle, quite a few ruined stone houses, even a standing circle of stones, and of course the sea was never too far away.

Back when I'd hoped to be coming to the Island of Lewis and Harris, I'd done my homework of course. I'd found the island on Google Earth, examined the mountains and the grasslands and tiny villages all dotted along the northern part of the coast where Hugh's family lived. And the beaches, there were terrific white sand beaches everywhere, as if a Caribbean paradise had been unmoored by the Gulf Stream and carried an ocean away to the outermost limits of Scotland.

I'd never heard of Scarp though, and had no idea what was in store. I searched the word on my phone and all I could find was a small mention of it along the western shore of the island we were presently travelling through. The satellite view showed nothing but a blur, as if a bank of fog hovered over it, deliberately hiding it from the all-seeing cameras of Google Earth.

After a couple of hours, we descended from high hills and set off down a single-lane track, still surrounded by thick mist. Sheep ruled supreme here, with dozens and dozens of them roaming freely. They owned the road too, or at least they thought they did, and in the lowering afternoon light the driver had to slow down from his frenetic pace more than once in order to avoid an accident.

It was about this time that I noted my fingers were tingling and my gut was churning as if a swarm of butterflies had taken roost there, an unmistakable sign of magic loose in the air somewhere. It began almost imperceptibly, but as the mist thickened to fog, so too did the magic in the atmosphere become more solid. We passed through the courtyard of a stately home, then by the stables, all in the middle of nowhere and we saw no people at all, just the endless ovine population, with a few highland cows thrown into the mix. But the magic all around us was growing ever stronger, that indefinable color in the air, almost a yellow smell I could taste, like the sulphurous atmosphere of a mill town.

Finally the driver pulled to a stop on the side of the road and we alit. To my left was a wide shore of white sand, a beach which stretched on without end into the fog.

'This is as far as I go,' he said in English for my benefit, and he nodded his head up to our right, away from the sea. 'Tak' the road to the other shore. I've told Miss Fergianna the way.'

He hefted out our bags and got back in the Land Rover. Within seconds he was gone, turned back the way we'd come, leaving us alone in that deserted spot.

Down below us was the empty beach, and to my right only sand dunes topped with high grass, with a small lane cut through them. Nothing else was visible through the grayness. The land was silent except for the whispering wash of the waves; no birds sang, no motors hummed.

My companion looked at my bags with contempt and sniffed loudly.

'You do know, whitever ye have in there, I've got to say it smells really bad.'

I had managed to smuggle the coin past Hugh, I knew he'd caught a whiff of the tainted magic on it as he hefted the bag into the luggage bay in Inverness, but in the rush of catching the bus, I'd thought I'd gotten away with it.

'My clothes are clean,' I replied shortly, although my eyes slid down to my purple flowered carry-on to check there was no evidence of the coin shining through.

'No, I mean the magic, in that bag there,' she replied as she nudged it with the toe of her scruffy black Doc Martens.

I stayed quiet while we both contemplated it.

'Is it your medium?'

'My *what?*'

'Your medium, your... familiar. What you use for casting spells.'

'No,' I said blankly. I'd never heard of such a thing. And Hugh had said that witches had no use for spells, for they could use the power of the mind.

'Then you probably don't want to bring it onto the island,' she said, her hands on her hips. 'Whatever it is, there's something wrong with it. *She* won't like it.'

I bit my bottom lip, not quite sure what was going on and what I should do about it.

'Ye can toss it, declare it or hide it,' Fergie told me in a kinder voice.

'Will they give it back to me? I mean, when I've finished here?'

She shook her head. 'Not a chance. It's gone forever if *she* gets her claws on it.'

'No.' The word was out of my mouth before I'd even thought about it. This coin was the only link to my mother, tainted magic or not, and it was too hard won from the sorcerer. No way I was going to risk losing it.

'Then I'm guessing you don't want to throw it away either.'

I looked all around me at the sand dunes and mist. 'Can I hide it here? Collect it afterwards, if I ever get away?' I meant, if I survived whatever awaited me at our destination.

Silence greeted that question.

'Do ye not feel all the loose magic in the air here?' she asked finally. 'You can leave it here, but the *beathach creaghe* will only snatch it up. They don't usually come this far from the water, but even a tainted morsel like that will attract them like vultures to a body three days dead.'

'I can't lose it,' I told her. 'Look, it was my mother's.... And it's the only link I have to her, it's the only thing that lets me hope she's not dead, like everyone thinks.'

My vision was blurring with unshed tears, and I blinked hard to hold them back.

She shifted her weight uneasily. 'Oh, shit, you're crying.'

With those words, the exhaustion of the past twenty-four hours caught up with me and the tap turned on. I stood there and sniffed as the tears let loose.

'Look,' she said, glancing around as if to ensure we were alone in the mist. 'Put a hiding spell on it, I won't tell on you.'

'I don't...' I began, then forced myself to speak through the despair. 'I don't know how to do spells.'

We looked at each other, then she broke the gaze and stared again at the purple carryon at our feet.

'Dammit,' she said eventually. 'I'll do it, if you promise me you'll not tell. We're not supposed to use any extra magic over there on Scarp, and if we're found out I'm in deep shite and will get thrown off the island. In order for me to help you, I need to trust you.'

'You can do that?' I breathed as I wiped my nose with my sleeve. 'Hide it?'

'It's a simple enough spell. But... you've got to be really careful, because it'll have *my* magic prints all over it.'

'I swear,' I told her fervently. 'If you can do this for me, I'll... I'll owe you big time, and I promise I won't let anyone find it. You don't know what this means to me.'

She clucked as if already having second thoughts. 'Well, hand it over then.'

'Do I need to give it to you?'

'I'll need to know what kind of spell to put on it, then, won't I? And I can't know that until I hold it.' Her voice was growing more impatient.

'I thought witches didn't use spells,' I said as I bent down to open my bag on the sandy road, working quickly before she changed her mind. I dug deep inside till my fingers closed over my medallion. It was pulsing in my hand, glowing like it had in Alt last month, probably because of all the untethered magic all around us.

'Indeed?'

'So I've been told...' I mumbled. That's what Hugh had said, not that I had any personal experience myself.

'Well you've been told wrong,' she said with an air of superiority as she reached out her hand. 'I'm a witch and I use spells all the time. It's far easier than that mind magic the Kin is always on about. Now then, we've got to get a move-on, the ferryman'll not be waiting for us.'

I felt humbled by my complete lack of knowledge, and put the coin in her waiting hand.

'Oh, my, then!' It lay in the flat of her palm, and her eyes widened as she examined it. 'That's no' good.'

'What? Why do you say that?'

She ignored me as she reached in her pocket and took out a piece of blue fabric, the size and shape of a handkerchief. It must have been pure silk, for the vibrant color glowed in the pale grayness all around us.

Fergie wrapped the coin with the fabric, then brushed two fingers of her right hand lightly over the small glowing bundle.

'*Nach fhaic duine seo, na leig le duine faireachdainn seo,*' she chanted softly.

She quickly unwrapped it and without touching the coin again, passed it back into my hand. The glimmer of the metal flickered on and off like an electric lamp right before the power is lost in a storm, then all of a sudden it became lifeless, just an ordinary, slightly tarnished piece of metal in my hand.

'Alright then,' she said, once the last flicker of life had gone from the object. 'That's good for a day or so, enough to get you on to the island. You'll have to think of something else when it wears off. You'll not want *her* getting a whiff of this, mind. You'd be kicked off the island and sent back to where you came from before you know it.'

5

I cradled the last remnant of my mother in my hand, no magic colors or tingle emanating from it now. 'That's amazing, it's like it was never magical at all now. I need you to teach me how you did that.'

'Yeah, sure,' she replied, absently wiping her hands on her jeans. 'I really don't know what they're thinking of, sending you to Scarp this unprepared. I think they're just setting you up for failure.'

I stiffened at those words, remembering my conversation with Cate. What Fergie feared was a distinct possibility, but it was too late for me to back out now.

'That coin, what's the story behind it? And how the hell did it end up with the likes of *you*?' She turned back along the sandy path. 'Never mind, don't tell me, it's been in places I don't even want to know about. Hide it back in your case now.'

After securing it deep amongst my clean underwear, I straightened up and pulled the handle out of my carry-on. 'Where do we go from here?'

'That's our road.' She hoisted her pack on her back and set off along the road cut into the dune. 'Ye'd better hurry, it's getting dark again and the *beathach creige* will be waking up,' she called back to me.

I followed her as fast as I could in the gathering gloom, but it was a hard struggle walking on the sand with my large knapsack on my back and carrying the other case. I was, however, feeling happier now the medallion was safely hidden by Fergie's spell. I now felt I wasn't alone, even if it was a reluctant partnership we shared.

After a long struggle through the path, the sand disappeared from under our feet and we walked down a rutted gravel path to meet a concrete boat slip rising from the sea. Familiar as I was with the action of salt water, I could tell the old pier had been there a long time, with its crumbled edges and the sea moss growing in the cracks.

We were in a sheltered cove, just an inlet to the sea between two cliffs of rock, and this was the end of the road. There was nothing around us but the hush of the waves, stone and mist.

'Hmph, the boat's not even here yet,' she grumbled. 'Bastards, leaving us to wait like this.'

All around us was stone in varying stages of decomposition – large boulders rubbed smooth by the actions of winter waves, small round pebbles lying in the cracks between them, and sand underlying it all. The rocks appeared dry enough except for the insidious dampness of the air. Fergie walked close to where the sea lapped the broken concrete and stared hard into the mist as if willing a ferry to appear.

'Mind your feet there,' I called out to her. 'The tide's coming in, you don't want a rogue wave to grab you.' I could see by the calmness of the small waves there was little chance of that happening, but I wanted to show Fergie I was not a total ignoramus. I might know little about magic, but I knew all about the treachery of the ocean.

I jumped off the slipway, heading for the largest boulder. We had not walked more than half a kilometer, but it had been a heavy trudge through the sand and I needed to take the weight off my feet.

She turned to look at me. 'Ye might want to watch yourself,' she said nastily. 'I warned you about the beasts, didn't I?'

'Is that what the *beathe... beathe* whatevers are? You mentioned them,' I said as I threw off my backpack and sat heavily on a particularly beautiful white and red granite boulder, one with soft black lines running through it. 'I don't see any monsters around here though.'

I lifted my eyes up to the top of the cliffs surrounding us. Nothing moved, no threatening creatures sidled over to peer at us, ready to make us their next meal. Speaking of which, I was pretty sure I had a bar of chocolate inside my knapsack, so I rummaged through it. Yes, as I thought, in the side pocket. Bliss.

'Gerroff it!' she screeched. 'You're feckin' sittin' on one! You're on a *beathach*!'

I could only gape at her as she had a mini-meltdown on the slip.

I was about to shout something rude back to her when the boulder shifted beneath my butt in a movement like a roiling wave, and I was off that rock in a second. But I didn't have the sense to run right then, I was too mesmerized by the sight of this solid stone moving in a way that wasn't natural for its kind. Ancient crepey eyelids flashed up to reveal liquid pools of oily black turning in their sockets until they found me; I could now see the face in the lines and wrinkles and colors of the rock. Two nubs I had thought to be natural outcroppings of erosion from eons of waves and wind perked up and swivelled toward me. The thing had ears, and now I could pick out the snout of it, lifting in my direction.

The beast focused on me and under that awful stare I felt my limbs growing heavy, thick and sluggish, as if the neurons of my brain were no longer sending out signals to the rest of me, and one part of my mind realized its gaze was petrifying me. I was becoming slowly, inexorably, like a rock myself.

'Don't look at it in the eye!'

But I couldn't tear my gaze away. It opened its mouth, and that was a terrible thing to behold, the rows of sharp flintlike teeth draped with green seaweed and the remains of a rotted fish tail still in the corner of its jaw.

As the boulder rose on its haunches, I knew I had to force myself into action or my bones would end up crunched and shredded and part of the white sand beneath the pebbles, yet I couldn't move.

The *craighe* moved fast for a rock, one great stone paw was reaching for me even as this realization screamed in my head; one swipe with that weight and I would be flat on the beach and it could munch at its leisure.

Fergie was not coming to my rescue; instead, she screamed shrill instructions at me from the safety of the concrete pier. Yeah, I agreed I should run away, but that's hard to do when your legs are solidifying into granite.

From the corner of my eye, I saw that her screaming had awoken other red white and black rock lumps and they were moving to join in on the feast of me, and now I was surrounded by a whole clan of the strange beasts, their black eyes gluing me into place and their jaws gearing up in anticipation. The whole beach was suddenly a seething mass of living granite.

The pier was too far away for me to escape to, even if I could command my increasingly numb legs to move. I had nowhere to go but up.

To this day, I have no idea how I did it, perhaps it was the surge of adrenaline in all my channels, for that was the only thing moving in my body by then. Perhaps it helped that I let loose a stream of invectives while I did so, naturally falling back into my Newfoundland roots and the colorful language I'd grown up hearing on the old streets by the harbor.

'*Goddamn-hangashore-bastard-sleveens*!' This was my mouth talking, while my heart and mind and soul thought 'Up!' and then I was there, hovering over the beasts out of their jaw reach by mere inches. As I teetered, trying to find my balance when there was none to be had in this new weightlessness, I watched as my last chocolate bar slipped out of my hand like it was all in slow motion, and it fell amongst the hungry stone clan below my feet.

'No!' But it was gone, a casualty in the clash of the rock beasts, and the largest of them shouldered out the littler ones to get at the shiny piece of foil that smelled so sweet.

With their eyes no longer holding me in petrification thrall, I was free to run away. Still with my knapsack in my hand, I hopped on the backs of the beasts, quickly placing my feet from one beast to another in a crazy zigzag pattern till I reached the safety of the concrete.

Fergie didn't offer me a hand up, leaving me to scrabble up the slippery cement face any way I could and when I reached the top she merely stared at me, her mouth wide open.

'You'll be letting in flies if you don't shut it,' I said, totally pissed at her lack of support during my danger, and at losing the last of my chocolate.

'How the feck did ye do that? You told me you had no spells.'

I'd done nothing but run away, yet if I'd learned one thing growing up with the bully kids of the Witch Kin, it was to never admit your weaknesses. When in doubt, waffle.

'What did you see?'

She turned back to the rock beasts who were now all morphing back to their slumbering stone state with the excitement over. Only one beast, the original, the largest moved slightly, and that was just to spit out the foil wrapper like an afterthought. The silver paper lay crumpled on the pebbles, all glistening and soggy with slime.

The creature bellowed, a lonely mournful sound like a foghorn, then it too settled back to its rock stance.

'I saw you rise in the air, you magicked yourself up with a spell I'd never heard before, and then you quieted the beasts enough to walk back over them. It was if they had no power over you.'

She was staring at me, her gray eyes wide.

I thought for a second, then nodded. Maybe that was what happened, maybe not. At the time, I thought it was the force of the stream of consciousness cursing which propelled me upwards. It had all happened in slow motion to my mind, just like when Wily E Coyote finds himself at the edge of a cliff with nowhere to go but down, but hasn't yet realized it.

I had, for those moments in time, floated myself above the danger. Gingerly, I did a mental check through my limbs, searching for any feeling of leftover magic, and I found it, faint traces still coursing like tingles at my fingertips.

I had flown, or at least hovered, and for real this time, not like when I'd projected my mind last September with Hugh by my side.

Fergie had missed the whole chocolate part, and thought I had calmed the beasts through some magical means. I wasn't going to disabuse her of the notion. With my reputation preceding me, I knew I was in sore need of street cred in this new place and I would grab it anywhere I found it. Besides, I was still blown away by this newfound talent.

So I shrugged and nodded, modestly saying, 'you do what you have to do, right?' I casually moved away from her as if to watch the mists over the sea.

'Get back here!' Her voice had deepened with anger, and I looked over my shoulder in surprise.

'Everyone says you have no training,' she shouted, her fists now on her hips. I could see the wheels turning in her mind, every thought reflecting on her freckled face, and steeled myself for the next lambasting. 'You tricked me into putting a hiding spell on that dirty coin!'

'Wait now,' I said, but with no force behind it. I could see where she was coming from, and it might be better for me if I confessed right now. 'It really wasn't like that...'

'That spell has my fingerprints all over it!' There was no stopping her. 'You're going to use it against me, and get me kicked off. You sneaky bitch! What an... an abominable thing to do!'

'No, no, I...'

'It's... absolutely fecking brilliant.' She still looked angry, despite her words.

I stared at her.

'I wish I'd thought of it,' she added, her shoulders slumped in her puffy coat. 'Damn. I haven't got a chance here on Scarp.'

'Hey,' I said, after a pause. I was feeling my way through this unknown territory. Everyone had talked about the Competition and hinted about the danger, but I'd had no idea what it really meant and I still didn't. Fergie obviously did, and thought me far more devious than I really was. 'Seriously, Fergie, that wasn't a spell, I was just cursing out loud and... and I'm not so sure I flew, I just jumped higher than I've ever jumped before.'

'What, you think I'd believe that, when I saw with my own eyes what happened?'

'I didn't trick you, and I'm really really grateful for that hiding spell.' I was practically begging her now. I wanted, no I needed, this woman back on my side. I'd been abandoned in a strange and confusing land with no map, no anchor, and my only directions were nebulous warnings of the dangers which lay ahead. I wanted to cling to this witch who'd given me her odd sort of kindness, for with that action she'd shown a heart big enough to shield me, and I would do almost anything to regain this comfort. I thought quickly.

'Fergie – we both know I don't have much of a chance in this Competition thing. So, why don't I work on helping you? That way I can learn from you, but help you at the same time? If I can help, and that's probably a big If.'

She stared at me in disbelief, then sank down to sit on her luggage, her lilac coat pulled tight across her hips.

'I'm serious,' I said as I sat next to her on my own suitcase. 'I'm going to need your help to get through this. All this competition stuff – Gawd, I don't know anything about magic working, let alone that, and I don't care, either. All I want is to learn to use my magic, and then go find a life for myself. If I can help you with the competition, I will.'

'That would sort of be cheating, maybe,' she said slowly, then thought some more before she shrugged. That was all the answer I was getting for the moment.

Neither of us had noticed a new sound introduced above the washing of the gentle waves in the little cove. It was barely recognizable, like an old memory, the creaking of ropes on wood. I looked up to see the prow of a small low-keeled boat parting the mists. With a single red sail, it drew silently along the slip where the water was deeper, a solitary black hooded figure at its helm.

'Get on then, if you're coming,' Fergie said without looking at me as she heaved her bag over the side and climbed aboard. 'He'll no' be waiting.'

I dragged my own bags over and dumped them in, then hesitated before I carefully grasped the railing and let myself over the side.

Once I was settled in, the small vessel turned back toward the open water. It had no motor, and there was no wind in its sail, yet it pushed silently forward through the water, leaving no wake behind it in the calm sea. Then all of a sudden we'd broken out of the mist; on one side of us a full moon rose, all bright and hard and silver in the deepening gloam of the sky, while on the other the last of the sun was fast heading toward the horizon. Above our heads, a path of stars came alive and directly in front of us rose a large black mass.

This, then, must be the island of Scarp, our destination.

I could see little in the dusk, just an outline of a castle rising from the flat land to the right with high hills looming behind it, and its windows lit and glowing from within. It was a welcome sight for my eyes.

Although the journey was smooth and the waves merely lapping in the calmness, my stomach was growing queasy as if my body were telling me not to trust the deep water, to get away to dry land as soon as I could. It didn't help that the magic all about us was thicker than the fog had been, building like a low pressure system before a storm as we slowly made our way across the strait to the castle; but unlike the tropical system that heralded the coming of hurricane-force winds back home, this was a cold pressure, the freeze burning on the lungs with every inhale.

None of us in the boat said a word as we passed to the other shore.

6

The last of the light still lingered on the south-western horizon when we pulled up to the small island onto another jetty much like the one across the water. Torches burned to give us light as we disembarked.

The magic in the air lifted the minute I stepped on dry land as if I'd passed through an unseen portal, and the air was suddenly crystal clean again, of moderate temperature, laced only with the familiar smells of salt and seaweed. I breathed deeply and with relish, only then realizing how heavy and oppressive the magic-laden air over the water had been.

A single person appeared on the pier to greet us before the ferryman slipped back into the night. I could make out a tall and lanky form in the dim light, and when he turned I saw his dreadlocks streaming effortlessly down his back. Fergie laughed and greeted him, the two of them hugging and cawing at each other like crows on the wharf, but something about the very intensity of her joviality made me think she felt uneasy, perhaps it was the way her voice tightened when she laughed too hard at his small joke.

Their greeting finished abruptly, and they both turned to me at the same time.

'Timothy, this is Dara,' Fergie said. A nervous tension remained in her voice, as if she wasn't totally sure of the welcome I would receive.

The torchlight showed his chiseled, perfect eyebrows rising just a tinge as he put on a noncommitted smile and looked me up and down. 'Well, here you are then.'

So word of my arrival to Scarp had preceded me, but Timothy sounded amused rather than offended at this half-blood's presence on the holy island of the Kin.

'Hey,' I said. I was not much for small talk at the best of times, and despite the lack of meanness in his tone, there was a supercilious note to his voice that set my hackles rising. And right now I was starving, too.

'You made it this far,' he noted, placing stress on the second last word. His accent was like cut glass, showing that he'd been educated at the most prestigious and expensive of schools in England. 'It will be entertaining to see how long you last.'

With that, he turned away and gallantly offered Fergie his arm. She flashed a look at me as he did so, a sort of apologetic grimace, as if to say 'sorry, but you're on your own now, kid'.

I trailed behind the pair as I lugged my carry-on over the cobblestone path, the uneven thumps and rolling sounding too loud in this quiet place and drowning out their hushed conversation.

We made our way up to the castle I'd seen coming across the water. From this aspect, it was unexpectedly graceful like something from a fairy tale, the bevelled glass panes of the grand entrance lit from within and shooting arcs of rainbows into the deepening twilight. The double doors stood open to allow us entrance, but before we reached it, I felt a disturbing rustle in my mind, faint like the echo of an evil chuckle. It was as chilling as the draft from an ill-fitted window in a wintery north wind, the icy fingers seeking out my most vulnerable spots and lingering, playing notes of discord and dread along my spine.

The hairs on the back of my neck rose and sweat prickled down my back, for I recognized the laugh of the Dutch sorcerer Willem, last seen on a steam ship heading out of Alt after wreaking his havoc with me and my home town. I had to pause my steps, it took all my effort to push this horror out of my mind.

Hugh had said I might have hallucinations, flashbacks, that they were side effects of my healing from the damage Willem had caused in my mind when he burned his way through last month.

'It's not real,' I whispered to myself. 'There's no way Willem could be here on Scarp, the very center of the Kin's universe. He's just a leftover echo in my head, brought on by the stress of the past twenty-four hours.'

When I just about had myself convinced, I pushed on again toward the castle.

·····•·····

The large entrance hall held two fireplaces, both glowing with welcoming heat, and for the first time I realized how frozen I had been in our journey across the water through the heavy bank of magic that cloaked the atmosphere around the island.

I paused to welcome the warmth and to defrost a little before following the other two through another set of large doors, into the castle proper.

I could only gawp and stare around me at first. The ceiling of that brightly lit hallway must have been twenty feet high, all arched wood with the plaster between the ribs painted to look like the night sky, complete with stars glowing goldenly. Doors led off on both sides and ahead of us rose a majestic staircase, all curves and polished wood glinting in the light of the many candles in the huge chandelier above. There was a pleasant fragrance of honey and lavender and beeswax in this space.

Timothy slipped off through a door in the back of the entrance, but my attention was caught by the familiar figure in black standing on the landing.

The pit of my stomach gave way and I thought I might pee myself right there and then. Hugh had warned me that something was not quite right with the whole situation, and now I was pretty sure I knew what that was. Here was the elder who had pronounced my sentence, her face still as expressionless as it had been that morning, her blonde hair set back from her face. Our eyes locked, and dread filled my heart.

'Johanna,' Fergie said in a timid voice as she drew next to me, looking up the staircase where the woman in black watched us. This, then, was the dreaded *she* that Fergie had spoken of. Johanna, the friend of Cate. The elder who'd sentenced me to Scarp.

The elder shifted her gaze to my companion.

'Fergianna McBride,' she replied in her crisp Scots accent. 'I'm glad to see you accepted the challenge. Your life has been an unusual journey thus far, but I'm delighted that you've been

49

able to overcome the obstacles of mind and circumstance to join us here on the island.'

Fergie bowed her head and stared at the ground. 'And I thank you for the opportunity,' she replied quickly. I could see her cheeks had reddened, but she kept her face hidden beneath the curls which had fallen forward.

'Dara Martin.' I gave a slight shiver, remembering the woman from that very morning. Had it been the same day? How the hell had Johanna reached the island before us, for she didn't look as if she'd been subjected to the rigors of public transportation. Undoubtedly Kin magic had been involved.

'Yes, ma'am,' I replied.

'Call me Johanna, please,' she said, briskly as she swept down the staircase. 'Ah, here's Pauline, your fellow student. This is Dara, and I believe you're already acquainted with Fergianna. Perhaps you will show our latest additions up to their room?'

Fergie said nothing, but I could feel her stiffen beside me. Pauline, whose name was pronounced with the accent on the first syllable, stepped out of the shadows. She was a dreary creature with her straight brown hair tied severely behind her head in a childish ponytail, and her bangs cut straight across and too high up her forehead. Her dark gray dress was shapeless, and her brown wool cardigan was buttoned right up to her neck; the only spark of color on her person was in the form of a large red letter 'C' embroidered on her sweater. Dark tights and sensible black low heeled oxfords completed her ensemble.

'Of course, Johanna,' she said primly.

After the elder had departed through a heavy carved wooden door, Pauline merely sniffed in reply to Fergie's reluctant greeting, and gave me the same look she might give a louse found lurking under her dinner plate. She led us through the green baize door set into the panelled walls, then down a rougher, poorly lit corridor and up a flight of stairs, all without saying a word to us. As we passed through the castle, it was like going back through time; whereas the grand entrance hall was luxuriously crafted, perhaps Victorian in all its embellishments, we soon transitioned into a much older part with bare stone walls and sconces burning smokily. The heavy doors leading off this corridor were all closed, the white wash on the wood not disguising the ancient bolts which studded each plank.

Pauline stopped before one of these and opened it. 'This is yours,' she said, finally opening her mouth. 'You two have to share a room.'

'A place this large and we've got to double up?' Fergie muttered.

'It's because of her.' Pauline gave a toss of her head. 'No one expected her to be coming here.'

'Bloody hell,' Fergie said as we peered into the small space. She didn't bother to keep her voice down this time. A small coal fire burned in the grate, not giving off any warmth that I could feel.

Pauline set the lit lantern on the table and the shadows jumped back a little to reveal two iron bedsteads stood on either side, blankets folded neatly on top of the blue striped ticking of the mattresses. There was a single table with two bentwood chairs, a small wardrobe, the tiniest sink I'd ever seen and not much else.

'This is shite,' Fergie continued. She looked furious. 'Not exactly comfortable, is it? This must be the worst room.'

Our escort Pauline cracked the first smile I'd seen from her yet, a thin mean line that didn't show her teeth. 'Sorry, this is the only one available. You should have come sooner, as the rest of us did. Doesn't auger well for your performance in the competitions, does it?

'Besides,' she added with a sneer. 'There is only ever supposed to be six of us. Six is the traditional number. With her here now, things are out of whack.' She jerked her head towards me without even having the grace to look my way. I felt as small as a smear of dogturd under her heel and just as unwanted.

'Feck off, Pauline.' Fergie turned on her, her voice matching the other's nastiness. 'You can just feck right off out of here.'

She stared our escort down till Pauline melted back into the shadows of the hall.

After she left the room, Fergie then turned her unfriendly look on me.

'I guess we're stuck together then,' she said, then let out a sigh of acceptance. 'It was all bad enough but of course *Pauline* had to end up here, too.'

Without explaining herself further, she plunked her bag onto the bed nearest the door and began to unpack, leaving me with the drafty window bed and, I later found, a scant six inches of space in the wardrobe.

7

Our quarters were in the older parts of the castle, the medieval ramparts with the Tudor additions; wonky staircases appeared randomly in narrow hallways and unexpectedly behind corners, and always the stone walls surrounded us at every turn. The place had originally been built for security, not comfort, and it showed, for these thick walls kept out everything but the cold dampness of the northern sea.

Only Johanna and the other Masters, I later found, inhabited the more genteel Victorian wing of the castle.

We found our way down to the Refectory where the communal meals were eaten. Here at least it was warmer, with a huge fireplace burning at one end of the room. The single long table had room for all of us and more, it could have held at least thirty people without crowding, but it was just us students, or competitors, whatever we were.

I found myself placed next to Pauline, who sat stiffly and still refused to acknowledge me. The last space at the table was taken by a late arrival who ran in at the last moment, all out of breath and bringing the fresh scent of the out-of-doors with him.

He was a short guy with thin hair all windswept and sorely in need of a trim, and the friendliest person I'd met on the island so far, giving me a wide smile as he took the last place setting. He was also the first person I'd ever seen to wear a kilt in non-formal circumstances. The olive green of his army-issue sweater clashed sorely with the yellow and blue of the tartan, and was unravelling from a hole in the arm.

'Hi, you must be Dara,' he said as he slipped into the seat across from me. His cheeks held the ruddiness of a life lived mostly out of doors. 'I'm Sandy.' He was so blithely cheerful, it was as if he didn't even notice that everyone else was ignoring me at the table, as if he didn't pick up on any tense vibes from our fellow diners.

The meal that followed was largely silent after that, each of us tackling the mutton stew while keeping watchful eyes on the others. After it was over, however, I had the opportunity to get to know the others; I'd thought the Witch Kin kids back home were rotten bastards, and they were, but they couldn't hold a candle to these, the supposed cream of the crop of the Kin.

'Here's to working together as a team,' Timothy sneered as he held out his water glass in a mock toast and lounged in the chair at the end of the table closest to the fireplace, his cafe-au-lait skin flushed with the warmth.

Fergie tittered at the sarcasm in his voice.

'Should be interesting. I've known most of you all my life but I never considered you competition before.' This came from a girl of Asian descent sitting next to Sandy. Her bowl was still full; she had tasted the soup, then let her spoon drop back to the bowl in disgust.

'You can't fool us, Win. We know that all you've ever thought about is competition.' This speaker occupied the chair between Win and Timothy, I thought his name was Oliver. He sat straight and easy, speaking in a perfectly pitched and educated English accent, and he was the most handsome man I'd ever seen, yes, even far better looking than Hugh. His blond hair was swept back from his face, his skin was smooth, and his dark eyes were deep-set above sharp cheekbones.

'I never thought I'd see the day when I'd be asked to work with a half-blood literally by my side.' This came from Pauline, our earlier guide, sitting next to me all tense and hunched.

I turned to defend myself from this direct insult, but anything I might have said was drowned out by the jeers and catcalls from all along the table. The others weren't exactly leaping to my defense, but it was heartening to see that not all of them seemed to hate me for my accident of birth.

'You Covenanters are so old-fashioned,' Win said, almost spitting out the words. 'Hasn't anyone told you it's the twenty-first century, and it's rude to show your prejudices?'

'Besides, Pauline, wasn't it your own father who sent her here?' Timothy drawled.

I wanted to speak out, remind them that I was right there, but the conversation was snapping and pinging all around me, and I thought it expedient to stay out of the line of fire.

Pauline placed her hands on the table to show she wasn't to be silenced. 'My father had no choice in the matter. It was *her* that insisted, and she over-ruled the voices of sanity in the Inquiry with her Modernist arguments. If it was up to my father, well, we wouldn't have any of this nonsense.'

'Burn the half-bloods at the stake, you mean,' Fergie said, a bitter note in her voice. 'That's one way to clean up the mess, eh, Pauline? Just like the good old days of 1591.'

'It is thanks to the supporters of the 1643 Covenant and the so-called Covenanters, that the Kin no longer act in such barbaric fashion, Fergianna,' Pauline hissed through thin lips. 'And I guess you probably don't want to look too closely at your own family tree, do you?'

My room-mate's face flashed bright red at this and she started up as if to jump across the table and claw Pauline's eyes out, but Oliver's voice cut through the furor.

'It is not her bloodlines that bother me, but the fact that she has no training what so ever, at least that's what I hear,' he said, turning his cool, assessing gaze on me. 'How can a witch with diluted blood and no formal background possibly survive the Competition?'

Oh God. He had to remind me? Were these gladiator games where we would fight to the death, as Cate had seemed to hint? And me with, as he had put it, no training what so ever?

'Perhaps they're allowing Natural Selection to take care of the problem?' Timothy was the only one to laugh at his own nasty joke.

'If I were you,' Win said to me, finally acknowledging my presence. She smiled cruelly at the terror she must have seen on my face. 'If I were you, I would request to have what little magic you have bound. It would be a far kinder thing.'

I saw Fergie hesitate, then bite her lip as she caught my eye speculatively. 'Actually...' But her voice was too quiet to be heard over the squabbling. I gave a short sharp shake of my head at her.

Don't tell them! I tried to convey to her, my eyes burning into hers. It was bad enough I'd been thrown amongst this crowd of vipers with no natural defences to assist me, I didn't want them to have a real reason to hate me. All I needed was to stay under the radar and hope to survive in that way. She slid her gaze away from me.

'Don't even think of burning her with your Dragon Magic, Win,' Pauline warned her as she thumped her fist on the wooden table. 'You can bet we'll all be keeping a close eye on that. I'll not have you cheating.'

'There's also no advantages given for family connections either, Pauline,' Oliver retorted. 'That, too, is considered cheating, and no doubt has you a little worried.'

Pauline huffed to her feet. 'I have no need of special consideration,' she said. 'I am the daughter of one of the most important of Scottish elders. Of course I will prevail in the Competitions. I am no mere Hedge Witch!'

Fergie's eyes flicked open with fear; this was cutting too close. I could see her scramble inside her head for a defensive tactic.

'Actually,' Fergie said again, louder this time. 'She's not powerless.' Her eyes met mine, and she gave a little shrug.

I stared at Fergie with horror; she had the grace to redden a little. She had just thrown me under the bus to divert attention from herself, after I'd promised to help her in any way I could. I could feel the eyes of all in the room sliding towards me, calculating the degree of the threat I represented. They were all Kin born and had been practicing magic since they could walk; there was no way I could ever compete against any of them, and they must know this. I had to think fast.

The others had all gone silent, and had turned their hunter's eyes on me.

'If it makes you all feel any better,' I said, looking at each of them. 'I had no desire to come here to Scarp, but it sure beats the alternative. I just want to learn how to use magic.'

I shook my head. 'I really don't think you need to worry about me in the Competitions.'

....

After the meal, the old thick door leading from the Victorian wing opened and Johanna walked in, her black robe swirling around her ankles. The subdued murmuring halted immediately as all six stood up, with me following a half-second behind the others. She looked at each of us in turn before speaking, as if fixing her gimlet eye into our very souls.

'Please, sit. I wanted to take this opportunity to welcome the newcomers into our midst,' she began. 'The Gateway term has now begun. Most of you know Fergianna already from the Kin community.'

Fergie smiled brightly at Johanna, then her eyes slid to Timothy's as if searching for approval. He gave her only a half a smile, but that seemed enough to satisfy her.

'Dara has come to us from across the water, and may not be familiar with our ways,' Johanna continued. 'I trust you will all have patience as she learns her way around.'

She turned her sharp gaze on me. I felt like a bug under a microscope, the scrutiny of her cool eyes laser sharp right into my head. Everyone else sat absolutely still, but I could feel them looking at me from the corners of their eyes.

Only Sandy grinned openly at me from across the table as he gave a small wink.

'You are aware of the privilege of having been chosen to study on Scarp,' Joanna continued. 'And you are all the fortunate recipients of a much coveted place. Your presence here means you are each counted amongst the most promising of this generation of witches.

'It is both an honour and a burden,' she stressed. 'You will be challenged here at Scarp through your tutorials and through the Competitions, which will be strenuous and test your every skill. Yet, it is not just your witch craft which is being measured.'

Here she paused and looked carefully at each of us in turn again, before settling her gaze on me. 'Dara. You may not be familiar with the purpose of the Competitions. Each year, one person is chosen from amongst the cream of the crop to apprentice to PANEC.'

I gaped at her, hardly hearing the rest of her words. Apprentice to PANEC? That was Hugh's organization. My dream job. All of a sudden, I very much wanted to take part in the Competition, even though my sensible mind knew I would never stand even half a chance.

·····••••·····

My mind was alight with excitement. I had to force myself to listen to the rest of her words.

'So, in order to be accepted for the apprenticeship, the winner must not only be skilled, intelligent and gifted. This person must also show an exceptional level-headedness under adversity and most importantly, the ability to work on a team.'

Johanna gave a small sigh as she continued. 'Unfortunately, we sometimes find that the more gifted a student is, the less able they are to work cooperatively. Your behaviour must at all times be exemplary and fitting to your future roles of leaders within the Kin community, for each of you, with your backgrounds and particular talents, each and every one of you will be contributors to the future.'

I could feel the tension around the table. Next to me, Pauline was sitting on the edge of her seat and almost quivering like a dog waiting to go to the hunt. Win was silent but every muscle in her seemed tense like a rattle-snake about to spring, and even languid, laid back Timothy's relaxed pose was forced; I could see he was working to keep up the pretence of breathing normally.

Johanna gave a small laugh and took a seat. 'Yes, you all want to know the details of this year's Competition. As you know, we debated about holding the Competition this year after last year's fiasco.'

She looked at me. 'A student died, Dara. And another was badly injured, possibly to the extent he will never practice magic again.' She let that sink in.

Jesus. What was I in for? Me, who had never been taught the basics of magic before, and she had thrown me into this pack of wolves with the stakes so high?

'That will never happen again,' she continued calmly, folding her hands before her. 'Instead, you may be happy to hear we've decided to keep the competition on a theoretical level.'

The entire table relaxed a notch and began to breathe again.

'I'm not sure I understand,' Oliver spoke out. He alone seemed a little disappointed. 'If it's only theoretical, how can we prove our abilities and stamina?'

She turned a sharp glance at him. 'We're looking for brain power, along with an understanding of magic principles.'

The others were casting sly eyes at each other, already sizing up the competition in the light of this news.

'What is the nature of this challenge?' Win burst out as if she couldn't hold it in anymore. 'And how meaningful can it be if it has no practical application?'

'Oh, it definitely has practical application.' Johanna gave another small secretive smile, then she leaned forward.

'I want you to try your best to divert the magical power of Scarp.'

A collective gasp went through the room. She looked around, satisfied that she had delivered the unexpected. No one could have been prepared for this one or seen this challenge coming.

'How...' Timothy had turned pale.

'That's for you to decide,' she said briskly. 'As I said, this does have a practical application. Much like hiring computer hackers to test a security system, we have decided to allow you free reign, theoretically, to take over, hijack, whatever, the power that is Scarp.'

'How could such a thing be imagined?' Pauline looked shocked and horrified. 'Scarp is holy, it's inviolable, nothing can get through the barriers erected by the Kin.'

'So we've believed,' Johanna observed. 'But nothing is totally safe, not in this day and age. Not with the sophistication of the enemies of the Kin. And don't fool yourselves, they are out there. The Kin has created powerful opponents through the ages.'

She stood up. 'Remember. This challenge is theoretical. I don't expect anyone to injure themselves trying to divert the power of Scarp, that will be unnecessary and we don't want further bloodshed on our hands. It will require thinking outside of the magical box, and most likely, teamwork. Whatever it takes, I set you this challenge. Any questions?'

Sandy spoke out. He wore a rather smug smile on his face. 'How long do we have to figure this out?'

'The Gateway term spans four months. This is the length of time you have too. The winner is not necessarily the first to pass the finish line, but the most ingenuous solution to this problem. I wish you all the best.

'You have Sandy to thank for suggesting this idea,' she added, smiling at him with what could have been fondness.

Johanna stood silent for a moment more, looking at each of us in turn, then gave a sharp nod. She had delivered her message and knew we understood what would be expected of us all. Her demeanour relaxed.

'Now, Dara, I will interview you in my study directly after breakfast tomorrow morning, in order to determine your strengths and your weaknesses,' she said. 'You will find my office at the top of the staircase in the new wing.'

In the silence that followed her departure, the air felt thick with suspicion as mistrustful glances slid around the table, no one meeting another's eyes. Johanna expected teamwork from this group?

Yet I for one was silently rejoicing – if there was to be no bloodshed, I would at least survive the whole Scarp experience. This was one less thing for me to worry about.

Not that I had any serious intentions of competing – no, none at all, not even with the prize I dearly wanted, for I knew I would perform inadequately compared to any of the others; I was happy just to keep my head down and stay out of their line of fire. It was true what I had told them earlier. How could I hope to compete with any of these witches? I was a half-blood, as Pauline had pointed out, so my magic should be diluted compared to theirs, not to mention the fact that I'd been actively discouraged from using my power all my life.

The prize, though; I yearned for that, and had since I'd first met Hugh. To work alongside him in the Pan European Council, doing whatever it was he did, that was still my dream. Even if it I knew it could never happen now, at least not as a result of my efforts in the dreaded Competition. I didn't even know what made Scarp so magical – how could I ever hope to learn to control the power of it?

My eyes fell on Fergie across the table, where she sat listening to Timothy's boasting with an ingratiating smile on her face. She wasn't such a complicated soul, really; I just hated that I could understand her position so well. With her common accent, she was obviously not from the same class and background of the others (I didn't count Sandy – he seemed to be in a league all of his own). Having been subjected to the snobberies and arrows of the Witch Kin kids myself, I knew where she came from. Not only could she not afford to show any support for me, the hated outsider, in front of the others – but she'd thrown me in their way as a decoy, to divert their unwanted attentions away from herself.

I shrugged to myself. None of it was important in the big scheme of things, anyway; not the Competition, not Fergie's friendship, not even working in PANEC alongside Hugh, despite how much I desired it. For me, what really mattered, what remained my ultimate goal, was to find my mother. The medallion was my only clue as to my mother's whereabouts, and finding her was my priority.

And for that, I only had to make it through the Scarp experience alive.

8

Sandy had been the only one not to take part in the bitching over supper, and it was he who took me in hand afterward. Everyone quickly left the table, including Fergie who had disappeared in Timothy's wake, and I must have looked rather lost as to what to be doing next. A cry and a nap in that order would have been lovely, but I wasn't quite sure how to get back to our shared room.

'Want to go for a walk?' he asked as he came up beside me. 'I figure you might be feeling the need for some support right about now.'

I nodded gratefully. Fresh air, a chance to stretch my legs and a friendly face suddenly sounded like a much better idea.

'There'll be cake and tea in the Common Room in an hour or so,' he said. 'Until then we just hang out, work on our practice, or whatever.'

'Practice? Is that for the Competitions?'

He nodded casually. 'Oh, yeah. You may have noticed, we're a competitive group. I'm sure most of us are hoping to nail it down within a week.'

A week? Dear God. How was I supposed to be in a position to compete with any of these witches with less than a week to learn what they'd learned over a lifetime? Win was right, I should just give up now.

I followed him outside into a walled garden. The unexpected rush of fresh air was like a balm to my senses, warm in comparison to the dank chill of the castle's interior, and the scents of oregano and other spices rose to greet us. I breathed in deeply, forgetting my exhaustion and confusion and feeling misplaced as we walked over to a wooden bench against one stone wall. The entire garden lay spread before us.

Silvery moonlight highlighted four statues of white marble, each standing on a quadrant of the space marked off by meandering walkways. Between the gravel paths and the plinths, plants grew, all contributing to the scents which filled the air. I sniffed the air again and recognized mint and rosemary and some others that I was familiar with from the overgrown and neglected herb garden back home.

'This is my favorite spot,' Sandy said. 'I like to come here and just sit, sometimes, and think.' The wool of his kilt rustled as he lifted his right leg over his knee and leaned back into the slats of the bench. There was no wind in this enclosed space, yet the taller plants swayed ever so slightly to a rhythm of their own.

'How long have you been here?' I had assumed the others had arrived not long before us as this was the start of the Gateway Term. It would hardly have given him time to find a favorite garden.

Sandy turned to face me, the pupils of his pale eyes huge in the reflected moonlight. 'This is my ancestral homeland.'

'You *live* here on Scarp?' I couldn't help the shiver that went down my back at the thought of living permanently on this isolated island; the comfortless castle, the lack of central heating and hot water, and the constant cold dampness of the stone walls. I couldn't imagine a place in the world where I'd less want to dwell.

He laughed softly and lifted his face up to the bright silver moon and breathed in deeply. 'No. I arrived two months ago. I wanted the time alone on the island, to prepare, and I've also volunteered to help with the sheep and livestock. They couldn't say no to me.'

'Oh. Is your father an elder, too?'

'Like Pauline's? Hardly.' He grimaced. 'You see, my family lived on Scarp for hundreds, thousands of years. Due to our historical association, the McClouds are the only clan to have a free pass to Scarp. The Kin can't deny me access to the island ever, no matter what spells and magic barriers they erect, for the island welcomes my blood, like iron to a magnet.'

Sandy paused then looked at me again. 'Of course, there aren't many of my clan left in the Outer Hebrides. I'm the last, the only one in this generation. But aside from that, I also earned my place here on Scarp, you know. No family connections to pull strings for me.'

'So when you were offered a place here, you jumped at the chance?'

'I could come here any time I wish, which is why I was allowed to come early,' he replied, a small boast creeping into his voice. 'Because of my clan's history. But yes, I wanted the chance to study and have access to what Scarp offers.'

A wisp of cloud passed over the moon right then and the silvery light shivered.

'This island has many secrets, and I may be the only witch who knows them all,' he said, a sly look coming over his face, then he whispered in such a low voice I almost didn't catch it. 'The Kin have forgotten that, arrogant fools that they are.'

Before I could ask him what that bit of creepiness meant, he turned back to me with his usual sunny smile. 'Let's give you a little tour before cake in the Common Room!'

We returned to the castle through a different door, a smaller one rounded at the top, with an arch of stones set all around it. When he opened it and stepped back to allow me to pass through first, I could see only that it led into a darkened corridor. I held back, and let him go in first into the windowless space. He closed the door behind me, then scared the hell out of me when he flicked his fingers twice and sconces flared into life along the short passage.

'Hey – are we allowed to just... I don't know, use magic whenever we want?' I stood and stared in awe at the flames that had seemingly come from nowhere. What a wonderful thing magic could be. Perhaps there also existed a spell to magic hot water out of the castle's taps.

He laughed and shrugged. 'Some rules were made to be broken, don't you think? We're not allowed to use magic on big things, you know, spells that require a lot of juice, because that's when the ley lines can really mess things up. Little fire spells like I just did, well, that was pretty straight forward, with not much room for shag-ups.'

To ask outright how he'd done what he considered a simple spell would be to admit my almost total ignorance in all things magic. On the other hand, everyone already knew I was a half-blood with no training, so it's not like it would be a great surprise to him.

'How'd you do it?'

'What, light the sconces?' He paused and looked over at me with his broad grin as if he was waiting for the punch line. When I remained silent, the smile slowly faltered, beginning with his eyes, and he gave a short whistle. 'They really didn't prepare you for this, did they?'

'Please, can you show me how you did that?' Although I spoke steadily with my head held high, I could feel my cheeks burning in anticipation of his mockery.

He paused as if to gather his words. 'You know, Dara, you don't need to feel embarrassed. I'm really not like any of them,' he told me in his oddly deep voice. 'The Kin.'

'Are you saying you're not part of the Kin?'

'I'll tell you about it some time,' he said slowly, then smiled. 'But first. You asked how I did this, so we'll have a lesson. Physical Magic 101. How much have you been taught of the Elementals?'

I let my blank face answer his question.

'Oh Lord, you're not going to make this easy for me, are you? Alright, then. There are the Four Elementals – Earth, Water, Fire, Air. Correct?'

Before I could answer that I didn't have a clue, he held up his hand as if to ward off my objections. 'I know, this is a very naive representation of the Elementals, but let's just keep it simple. Agreed?'

I nodded.

'The basis of elemental magic is how they are combined in different ways. Sort of like chemistry, but using the elemental forces. Do you follow me so far? Let me know if I'm being too simplistic.'

'No, you're good,' I said. One of the few science things I liked in high school was Chem Lab, so I could sort of see what he meant.

'So – to light a torch on a wall, we require Fire, naturally, along with Air. A little Earth to keep it grounded, but Water, not at all.'

'And how do you mix them? I mean, you didn't have Fire and Air in your hands or anything, it looked like you just thought it and it all showed up in the right proportions.'

'Exactly. The thought, or Intention, is what does the trick. Despite the name, Physical Magic usually requires Mind at all times.'

This was ringing a bell, for last September Hugh had discussed intention as the basis of all magic. 'So, I intend on creating the fire, and it happens?'

Sandy barked with laughter. 'If it could be that easy, the whole world would be witches,' he said. 'No, it's much more complicated. Intention can be the very devil, you know, for you may *think* you intend something, but your mind doesn't actually interpret it that way.'

'You're losing me again.'

He sighed and thought about it for a couple of seconds. 'Okay, the best way to do it is to let you experience it yourself. I'll turn one of these off, and you re-light it.' He clicked his fingers once and half the light in the corridor disappeared.

'Now, you need to hold the balance of the necessary Elementals in your mind, while simultaneously Intending the sconce to light. Don't worry if you're not successful in the beginning, for you will be eventually, and after that a lot of things will come more easily. And if necessary, I can give you an incantation, that often helps.' He stood back, well out of my way.

I tried to do it as he said, but I guess I didn't have enough understanding of the Elementals and the Intending that he was talking about, and I really didn't have a clue how to balance them. Nothing happened, a state which continued for too long, and after a full and intense two minutes, I let out a grunt of frustration.

'Oh, just light, would you?' I glared at the lifeless sconce as I clicked my fingers, like he had done.

And to my utmost surprise it worked. With a whoosh of flame and a distinct smell of burning oil, the sconce exploded into a brilliant flare, with a cascade of blue sparks rising from it like spray from a waterfall. I stepped back involuntarily and gasped, for I hadn't done it at all in the way he'd instructed. I looked over at Sandy to gauge his reaction.

He was staring at the burning torch with his jaw opened wide until the flame settled back down to its normal slow burn, then he wrenched his eyes to look at me. I could almost swear I saw a look of annoyance flash over his face.

'Really,' he said, his tone flat and devoid of emotion. 'So funny, aren't you? You had me going there, thinking I could help you.'

His reaction wasn't so different from Fergie's when she thought I'd flown, earlier that afternoon. I couldn't let him get mad at me, too.

'Sandy,' I said, grabbing him by the arm as he made to turn away. 'Wait. I've never done that before, I never thought it was possible, and I didn't do it the way you told me to, I just... I don't know...'

He shook off my arm and leaned back against the stone wall, and looked across at the sconce I'd just lit, and then looked at me again moving only his eyes.

'For some reason, against all logic, I find myself believing you,' he said slowly. 'But it just doesn't make sense, any of it.'

After a long moment he asked. 'How *did* you do it?'

I bit my lip and tried to think. 'I was really annoyed that it wouldn't work for me, and I really wanted it to, so when I clicked my fingers I sort of sent a stream of ... pissed-offness at the sconce.'

After he thought about it for a while, he nodded slowly. 'Yeah, okay. Alright.' After another half minute he asked, 'Can I give you some advice, Dara?'

'Anything,' I said. 'Anything to help me get through all this.'

'Don't tell anyone what just happened,' he said. 'If any of this crew find out you're a bloody Wunderkind, your life may be in danger. Yes, they are that competitive. Stick with me, and I'll help keep you safe.'

Our eyes met, and in the wavering light of the sconces I could see that he was deadly serious. He was silent for a long moment after dropping that bomb in my lap, but then roused himself as if with a new purpose.

'It'll soon be time for cake,' he said as he pushed himself away from the wall.

9

All five of the others were already gathered there in the small Common Room which, despite the shoddiness of the furnishings, was the most comfortable place I'd yet found in the castle. The stone walls were covered in a hodgepodge of fabric hangings, their faded embroideries telling tales of myths and magic and lore, and the lumpy old sofas both faced the logs burning in the fireplace.

'Whose turn is it to make tea?' asked Timothy in his languid drawl as we entered.

'It should be hers,' Win replied, jerking her thumb towards me. 'But she probably doesn't know how to boil the kettle.'

'Tea is hardly rocket science,' I told her shortly and I looked about me for the makings of it. There was a huge iron sink with a single tap and a shelf above it over to the side, but no kettle and no teabags. And no electrical outlets of course, not here on Scarp in the old wing of the castle. This might be a little more difficult than I thought. Was I expected to magick up the brew?

'I'll show you,' Sandy said and he led me towards the sink. He measured loose tea into a large teapot, and brought it over to the fireplace where, with a big mitten on his hand, he lifted a heavy black kettle off its hook.

'Remember, don't let on to anyone about what happened with the sconce,' he said in a quiet voice as he poured hot water into the teapot. 'They'd tear you to pieces if they knew the kind of raw power you hold.'

He turned away to load up the tray, leaving me with my jaw dropping behind him. Raw power? What could he be on about? Whether I had power or not, I was in total agreement, of course, for I had no desire to be the target of attention, not with this crowd of wolves.

'Now,' Sandy said. 'If you wouldn't mind bringing over the scones, we'll be all set.' He placed the over-sized brown teapot on a wooden tray which already held cups and saucers and milk jug and spoons, and brought it all over to the low table in front of the sofas.

'I'll be Mother, shall I?' Timothy said, sending a brittle smile around as he proceeded to pour.

After the nasty supper hour we'd shared, I was glad to have Sandy by my side. I was even gladder of his advice, for I wasn't sure the others had believed me when I told them I had no intention of threatening their competitions.

Given the hour, the warmth of the room and the fresh-ness of the scones, there should have been a cozy feeling of fellowship, all seven of us young witches grouped round the fireplace and sipping tea, but despite everyone's pretenses at good natured bantering, it was an uncomfortable affair with each of the students playing mind games and no one letting down their guard.

And it wasn't long before the sniping began.

'Did you see the rainbow I created over the castle today?' Timothy asked as if just making conversation to fill the empty space, but everyone knew it was an attempt at intimidation. 'I managed to create the ninth colour. It does exist, after all!'

Win's face took on a sour expression.

'I've always thought the illusions of fae-touched magic a facetious use of power,' Pauline quickly shot, her straight eyebrows managing to convey her disdain. 'It fact, there's not much meaningful use for any of that, is there? Doesn't make a noticeable difference to the world.'

'And not a lot of use in the Competition, I'm afraid.' Oliver jumped into the fray, smiling as if in sympathy.

Win snorted. 'Yeah Timothy, you keep working on those pretty colours if it makes you feel good, but the judges will be looking for talents that will help in the real world.'

'My magic is not fae-touched! And it's a damn sight more useful than Dragon magic in the real world, Win, illusions are far more subtle than scorching with fire.'

Oliver chuckled sadly. 'I think the Kin need practitioners of Pure Mind, for that is the way of the future. Did you know I am able to enter the Matrix?'

On the sofa next to me, Sandy shifted uncomfortably, as if itching to get up but something held him back.

'I believe you told us that already Oliver,' Pauline spit out. 'Once or twice. Although seems to me that any Normal hacker worth his salt could do what you're doing with none of the drama and at a quarter of the wage.'

'How are the earth spells going, Pauline? Thought I saw you getting a little bogged down there today,' Timothy drawled. 'I think the heavy sheepshit component in the local dirt doesn't help.'

'Metallurgy, Timothy!' Pauline turned on him. 'Is it so difficult for you to understand the difference?'

I kept my mouth shut to stay out of the line of fire, for they'd already had a go at me today. Fergie too, was staying quiet; she kept a supercilious sneer on her face as if above all the nastiness, but the tendons of her neck were straining with the effort. She refused to catch my eye.

Sandy however, was turning red in the face and he finally burst through the nasty quibbling, his voice deep and sonorous.

'Dragon Magic, Mind, Physical – all of these are just aspects of the one!' He looked around at the others. 'None of these distinctions are important, do none of you see this? What matters is that we are here, on Scarp, in such close proximity to the Crystal Charm Stone – this is an opportunity like no other. Why aren't we all making the best use of our time to do what is right for the future?'

He sure knew how to change the mood in a room, for after a long silence, all the other five broke into laughter. But it wasn't the camaraderie of humor that drew them together; no, they were united in sneering at the small Scotsman and the fervency of his unfashionable beliefs.

'The Crystal Charm Stone?' Timothy sputtered when he could catch his breath.

'I think I read about that one – was it in Harry Potter or T H White?' Oliver asked. Timothy smacked him on the arm and keeled over laughing again.

'Isn't the Stone kept in Avalon these days?' Even Fergie was having fun now that the pack had found a common victim and there was no possibility the attention could be turned on her.

Pauline was the first to draw the knives out and make a serious cut. 'The Stone is just a legend, Sandy,' she said. 'It's never existed, any more than Arthur and his sword in the stone.'

'Is not!' He was furious. 'I should know, my ancestors were the Keepers of the Stone for centuries!'

'Your ancestors were sheep herders and raiders who lived in sod huts,' Oliver said. 'I believe they were actually kicked off the island for their lawless ways, because they couldn't stop with the blood sports. The McClouds of Scarp are the ones who gave all Scottish clans a bad name.'

'The original Nac Mac Feegles!' Timothy was still chortling, reluctant to let go of the literary barbs.

At this last thrust, Sandy stood up and stalked out of the room, his kilt swishing against his legs. As the others still giggled and bitched amongst themselves, I too left, but quietly, without inviting their nasty attentions.

....

There wasn't a great deal of cell reception on this island so far away from civilization, but I managed to find a spot in a corner of the attic down the corridor from our room. I wasn't phoning home this time. I was phoning the one person who might understand what I was going through.

How had Hugh allowed this to happen? He'd known what I would be getting into here on this island; he'd expressed concern but had not done a thing to stop this train wreck from hurtling on its course.

'Dara,' he said. I heard movement over the phone, then the clicking of a door closing in the background. 'You made it then?'

'Hugh.' I breathed out a heavy sigh. 'What the frig have you gotten me into?'

He hesitated before answering. 'It's not as bad as it could be, that's something anyway.'

'Oh?'

'Yes.' His voice began to warm with enthusiasm. 'I heard that the Competition isn't to be a bloodbath, just a theoretical challenge. That's a very good thing, wouldn't you agree? I'm certainly relieved for you.'

'Oh, yes, there's a chance I won't be killed in the challenge, that is certainly a load off my mind. But not to say it's a certainty, for you haven't met this crowd.'

He laughed as if my sarcasm hadn't made it through the phone line. 'Look, this will all turn out okay,' he said in a jollying-along kind of voice. 'You just keep your head down and soak up what you can while on Scarp. You don't need to worry about competing – leave that for the others.'

'I have no intention of trying to best any of them, believe me,' I said. I turned to face the wall and wrapped my free arm around myself. 'But they already hated me before they even met me. I thought you said there was no prejudice against half-bloods here in Scotland.'

'Yes, hmmm,' he said. 'Well, if you'd gone to my own community, as we had originally planned, there isn't. Your fellow students are not from the Hebrides, unfortunately. The Isle of

Lewis and Harris is an anomaly though, of course, as you've discovered.'

'And Johanna, what's up with her?' I whispered now, for fear of being overheard. 'She's a friend of Cate's. Why has she sent me here, what's her real agenda?'

Hugh was obviously taken aback. 'There's nothing to fear from Johanna,' he replied at last, amazement in his voice. 'She is one of the most reasonable, level-headed people you'll ever meet in the Kin. She's one of the good guys, Dara.'

Our conversation petered out after that, for I couldn't accept his hearty endorsement of Johanna or his positive spin on my situation. Chills went up my spine as I hung up. No matter how much he insisted, I could not for one minute believe the elder meant me well.

....

'God, that was tense!' Fergie burst through the door and threw herself on her bed, the iron springs creaking. 'I'll be so glad when all this is over, but it's only just begun.' She sat on the cot with her head in her hands, allowing her hair to hide her face.

I'd just changed into my flannel PJs and heavy wool socks, trying to get up the nerve to crawl between the cold covers.

'Such a bloody nest of vipers,' she added, her voice muffled. 'What have I signed up for?'

I sat cross-legged on my own bed with the blankets wrapped around my shoulders, watching her despair with cool eyes. In her desperation to avoid the negative attention of the Kin, she had thrown me under the bus with no thought as to my welfare. She had totally ignored me at supper, yet I remembered how she'd shown herself to be a bit of a rebel in helping me smuggle the medallion on to Scarp. There were bits about her that I couldn't help but like; I even liked that she got annoyed when she thought I was lying about knowing how to use magic after she'd given me assistance. Fergie had guts, although she didn't realize it herself. If we'd met under different circumstances, away from the sphere of the Kin, say in a bar on George Street on a Friday night, we'd probably have a lot in common.

'Fergie,' I began, but hesitated.

She lifted her head a little and peeked through her mass of curls. 'What?'

'How well do you know all of them?'

'The Kin?'

'Yeah.'

'The witch community in Scotland is small enough,' she said with a shrug. 'You meet up at the solstice gatherings, things like that. Timothy and Pauline, I've run into them a lot over the years. Why?'

'Well,' I began, trying to find the words so as not to cause offense. 'You're not really like them down there, the rest of them. Are you? I mean, you didn't really join in to the meanness, the tearing each other down.'

'You're talking about the utterly bitchy displays of bad behavior?'

We both giggled a little, and this shared laughter lightened the mood. After a moment she looked up at me again, apprehensively this time, as if wondering how much she could trust me.

'Believe me, that's what I expected of the Kin,' I said, allowing a tinge of bitterness to creep into my voice. 'You're talking to a half-blood, remember? Growing up, my Dad's legitimate family took every opportunity they could to let me know I didn't belong.'

She nodded with understanding, then she loosened up enough to share a little of her own story.

'You may have noticed my background is a little different from them downstairs,' she said. 'My Mum and Dad aren't rock stars or models or trust fund babies or even on the Council of Elders. Hell, I've not seen him for fifteen years. He got himself banished for some drunken foolery, and Mum, well, she tried her best, but the magic life's not so easy when you don't have money behind you. She's made a living reading cards, but half of it's fake. She lost the heart for magic when m'Dad left.'

I'd never heard tell of members of the Kin who weren't fabulously wealthy and entitled; Fergie may have been the first one I'd ever met. I leaned forward on the bed, my elbows on my knees.

'How did that work? I mean, did you go to the same schools as the other Kin kids?'

'Nah,' she said, shaking her head. 'There's not so much organized Kin in Glasgow, they all want to live in hoity-toity Edinburgh. Growing up, we had an after-school program run by a pair of elderly witches round the corner from where we lived, that's where I picked up all my knowledge. Hedge Witchery, really, that's all it is.'

'So how did you come to be here?'

'Johanna,' Fergie said simply, looking at me straight in the eye. 'She insisted. That witch scares me half to death, but when she tells you to do something, you do it, no matter how much you don't want to.'

Johanna again. 'She must think you have potential.'

Fergie sighed. 'That's what she said, and she also said I needed this experience to bolster my confidence. Don't see that happening yet.'

We snuffed out the candles soon after that. I was exhausted from my travel and the trial – had it all taken place in the same twenty-four hours? Felt more like a week had gone by.

A thought struck me as my body slowly relaxed enough to allow sleep in. Fergie's situation was not so very different from my own. We were both far out of our comfort zones, like fish out of water. I began to understand a little of her harsh behavior towards me when she deflected the attention of the Kin towards me; I recognized the absolute and sheer terror that lay behind it.

The fear of the bullied.

The last thought I remember having that night was the medallion. I would have to come up with a solution to hide it properly on the island somewhere. Fergie had already gone out on a limb for me once, and with this delicate truce between us, I couldn't ask more from her.

10

Lying in the darkness the next morning in that timeless space between sleep and waking, I was conscious of a ringing sound coming from a long way off, but loud enough to reverberate through the stone walls. When it rang again, I recognized it as the sound made by a large gong.

I looked over to where Fergie's body was still lying in bed.

'Fergie,' I said. 'Fergie! Do we have to get up now?'

'Urghhh,' she said as she lifted her head. 'Is it feckin' morning already?'

She stretched and then pushed herself off her cot.

'Better make a move on,' she said. 'Or the gruel will be cold.'

She shoved on her jeans and sweater where she had left them on the chair last night and we took turns scrubbing our faces at the sink with the scratchy face cloths and towels supplied.

The flagstone floor was freezing even through my socks, but hunger was driving me, so I forced myself to move quickly.

Downstairs the Refectory was cold and dark still, despite the fire burning, and the windows showed not a hint of sunlight so early on a January morning. I was glad of the heavy socks inside my boots but shivered as the damp-cold came through the seat of my jeans.

Turned out breakfast was a serve-yourself buffet of porridge and berries and cream, not too bad really, for the fruit was sweet and the cream unpasteurized.

We all seven of us sat together in the same places as we'd taken at supper the previous night. It was a silent meal, and although I was still bursting with questions about Scarp, I couldn't ask this crowd for fear of being held up to ridicule. I would have to trust my questions would be answered in time.

Besides, none of us seemed to be morning people with the exception of Sandy. He must have been up and out with the sheep long before the dawn, for again he brought the freshness of the outside world into the castle with him, along with a strong whiff of manure.

The large clock behind me said it was ten minutes to eight as I scraped the last of the porridge from my bowl. There was no coffee, but I helped myself to a mug of strong tea from the sideboard, and as I sipped it standing up, I watched Fergie finish her silent meal. Her red curls stood out fluffed all over her head this morning, and I saw that without all the make-up coating her face she was quite pretty, her skin creamy and flawless under the freckles, and her eyes looked softer.

....

I found Joanna's lair upstairs, across from the grand stairway in the newer, Victorian wing of the castle, and I knocked on the heavy panelled door with some trepidation. I had almost been dreading this interview with Johanna – those hours of staring at her across the court room may have skewed my opinion of her and my fear for her. Yet, now that I didn't feel so alone, now I felt I had Sandy and to some extent Fergie on my side, I felt better about a lot of things.

'Enter.' That was Johanna's voice, so I turned the large crystal and brass doorknob and let myself in.

Oh, now this was a room. I forgot my fears as I took in these surroundings, for it was everything a room should be. Tall bookcases covered almost every available wall space, with warm wooden panelling everywhere else except for the three long windows arching toward the ceiling where wide moldings offset intricately carved plaster rosettes. Two chandeliers hung from the ceiling, unlit at present, but there was no need for their candles here as electric lights blazed from sconces and from the green banker's light on her desk. A fire burned in the grate and its heat filled the room, while a red carpet warmed the entire floor.

It reminded me a little of the library back in our family home, how it used to be in the days when Mom was still around before the house started falling apart, but Johanna's room was much grander.

Still dressed in her black robe, Johanna sat behind the biggest desk I'd ever seen, folding down the cover of a lap top as I entered. So there must also be wifi here along with the iffy cell reception, a fact I stored away in my mind for later consideration.

'Good morning, Dara,' she said. There was no trace of welcome in her severe Scottish accent, but there was no anger or distaste or mockery either. 'Please sit.'

I took the large leather armchair she indicated; it was a high winged one, the kind that sort of hugged you when you sat in it. She regarded me silently for a long moment.

'You must have many questions,' she said finally.

I nodded dumbly, unable to trust myself to speak. Oh yes, I had a lot of questions and they weren't all about the island and the Competition and how my complete lack of training in all things magic was not in my favor. I wanted to know what she, as Cate's friend, had planned for me, and why she had really brought me here. I had to know if she hated me as much as Dad's wife did. But I didn't know how to broach the subject.

'I understand Hugh did not have the opportunity to explain about Scarp yesterday,' she observed. 'The bus and ferry schedule did not allow for delays.'

She continued on, not giving me space to air my questions. 'You see, what Hugh perhaps did not have a chance to tell you, is that Scarp is a holy place for the Kin,' she continued. 'It is the center of our world. In my position of Chief Elder of the Scots Kin, I am also the Master of Scarp.'

Johanna was watching me very carefully as she spoke. 'This is... a very special environment here. A very magical place,' she added. 'Which is why we allow our most promising young witches to study here, in order to absorb the island's atmosphere.'

'I thought it was all about the Competition,' I said cautiously. The Competition were my biggest worry for first Hugh had warned me, then Fergie. If Johanna really was in cahoots with my father's wife, then it seemed entirely rational that she might have gotten me here with the sole intent to have me killed or worse, even if she said there was to be no violence.

'Oh, yes, that's an important part of the Scarp year for many,' she said with a slight smile. 'Every year, as I said last night, PANEC takes on apprentices from all over the Kin world, and we choose our delegate from amongst those attending Scarp. Of course, only one can apprentice, but everyone here has the opportunity to do whatever they wish with their lives once they finish their term. Time spent at Scarp is a ticket to any career you wish in the Kin world.'

She was making it sound like a positive thing for me to be here on the island.

'Hugh said only the best and brightest of witches come to Scarp,' I said, still hesitant, fearful of hearing mocking laughter in response.

Johanna nodded. 'And you're wondering why, with your lack of training, you are here?'

'Instead of having my magic bound for the things I did, yes.'

Even though I was looking down at my lap, I could feel her cool gray eyes on me.

'Dara, what you did... how can I say this? Yes, you made wrong choices, but I didn't feel we should allow that to define the rest of your life. You show great promise, a wonderful and unique power, and can contribute much to our world. That is one of the reasons why, in the face of considerable protest, I made the decision to bring you here.'

These words made me sit up straighter. I lifted my head, and could see that she wasn't being mean or sarcastic or making fun of me.

'In your particular case, the Kin is certainly taking a risk,' she said. 'Under normal circumstances and for a witch who had the benefits of a classical education, the incidents of last December would call for immediate action on our part to prevent a similar occurrence. Indeed, there was one such, years ago... and we didn't take appropriate action at the time. That was a very sad story, but it is relevant to your experience, and it goes a long way toward explaining the backlash against my decision to bring you here.'

She drew in a deep breath before continuing on a different vein.

'This sorcerer, Willem de Vriejz,' she said slowly. 'During the Inquiry, you gave evidence that he entered your mind, burrowed in to it, so to speak.'

I nodded, swallowing. Willem, the failed sorcerer who had gotten me into that whole mess in December. If it wasn't for him, I'd be settled away on Hugh's family estate, learning the basics of magic properly. Well, okay I had gotten myself mixed up with him, but I was only guilty of making bad choices, as Johanna so kindly put it. My heart was beginning to thaw towards her.

'A similar thing happened, as I said, years ago, to a witch with more experience than you,' she said. 'Different times, different players, but we weren't aware and the outcome wa s... bad. Sorcerer's magic can be a terrible thing in the wrong hands, which is why they are so strict with their moral regulations.'

'Willem didn't make it through,' I said. 'He's not a licensed Sorcerer.'

'No, he was caught cheating, and that is unforgivable to the Sorcerer's Guild,' she agreed. 'However, he is a sorcerer in all but name, with the full power and training behind him, yet not bound to their moral code. He's been on the run for years.'

She sighed as she looked at the fire, and a look of irritation crossed her face. 'I do wish the Sorcerer's would clean up their own messes instead of leaving it to the Kin each time.'

'At any rate.' Her face was calm again when she turned back to me. 'I believe Hugh explained about your need to heal from your encounter with that wizard. Willem burrowed himself deeply inside of you, and we will do extensive testing after you've had sufficient time to get well, to ensure that there are no lingering holes under the scar tissue. What he did to you was reprehensible.'

I nodded in agreement, a little embarrassed, truth be told, although I'd already laid it all out in painful detail for the Inquiry. This was a more intimate setting, just me and Johanna, and I had to look her in the eye.

'About the Competition,' I said, partly to change the subject. 'I guess I'm not expected to take part in it, right? I mean, look what I'm up against.'

And Fergie said people had died in these wars.

'Of course you will,' Johanna replied, her eyebrows raised in surprise. 'You need this atmosphere, all of it, as I said. I think you will find the competitive atmosphere will spur your learning.'

She must have sensed my discomfort, for she leaned forward. 'Just concentrate on developing your own self,' she said. 'Don't worry about the politics.'

I nodded again, but without conviction. It was easy for her to say, perhaps, but she hadn't witnessed the warm-up exercises in the Common Room last night.

Johanna sighed and sat back into her chair. 'I am well aware that you were wronged by Jon, your father,' she said. 'He of all people, should have recognized the need to help you deal with your power.'

'I think Cate had a lot to do with that.' The words were out of my mouth before the thought registered in my brain, but I didn't try to take them back or lessen the sting. Johanna might be a friend to the bitch, yet I had to lay blame squarely where it belonged.

'Perhaps.' Her voice was heavy with regret. 'There is still a lot of prejudice against half-blood witches in your home country, I believe. That's unfortunate. However, I feel that Scarp is the best place for you to recover, to allow that part of your mind to scab over, so to speak, to let it heal from within without disturbance.'

So I was to heal while at the same time learning how to wield my power and competing against my terrifying class-mates? I didn't see how it would be possible.

'And I am staking my own reputation on your rehabilitation and performance, based on my assessment of you.'

Was it in fact her own assessment, or was it Cate's sly suggestions whispered down the telephone line?

'You don't feel too pressured, then? You realize that, at any hint that this is not successful, we will be forced to renege on this agreement,' she said. 'And that means returning to the recommendations of the others of the Kin Council from yesterday.'

Damned if I do, and damned if I don't, in other words. There was no way I could win in this situation; either I would be destroyed in the Competition by those vicious Kin, or I would prove myself to be unworthy. Why not just bind my magic now and have it over with, I wondered bitterly even as I realized that my entire future lay in the hands of this woman.

'But on the other hand,' I said, not wanting to give that dark possibility a chance of life. 'If I survive the Competition... and can develop my powers, do everything I need to do, I could actually find a place working with the Kin?'

Johanna allowed herself a small smile. 'Oh yes. Provided also that you fully heal from your entanglement with Willem.'

'How will I know? I mean, if I've fully recovered?'

'He won't be in your brain.'

'Hugh said there might be residual ... illusions.' Like the auditory hallucination I'd experienced on entering the island.

She nodded. 'Yes, more than likely. Have you experienced anything so far?'

If I told her the truth right now, what action would she take? I could tell her that I'd felt the whispers in my head right before I entered the castle, just the previous evening. It may have been just my imagination, a side effect of all the magic in the air combined with my own exhaustion. I could tell her, but then what would happen?

'No,' I told her. 'There's been nothing.'

Besides, Hugh said the hallucinations would only be temporary and harmless.

She cleared her throat discreetly and opened her laptop again. 'Well, if that is all...'

'Just... one thing?'

Johanna looked back up at me.

'Last night, the others were talking about different kinds of magic. Dragon Magic, Mind, Hedge Witchery even, and I can't remember what the others were. Seems like they each have an affinity to one or the other. I'd never heard of all this before.'

She looked at me long and hard before continuing in a very kind voice. 'These special affinities are mostly a result

91

of nurture, as opposed to nature. A witch is usually trained in one or the other from their early years, depending on the background they come from, so this will be the magic form they practice as an adult.'

'Do you... do you think I have one? A special affinity?'

'Have you noticed anything yourself?'

I thought about it, then shook my head.

'Because of your special circumstances, you have not yet had the opportunity to delve into the reaches of your innate power. This exploratory work is usually done in the early years, and I fear you will have enough on your plate with learning the basics here on Scarp. I expect that any special talents you have will arise in the course of your work. But you are a peculiar case, having had no training. It will be interesting to see which form of magic you gravitate towards.'

She stood then, indicating that my interview was over. 'Anything further?'

I stood too. 'Yes, one more thing,' I said, then hesitated. She hadn't bitten when I'd blurted out Cate's name before, but I still needed to know what part my father's wife had played in having me sent to Scarp, to find out if there was a nefarious reason behind her action. Why had she wanted me to come here? There had to be an ulterior motive; I had to sound her out somehow.

'Cate said to send her best regards.' I kept my voice casual.

The small smile on Johanna's face changed not a whit; I could not read her expression at all.

'Dear Cate.' She left it at that, and I had no way of telling if Johanna was friend or foe.

'Oh, also,' she said as I opened the door to leave.

I turned to face her.

'I will remind you that you should use no magic here on Scarp, as the ley lines will interfere with it. The only exceptions are in the specially sanctioned areas with your tutors,' she said. 'And that means none. No charms, no... hiding spells, for example, nothing.'

I froze. Did she know? I was left speechless, searching her face but it remained blandly pleasant, no clue as to whether she was aware of Fergie's magical help.

'Is there anything you'd like to tell me?' I realized I had been standing before her for a second too long.

I could only shake my head and mumble something about understanding, but after I'd left her office, I sank down on the nearest hard chair in the hallway.

Why had she so pointedly added that - was she even now aware of the coin's existence, or of the spell Fergie had cast to hide it? I broke out into a sweat in that chilly corridor, although it was such a small thing, really.

Small, but not unimportant, for if Fergie's hiding spell were discovered, the consequences could be dire for both of us. I could take responsibility for myself, but there's no way I could allow Fergie's future to be compromised. This was her ticket out of the slums of Glasgow, and I was determined to help her in any way I could.

Or at least, I would try my best not to screw things up for her.

11

I found her in the library, seated at a table flicking through a thick book in a listless, woebegone manner. She seemed happy enough for the interruption.

'Listen.' I repeated Johanna's last words to me. 'I think she knows about the coin, and the hiding spell you put on it.'

Her face had slowly blanched as I spoke. 'Damn,' she said, her shoulders hunching. 'I can't risk that. How the hell'd she find out? I had it covered up pretty well. Unless...'

She shot a suspicious look at me. 'Did you tell her? Dara, did you rat on me?'

'No! I wouldn't do that.'

'Did she... read your mind?'

'Fergie, I promise she didn't get anywhere near my mind, I swear. Believe me, I know what that feels like.'

I sure did. It had been bad enough when Hugh could read my mind like a TV screen – I'd learned to shut that broadcast down pretty fast. But when Willem had wormed his way into my head last month, touching me with his cold little fingers,

94

searing a part of me deep within that might never heal, that responded to him even when I saw the depths of destruction he'd wrought in my home town – well, yes, I would know if that happened, and Johanna had not crossed any boundaries.

'Right,' Fergie replied slowly, suspicion warring with fear on her face. 'I doubt that. You must have given her some reason to suspect, and you're no match for the likes of Johanna.'

She slammed her book shut. 'What possessed me to put that stupid spell on it in the first place? What was I thinking?'

'You were helping me,' I pointed out.

'Yes, and then it turned out you didn't need my assistance, you've got enough power of your own if you would just bloody well use it!' She stood up. 'Well, you're going to have to find something else for that medallion, I'm no longer involved in this.'

With that, she withdrew into herself, and after a moment opened up her eyes.

'That's it then, not my problem anymore. The hiding spell's totally erased.'

'Just like that? No hocus-pocus with the cloth, you just blink your eyes and it's gone?' Kin magic could be so quiet, so unimpressive, unless you knew what was happening.

'Shouldn't even be a smidgeon of my magic on it anymore.' She lifted the book from the table and turned to go.

'I need to hide it now, can you help me find a spot where it won't be found?"

'What, in the castle?'

'Or anywhere on the island. There must be some out of the way little spot I can put it till I leave again.'

'As if!'

'What, you won't help me now?'

'No!' she said. 'I'm not getting my magic prints on anything illegal here on Scarp. I shouldn't have done it in the first place. I don't even know if I can trust you!'

'Maybe there's somewhere outside, come with me to have a look,' I cajoled her. Yes, I was begging her.

'As for the rest of the island, I haven't a clue. I only know there are sheep out there, and that's enough to make me stay within the grounds.'

'Don't tell me you're scared of sheep!'

'I'm no' afraid of sheep,' she hissed at me. 'But the damn things are evil. Can't you see it in their eyes? Niver cross a sheep, they're the devil's own breed.'

....

My blossoming friendship with Fergie appeared to be withering before it had a chance to thrive, and I knew it would take some work to get her back on side with me. However, I had to prioritize, and hiding the medallion was the most important thing on my list right now.

Sandy. He would help me, not that I wanted to involve him, but I had no choice; he knew the island. It was just a matter of finding him.

The winding castle passages eventually led me back to the room I shared with Fergie, and I dug deep into my carry-on where I'd buried the medallion.

Even before I touched it, I could feel the power it held now that the hiding spell had been removed. Here in this land where magic was all around us, the metal glowed through the mess of clothes in the case.

Yet it didn't burn my hand – the golden medallion pulsed as if it had a life of its own, and it was warm and almost liquid on my skin, the letters and figures impressed on it now clearer than ever, as if I was looking at it through a magnifying lens.

Brin the elf had returned it to me before I left. He'd spent Christmas with us at Richmond Cottage, in fact he now appeared to be a semi-permanent fixture in our family home, having won the heart of Aunt Edna while making himself useful painting the ceilings and doing other renovation jobs which made use of his height and long limbs. I wondered what he was up to, how he was adjusting to his new world, and how he would make a living when he had no social insurance number, no identity papers. He was a non-entity, but he still had to eat, and living with my family could not be a long-term plan. Once it all came out that I'd allowed him to escape into the real time out of his home in Alt, I was surprised that the Witch Kin hadn't forced him back. It had something to do with supernatural refugee status and the recent Rights of Being legislation. I could only hope they would follow through with their promises of assistance to him, so that he and my best friend Alice could be together forever.

I'd spent hours searching the coin for clues over the endless Christmas week, that week of time when time stands still and you're never really sure what day it is. It hadn't told me anything, though, never again gave me a hint of Mom, not like the night Willem had torn the veil between Alt and real time and I'd felt her presence almost as if she'd been next to me.

A Google search had not turned up anything about the letters embossed on both faces of it; they were similar to Nordic runes but not the same, and that's as far as I got with it.

I hadn't wanted to take the medallion with me when I left to go to the Inquiry on the second of January, but Brin had insisted, going on and on about how hard won this had been and how I might find answers, and even if the worst came about I would still have it on me, and it might make me remember even if the Kin wiped my magical memory. I had to agree because he was so fervent he looked like he was getting ready to break out into a song about it all, and elf songs are the worst. At the time, I'd have agreed to almost anything to avoid that; now, I was feeling such homesickness that even an elf song would have been joy to my ears, because it would mean that I was home.

....

And there was Sandy, doing up his winter coat and donning his hat, preparing to go outside. What perfect timing.

Even in this cool weather, his knees were bare beneath his kilt.

'Hi.' I skipped up next to him and started to do up my own jacket. I kept it on in the castle because the stone walls made everything so damp and cold. 'Going out?'

He whirled around to face me.

'Dara,' he said in a less than welcoming tone. 'Yeah, I'm just heading out again to the barn.'

We both looked out the door he had just opened. The mists of the early morning were dissipating under the weak northern sun, but still lay thick in the shadowy corners, blurring the garden walls.

'You probably don't want to join me, it's a messy business,' he said firmly.

'I don't mind a bit of animal smell,' I said as I went out the door ahead of him. 'Besides, you probably could use someone else out there with you, it's still a little misty out there. Don't want you getting lost, right?'

'I won't get lost,' he said, looking a little discomfited. 'I'm just going to the barn, as I said. Really, I think you should stay back here.'

'It's not a problem,' I assured him. I could probably hide the coin in the barn, surely there would be a hidden corner in that large building, in which case I wouldn't even need to ask Sandy for assistance.

Outside the door were two large tin pails. He hefted one in each hand, brushing aside my offer to help.

'I'm fine, I don't need you,' he insisted as he set off through the garden.

I followed him in silence till we reached the garden wall, then once we were shot of the castle I began to speak again. He'd been so friendly to me last night, but right now his mood seemed sour.

'Are you okay?' I asked him tentatively.

The barn was a distance from the castle proper, through a vegetable patch lying fallow for the season, past a root cellar dug deep into the peat. He paused and set down the pails, chafing his hands together. The handles of the buckets were little more than thin wire. I grabbed one with both hands, glad of my protective felted mittens which cushioned the sharpness, for the metal pail and its contents were heavy.

He looked at me darkly but this time accepted my help, and we set off again through the thick wet air in the direction of the wooden raftered barn.

'I shouldn't take it out on you,' he said finally. 'You're not part of them. They made me so angry.'

'They're a pretty rotten bunch, all told.'

He shook his head. 'But they'll see. I'll show them, and we'll be all the harder on them, the bastards.'

An odd answer, and I was going to question him further when at last the barn hove into view, but I saw we weren't alone. A figure lingered by the entrance, one dressed in a robe, brown this time, unlike Johanna's black one, with its hood up against the damp.

'Who's that?' I shifted the pail into one hand and pointed with my free one.

The person must have heard my voice, for sound carried easily through the moisture-laden air and the figure looked up sharply before slinking away around the side of the barn.

Yet our eyes had made brief contact through the mist, and my heart dropped to my boots for the second time that day. I recognized the set of the head, the pale eyes boring out from beneath the hood, and I thought I saw a terrible, thin smile. If this was right, then I had reason to feel afraid, very afraid.

Willem the failed sorcerer, last seen disappearing into the veil of Alt on a wooden steamship in the midst of a snow storm an ocean away, was now here on Scarp, the holy island of the Witch Kin.

I dropped the pail, wanting dearly to chase after him and tackle him down and beat him within an inch of his life but I found my feet refusing to follow instructions. 'That's... that's...' I sputtered.

'That's the shepherd,' Sandy said dismissively. 'You'll have to excuse him, he's a hermit and really doesn't like people much, he says they give him headaches.'

'Are you sure about that, Sandy? He looked... he looked familiar.' I swallowed my next words, for if it really had been Willem then as sure as shooting, I was the one who had attracted him to the island. Sandy was so upset about the mockery he'd experienced last night at the hands of the others, that perhaps he wasn't concentrating, and was seeing only who he expected to see.

'I'm sure you've never met him before,' Sandy said, and then went on to scold me. 'But I wish you'd listened to me and stayed in the castle. Do you see now why I didn't want you to come? You've probably scared him off and I won't see him for days again, and I really need to ask him about a ewe who might be in for an early lambing.'

'I need to speak with him.' I could hear the determination in my own voice.

'Not going to happen, never.' Was it my imagination, or was my friend sounding a little apprehensive?

'Can't he make an exception for once? I'm pretty harmless.' If I'd been wrong and it wasn't Willem, then no harm done. I could dismiss the sighting as a visual hallucination, and know that it was just a side effect of my healing.

If, on the other hand, it really was Willem, then it would be good to know what I was up against.

'No,' Sandy said with a shakiness that hadn't been present before, laced with an edge of panic. 'You need to leave him alone, do you hear me? He's a hermit, he hates people, and he won't forgive me if I bring you to him!'

'Okay, okay, calm down,' I said, then crossed my fingers. 'I won't go bothering your hermit.'

As if. I was going to find that shepherd if I had to rake the entire island with a fine tooth comb.

12

I still had an hour before we met for our first class, so I left
Sandy to his animal chores and set off up the hillside in the
only logical direction the shepherd might have taken.

The mist was burning off quickly, and it was becoming
a beautiful clear day; the wind was chilly but fresh on my
cheeks, and hiking the mountain felt good on my body still
recovering from the travel and tension of yesterday. From
here, I could see over the water to Lewis, to the sandy road
and concrete slip which had been shrouded in fog the previous day, and then all along the coast with its white sand
beaches and the purple hills rising to the northeast. Far off
clouds hurried across the sky, but they were white and not
threatening to lower.

Then I saw a strange thing in the landscape, and it took
me a second before I recognized the misplaced landmark.
Below me on my hilly perch lay a flat parcel of land with a
large concrete square spread out on the ground, painted white
around its perimeter with a large white X in the middle.

A helicopter landing pad. An unexpected thing to see in the medievelish world of Scarp, but at least now I'd solved the puzzle of how Johanna had reached the island before us the previous day, and had managed not to be worn out through the stress of public transportation and that bumpy long ride through the mountains of the Island of Lewis and Harris.

I continued on and wandered further than I meant to in my search for the shepherd Willem, following a sheep path across the hillside, and I didn't notice I'd turned a couple of corners until, looking back along my path, I realized the castle was out of sight. Here, there was no sign of human habitation, past or present; I'd almost forgotten about finding anyone by now or returning in time for class, because the heathery scented air had a headiness here in the freedom of these hills and, filled with an inexplicable rush of joy, I continued my meandering way across a stream and on again to the rise of the next slope.

And then I saw something even stranger before me, in the middle of this wild country, a straight sided tower reaching high up into the sky above. It was huge, a man-made structure, built of stones pieced together on a perfectly slanted rise to the heavens, and I could tell by the golden lichen spreading up the north face of it that it was ancient. No windows pierced the sides, I couldn't guess at the purpose of this monument standing on its own little rise away from the mountains which defined the island.

I couldn't not go to it; like a beacon it called me and I forced my way through heather and gorse and loose scree underfoot, ignoring the scratches on my hands from the brambles surrounding the base of the structure like a fairy tale princess's home.

Once there, I laid my hand on the warm stone, feeling the living rock pulse beneath my touch and I rested my cheek against its solid roughness, breathing in deeply of the dry stone smell. I became rejuvenated, empowered, feeling the energy running in my body along ancient paths determined long ago in my genetic witch heritage.

I felt at home for the first time in my life, enervated and renewed with every cell in my body crying out 'At last!'

I don't know how long I stayed like this, totally lost in this unexpected homecoming. I was outside time itself, there on that rocky and brambled hillside, until I dimly became aware of the heat coming from the pocket of my jeans where I'd stuffed the coin and curious, I took it out.

It glowed even in the bright sunlight, the metal sparkling as if it was lit within, and the runic characters were clearer than they'd ever been. More than three dimensional, they were moving and vibrating and morphing before my eyes, as if urgently trying to give me a message. But I couldn't understand their meaning.

Then right beside me, so close I could almost feel their breath on my neck, someone spoke my name.

Dara?

That voice transported me back to hot lazy summer days in our walled garden, a frosty lemonade in hand and Mom prancing, fooling, whirling in Great-Aunt Sadie's flowered dress six sizes too big; and to marshmallows melting in the red mugs full of hot chocolate before the fireplace, and us wrapped in home-made quilts, yet even in the dead of winter she brought sunshine, always sunshine in that voice.

'Mom?'

Dara! My darling, my dear one. That's you finally! How I've missed you.

I whipped around but couldn't see her, not behind the bushes, not on the scree, not by the stone tower.

'Mom, is this you? Where are you? Oh my God, you're alive! I knew you were, oh God, I've missed you too, you don't know how much, for all these years.' I was babbling, yes.

Has it been a long time then? Her voice was sad. *Time passes differently here, I think.*

My hand reached out to the rock wall before me, the warm stone unyielding; windowless, doorless, no way in or out.

'Where are you?' I asked again. 'Are you in there? In the tower?'

Tower? I could hear the confusion in her voice. *I'm here in the ice, it's so cold, Dara, I need your help.*

I stared up at the immensity of the wall before me, then again I began to walk all around it. Surely I'd missed the opening.

'I can't get in Mom,' I said. 'How did you get there, why are you inside the tower?'

Dara, it's not what you think. Get Jon to help. Call Jon, he'll know what to do.

Jonathon de Teilhard. Dad. The man who gave me my genetic magic but not his name; my heart hardened at the very thought of him. He'd driven me to the airport two nights ago, not out of affection but to ensure I got on the plane to the judgement awaiting me in Inverness. No words of love to soothe my fears though he must have known how scared I was feeling, leaving home for the first time with the ordeal looming ahead, no comforting hug as I left to go through Security. Just that hardness in his eye, and a final admonition to do whatever was requested of me and tell the truth and accept the consequences. He didn't tell me outright not to embarrass him further, but he didn't need to. Dysfunctional families each have their own unspoken language, the secret meanings behind the words, meanings forged in skirmishes and arguments and strife and anger till the communication has been winnowed down to a glance, a sniff, a shake of the head. The words no longer need to be said out loud for each player to express his lines.

'Dad is thousands of miles away, Mom,' I said to the stone wall. 'I don't think he'd help even if he was here.'

Give it up, Dara! The two of you are so much the same, you can't see it! She was almost laughing through the tears in her voice. *You two are going to have to work together for a change. I can't reach him from here, don't you understand? I need both of you.*

'I'll find a way in, Mom, I'll get you,' I insisted. I searched again the entirety of the stone tower for a break in its surface, something, anything, but it was too solid.

Perhaps I could climb to the top? I stepped back and looked way, way up to where the sun was just cresting behind the very top of the structure, and I shaded my eyes to peer closely. There might be hidden footholds. So happy was I to hear my mother's voice for the first time in years, so desperate to scrabble my way inside, that I didn't wonder why I could hear her if she was locked inside a solid stone tower.

I rapped a few times to find a hollow spot, perhaps a hidden doorway, but all I got was sore knuckles. 'Help me with this Mom,' I cried. 'Help me get to you!'

It's no use, Dara. You can't reach me where you are. The portal is closing, they're coming back. Get Jon, he'll know...

'Mom?'

And her voice was gone, just like that. I raced around the base again, searching high and low, and then I knew it was no good. Had her captors silenced her? What portal was she talking about?

I slumped against the stone wall, the tears spilling out and raining down my face unchecked, overcome by that terrible deep feeling of loss, of losing my mother all over again. I let my body slide down until I sat on the hard ground beneath it, staying in close contact with the wall and unable to tear myself away from it.

After the flow of grief had passed I came back to myself slowly, and with this return I realized the unlikelihood of what I believed had happened.

Mom locked in a stone tower on Scarp, and I just happen to be sent here? No, maybe in fiction, but not in real life, such a thing was not believable.

Yet I had long suspected Cate of having a hand in my mother's disappearance and she'd made a point of telling me what a good friend Johanna was. And Johanna ruled this island. It was not such a foolish leap in thought as it might seem.

Was I the next to be caught in Cate's web? The next one to be trapped in the tower? It hardly seemed feasible, but if it had happened to Mom...

I took a deep breath and sat up, forcing my mind to work in a logical fashion. I had happened upon this stone tower in the middle of nowhere, and I'd immediately felt comforted, at home, as if I'd reached the center of my own universe after living all my life on the edges of it. I'd heard her voice like she were standing right next to me and we conversed; it wasn't a memory or an echo, it was her and she was here.

My glance fell to the medallion still clutched in my hand and my fingers opened slowly. It glowed and sparkled in the sun, the magic unfettered on this island, but the runes were quiet now. Mom had somehow imprinted herself on this item all those years ago, yet how? She was Normal, supposedly, with no magic in her genes.

Perhaps the coin's magnified power had allowed the solidity of the stone to evaporate so that me and she could speak, the soundwaves travelling effortlessly on some supernatural band width?

I scrabbled to my feet again and searched, but there was still no way into the tower that I could see. I leaned against it for a long moment, the warmth of the late morning quickly ebbing out of the stone. I would return here, but I was going to need assistance.

This was as good a hiding place as any, here at the base of this landmark. There were no signs that people frequented the place, no paths worn through the brambles at its base save that which I myself had cut through. Mom's medallion would be safe here.

I scrabbled in the dirt by the bottom of the stone structure till I found a crevice and slid the coin into it, mounding pebbles from the scree over it so I would easily find this hiding place again. I definitely couldn't risk having it found and confiscated now, not for all the world.

13

I was late for my first ever class on Scarp. I raced back to the castle in a panic, yet at the same time my feet felt as light as the cool sun as they flew over the hillside paths, my heart infused with joy and hope. My mother, long thought to be lost to me, was on this island, and I would somehow get into that doorless stone tower and release her from whatever demons held her captive.

Just as I reached the back entrance of the castle, my steps faltered for I saw where this train of logic inevitably led to. This island belonged to the Kin and Johanna, and anyone held here would be here with the full knowledge of her. My mother was trapped by the Kin themselves.

She'd asked me to tell Dad, but how could he not be aware of her prison? He was the leader of the Kin back home – a small community yes, but they were an old family and had been established there for hundreds of years, and they kept to the old ways. The Avalon Witch Kin were not an insignificant body in the world of witchery.

So it had to be Cate, all along, the horrid wife of my father. What had finally set her off to be threatened enough by Mom to lock her in a tower on this lonely island off Scotland's north coast? And how could he not know?

And why did she allow me to be sent here? I had no doubt she could have stopped the process at any step along the way.

I would have to walk very carefully through this twisted maze of intrigue and not allow myself to be captured in the same way. The clouds were lowering now, covering the sun, and the wind stepped up, cutting through my jacket. Shivering into my hunched shoulders, I hurried back into the shadows of the castle.

The man in the front of the room stopped his mono-logue mid-sentence and stared in dramatic outrage at me as I opened the door, intent on sneaking into the back of the room. It didn't help that the door emitted a loud and painful squeak, or that there were only seven of us in his class. My absence had been noted.

'What is this?' He spoke like a member of the English Royals, his accent so sharp it could cut glass, but his voice was a high-pitched whine. It sounded strange coming from such a rotund body. He slapped down the book he'd been holding. The sound echoed off the desk and around the circular tower room.

Everyone else was already present; I could feel their eyes swivel in my direction. I took the last seat in the half-circle surrounding the podium and Professor Durand.

'I'm so sorry,' I mumbled. I glanced over to Sandy at the next desk. He had paper and pens in front of him. I had nothing.

'Did it speak?'

My head jerked up. Did he just...

Yes, he did. He was staring at me, his hands where his hips should be, and a sneer painted on his face. The red 'C' embroidered on his black robe announced he was of the Covenanter persuasion, and my heart sank even further. Not only was I late for his class, but in his eyes I would be the unwanted half-witch who didn't deserve a place here anyway; I could tell by the gleam in his eyes that he had me exactly where he wanted me.

Annoyance flared from deep within me. I didn't care who he thought he was, he had no right to treat me in this fashion. This half-witch was going to fight him back every inch of the way.

'I'm sorry for being late,' I said clearly with my head held high and shoulders straight.

'Who are you?'

He knew damn well who I was.

'Dara Martin,' I said proudly, then added, 'De Teilhard.' It couldn't hurt to throw my Dad's name around, even if he'd never officially given it to me.

Durand sniffed. 'The half-blood.'

I felt no need to respond to that remark.

'The errant half-witch whom Johanna has thrust among us,' he continued. 'The one with the supposedly extraordinary untapped powers. Well, shall we discover the depths of your magical training, then?'

'I haven't had formal training,' I said, as if everyone present didn't know that already.

'Well, Dara Martin, time is wasting,' he said as if I hadn't spoken. 'Come up to the front, and we'll take this opportunity to show everyone what wonderful talents you have.'

It may have been Win who snickered first, opening the door to the round of tittering that followed. They were enjoying this, the Kin students, and they sat back in their seats to watch me be flayed alive by this despicable witch.

I glanced around at the semi-circle of my cohorts as I stood. Fergie was studiously checking her manicure, while Sandy, bless him, peeked up at me and gave a small smile of encouragement. It felt a long way up to Durant's desk, but was really just a few short steps.

'Sit.' He pointed to the seat behind the desk, so that I would be on full display to the others as he carried out his humiliation.

'You have absolutely no formal training in magic, you say? I can't imagine what Johanna is thinking, sending you to waste my time.' He was enjoying his role of tormentor, throwing himself into the spirit of it all like an actor in a badly written pantomime.

He gave a snort and finally looked at me fully for the first time, his eyes suspicious as he took my measure. He sniffed with distaste as if there was a bad odor assaulting his nose. 'So you know nothing about magic, eh?'

'I didn't say that, I just haven't had training...'

'No magic,' he interrupted me as he announced to the class. 'I am sent an untrained neophyte and am expected to teach her the ABCs of Mind. Hah!'

More titters followed, but I was gratified to see a dark expression forming on Fergie's face.

'What was Johanna thinking? How could she imagine any-thing good will come of this?'

Pauline muttered something in agreement.

Durand paced, fully playing to his audience now, building them up for the drama of my failure.

'I disagree with the decision of the Inquiry. Rules are rules, and no matter whose bastard offspring she is, this is an inappropriate placement and I intend to make my complaints known. According to the Convention of 1945, she should have had her magic bound, for we don't want to see a reoccurrence on that level again. Memories are short, but we must never forget!'

He was composing his official letter of complaint against Johanna right there and then. I forced myself not to slink down into the seat.

'And to ask me – me! A Witch of my stature! To coddle her along with teachings she should have learned in the nursery. A waste of my valuable time. This is too much. Too much, I say!'

He whirled on his toes, lightly for such a heavy man and leaned in so close to me that I could smell his breakfast egg and coffee. 'Do you know that I hold the title of Grand Master Witch of Pure Mind?' He stood back and watched the effect of his words, his nostrils flaring. Something whistled in his nose.

I'd never heard of such a title of course, although I could tell he thought it was a very important office, and he watched as all this formed on my face.

'You're nothing better than a heathen,' he muttered as he turned back to his desk. 'So, Dara Martin of No Kin, I am to test your limits of practice. Humph!'

I'd never heard anyone actually say that word, but he enunciated it carefully, even to the exclamation point. He was not going to make this easy for me. I sat back in the chair and readied myself. I could hear the others rustling in anticipation.

'Pick up that pen,' he commanded me.

I reached over to take up his writing tool only to have his wooden wand smack sharply on the desk top, missing my fingers with mere inches to spare. For the first time, a look of satisfaction came on his face, especially as mine began to burn with humiliation at this public ill treatment.

'Not with your hand,' he said, sarcasm dripping from his tone. 'Your mind, woman, your mind! That's what you're here for, after all.'

It was a heavy gold pen, the old-fashioned kind with a nib that required hours of practice to perfect its use. The perfectly pretentious tool for a witch like him.

I focused and concentrated, and focused some more. I used to be able to do this no problem, back when I was a kid with a child's flexible mind muscles. Finally, it lifted an inch from the desktop, then two. It hovered there, trembling a little with the effort.

'You can drop it now,' he said with fake patience. 'A poor showing, but you've made your point.'

The next test was a thick old book which, with a nod from him, lifted itself off a shelf and flew to land gracefully in front of me. I glanced from it to him, where he sat looking down his nose at me.

'Open it,' he said, nodding at the tome. 'Page four zero six.'

I didn't make the mistake of using my hand this time, but funnily enough, I'd never attempted to open a book with my mind before. I took a deep breath and bit my lip; how difficult could it be?

This was a different feeling from picking up an object, yet in fact, it didn't turn out to be difficult at all. I pictured the front cover opening like a pirate's chest, the cover revealing all the wonderful secrets inside. Only, these weren't secrets, the book was a dictionary of sorts, filled with magical terms and illustrations of fantastic beasts. I wouldn't mind having a few hours alone with it sometime without Durand looming over me.

The cover opened easily enough, and then like a breeze I rifled through the pages until I found the one he had asked for. He didn't allow me a second to read the contents.

'Close it,' he said shortly. 'You have very bad form. I asked you to open to a specific page, and you were unable to do so, you physically had to flick through the pages to find the right one.'

'But I did it with my mind power. And to be fair, I've never done this before.'

He dismissed my objections with a loud sniff.

'Tell me what is on page three nine three.'

I put the number firmly in my mind as the cover began to open again, asking the book to open to the right page. I was determined not to disappoint him again.

Again the wand cracked down, this time on the book. I winced at the sound, and the book itself seemed to flinch too.

'Did I ask you to open it?'

'Well, I thought you were...'

'No. You have already shown me you are unable to do that simple task,' he said. 'We are moving on to determine the full details of your pathetic lack of education. I am asking you to tell me what are the contents of the book's page.'

'Without reading it?'

'Use your mind!'

I took a deep breath. I was totally out to sea with this one; out of my depths and without a paddle board. And the shark was circling closely around, just waiting for me to put a foot wrong.

I stared at the book lying lifeless in front of me. How could one read a book without reading it? I closed my eyes and imagined sifting through the pages, feeling the softness of the well-thumbed old paper, the smell of the ink still present from the old-fashioned printing press. I thought with longing how I'd rather just be curled up on the sofa in the Common Room with the fire burning in the grate, just me and that book and all the knowledge it held, it telling me its stories and me soaking them up as if the book was an old, beloved friend.

Durand was huffing and jangling the chain of his watch, and I could hear mocking whispers from the others.

But then something happened. Even as I kept my eyes closed, page 393 appeared before me in my mind like a sepia colored photograph. There were words mixed in with the pictures, but at the very top of the page was the heading PANLONG. Beneath it, an illustration of a water dragon from China; as I looked with delight from my mind's eye, the dragon turned to me and gave me a sly grin and a wink.

I laughed out loud with delight and opened my eyes to see Durand's face turning beet red with annoyance.

'Panlong, the Chinese water dragon. That's at the top of the page.'

He harrumphed to cover his surprise.

'Parlor tricks,' he muttered as he sent me a look full of vociferous dislike. He blew his nose strongly into a handkerchief to show his disdain.

But as he took the linen from his nose, he grew very still, and he cautiously sniffed the air. 'What is that?'

I took a hesitant sniff, but all I could smell was the wood burning in the fireplace and the smell of a fusty old witch who rarely bathed, but drawing attention to his lack of hygiene would not earn me brownie points.

His nose quivered, dancing around all directions of the compass until it was pointing right at me.

'You.'

Now what? Was he objecting to the smell of my shampoo or my general air of cleanliness despite the primitive washing facilities of the castle?

'Have you drunk from the Water of the Well?' He sounded truly shocked now, he wasn't just spreading his feathers and squawking like a peacock on a stage. His eyes bore into mine and he leaned across the desk. I heard a collective gasp from the others.

'There is an unmistakable odor of magic coming from you, the smell of the very magic of Scarp.'

I shifted back in my chair without a clue as to what he was talking about, but it sounded like I'd committed a venal sin.

'So you'll claim ignorance about the Courtyard Well?'

'The what?' This came out as a whisper.

'I can see you must have helped yourself to the waters therein,' he said. 'This would be obvious to any witch.'

'I don't know any Well,' I said. Wait – there had been some sort of water feature in a courtyard I'd stumbled upon earlier, but I hadn't touched it, hadn't even known it was a Well with a capital W.

'It is forbidden,' he continued, ignoring my protests. 'The Water can only, should only, be used by advanced practitioners of magic, those who know what they're doing.' He stood before me with his hands folded across his rotund chest.

117

'I didn't go near the Well.' I was starting to feel exasperated with the man.

Professor Durand selected a different wand from a selection hanging on the wall in a case and turned back to me.

'Explain this then,' he said as he touched the wood to my cheek and watched triumphantly as blue static fizzled and cracked all around me.

'Ouch!' I jumped up from the chair, my hand going to my face. 'That hurt!'

'Well?'

'Well what?'

'Do you still claim not to have imbibed the forbidden Waters?'

'Yes! I mean, no, I haven't gone near them.'

'Then kindly explain to me the excess of magic energy emoting from you. How else can you have absorbed so much of the life blood of this island? You do know there is to be no magic practiced except under circumstances dictated by a tutor?'

I stared at him in horror. The medallion was definitely infused with magic and over here on Scarp, in this strange land with no separation between Alt and real, there was nothing to stop its full-on force. Had the medallion charged me up with magic?

At least I'd hidden the thing at the base of that old tower – the area seemed to be little used by people, so it shouldn't be found. And hopefully it wouldn't be, for it could definitely be traced back to me.

'I have no time for this,' Durand was querulously speaking in a low voice, then he turned to me. 'Be off with you then, I refuse to work with one who lies and denies what is obvious. The Kin shall hear of this. Leave, leave now! Everyone, out!'

He flapped his short arms at me and not needing to be told again, I was off through the heavy wooden door like a flash of magic myself.

14

I took off down those circular stairs like a scalded cat and didn't stop till I'd found a nook in the old walls in which to crawl into and hide myself and my fear and confusion and humiliation. What nightmare had I been thrown into? And how could something that felt so good, that beautiful feeling of magic I'd felt from the coin, how could that be so bad in the eyes of Professor Durand?

Not only did the Kin have my mother locked up in a lonely stone tower with no doors or windows, but they'd brought me here too, for seemingly no other reason than to humiliate and torture me. The tears which flowed so easily out on the moor threatened to return.

'Dara?' A soft Scottish accent was whispering my name and someone was blocking the faint light. I looked up to see wide blue eyes looking into my own.

'Sandy.' I sniffed back the tears and wiped my nose on my sleeve.

'Oh, Dara,' he said sadly.

'You'd better not be seen hanging out with me,' I said, my voice still shaky. 'Or they'll go after you too.'

He shook his head and reached in his hand to my shoulder. 'You did amazingly well,' he said softly. 'Under all that pressure.'

'He's a bastard, Sandy. They all are.'

My friend nodded. 'Yes,' he said. He reached into his deep coat pocket and drew out a small tin. He removed the top to show an assortment of real butter shortbread fingers, all half-dipped in chocolate. 'Will this make you feel better?'

I could hug the guy for knowing that butter and chocolate had the potential to solve many of the world's problems, especially the emotionally charged ones.

'Where'd you get them?' I asked as I crammed one into my mouth to let it melt on my tongue.

'I brought supplies with me when I came,' he replied. 'The quality of food here is legendary. Have another, or two.'

Life was already looking brighter.

'But you showed Durand,' he continued. 'Never mind the bit at the end – you really aced that trial.'

I shook my head, my heart starting to slow down now as the adrenalin began to work its way out of my system and the crispy butter biscuits soothed my ruffled pride.

He brushed off the last of the loose blue magic from my hoody, then shook his hands to let the particles float off. Then he looked at me again, an expression of awe on his face. 'What happened? How *did* you get this magic all over you? I can't believe you actually did what he claims.'

'I didn't! I didn't drink at the stupid well, I didn't even stop near it,' I said.

'Where did all that come from then?' We watched as the last of the energy fizzed against a cobweb far above our heads.

'Honestly, Sandy, I don't know,' I said. 'I was just out on the mountain before I came here, and, and something weird happened to me.' I watched him closely. How much could I trust him?

Of all the people on this island, Sandy might be the only one I could confide in. I took a deep breath, wanting to tell all, to unburden myself, but he didn't give me the chance.

'You were out on the hills?' He broke in sharply. 'How far did you go?'

'I came to this stone tower, do you know it? It was the oddest...'

He grabbed my arm before I could finish and hustled me out of my safe nook. He rushed me away from the circular tower and down a dark corridor, little used, judging by the amount of dust on the floor, until we came to a door and he thrust us both in. We were in some kind of medieval broom closet or lavatory, I couldn't tell, but it stunk bad in there and was really dark.

'You didn't go to the Broch?' He hissed, his mouth almost on my ear.

'The *what*?'

'The tower! Did you touch the tower?' The urgency in his whisper was unmistakable.

Touch it? I'd hugged the damn thing when I'd reached it; the memory of the feeling of coming home swam over me again.

'Yeah, sort of,' I said. 'But why? What's wrong with that?'

'We really need to talk,' he said in a firm whisper. 'But not within the walls of the castle.'

···········

He led me out of the closet, down through the stone corridors, along the passage we'd walked the previous evening, and out into the walled garden again. But he didn't stop there – we continued through a door leading out of the stone courtyard, and then out along the beach to a large rock overlooking the sea.

I sat gingerly on the boulder, remembering the rock beast from yesterday, but this one was safe. Or at least, if it was alive, it was sleeping soundly. Besides, the beast had been on the other side of the strait of water. Rocks couldn't swim, could they?

Sandy stood before me, worry etched onto his broad face. 'If you'd touched the broch, that would explain the loose magic on you,' he said. 'Hardly anyone knows about the Broch, and the ones who do know, would be unhappy that you've discovered it.'

'But why? And who built it? What's it doing out there in the middle of nowhere?'

He drew himself up to his full height, which wasn't very much, yet still he had an air of pride as he began his story.

'The Broch was built by my distant ancestors, the clan before the McClouds,' he said. 'Thousands of years ago, that's how long we'd been here on Scarp. The Broch is very special.'

I waited.

'It holds the Crystal Charm Stone,' he said, his pale blue eyes boring into mine.

Timothy, the Englishman, the Southerner, had scoffed at the story of the stone, and so had the others, so much that Sandy had walked off in a rage.

'The Crystal Charm Stone,' I repeated for lack of anything else to say. The others said it was a legend, no more than a fairy tale, but he believed in it strongly.

He nodded solemnly. 'The *Clach Seun*.'

'What's that supposed to be?'

'Ye've niver heard of the *Clach Seun*?'

Why was it with Scottish people that whenever they get their knickers in a knot, their accent became so strong? I'd noticed it with Hugh, and Fergie too. Sandy was beginning to sound like a parody of himself.

'Calm down,' I said, placing my hand on his arm. 'I'm not like the others, okay? I'm not just out to make fun of you. I've never heard of this stone you're talking about before coming here. Have you... seen it?'

He didn't answer, just watched as a slow wave broke upon the pebbled beach, the water catching the sunlight as it trickled back to the sea.

'It's true.' His bottom lip was jutting out in a pout. 'It's not made up. I swear on my clan's name.'

'Why do you think this stone is in the tower?'

'It's not a tower, it's a Broch.'

'Fine. Broch, then.'

'I'll tell you the story.' He sighed soulfully and placed himself on the boulder next to me, staring out to the coastline across the water.

I was getting just a tad impatient. I wanted, no I needed to tell Sandy about my mother locked up in this tower, and to marshal his help in rescuing her, but it looked like I'd have to pay my dues by sitting through his story first. I gave a sigh to match his and grabbed a couple more shortbread from his tin as I prepared to wait, but then, out of the corner of my eye I saw a slight movement on the beach, the tiniest shift of a white granite boulder.

After yesterday's run in with the living rock, it was only natural I gave a start. Sandy hadn't noticed a thing, gazing off into the distance as he was and setting the scene for his story.

'Um,' I said, lifting my feet off the beach as if that would save me. I watched as the boulder moved again, yes it was definitely coming my way, and I recognized the glint as the black eye opened, so like a seal but made of pure living rock.

It was the same beast I'd had the run-in with yesterday, I was pretty sure I recognized the pattern of black and pink markings around its snout, and it was making a beeline straight for me. So they could swim after all or, if not able to float, they might crawl across the sea bed.

'The Crystal Charm Stone, no one knows how it was originally created,' Sandy began in his deep voice, his cadence beating with the wash of the waves upon the stony beach, totally unaware of the small drama taking place right next to him.

I attempted to shoo the creature away but the attention only seemed to encourage it. The beast came right up to me, and I could swear it was sniffing all around me like a cat would. A hungry feline, but I wasn't its prey.

No, the darned rock had its beady eye on my chocolate shortbread! It gave a little mewl (such a small sound from the large boulder) and nudged the hand with the tin in it; it felt like my hand was being pushed with a brick. I carefully lifted the plastic holder out of the tin and set it down on the ground with the remaining shortbread, nudging it over to the beast with my foot.

'The Crystal Charm Stone came from the North Kingdom as the dowry of a princess whom my ancestors captured. So it was brought to the island after a successful raid.' Sandy hadn't noticed a thing.

I watched in silence as the beast slavered and gobbled the chocolate and buttery goodness along with the plastic liner. It was all gone within seconds. The beast swallowed, then gave a small cough, which became a bigger one as it hunched its shoulders like a cat with a hairball stuck in its throat. I watched fascinated, as the creature urged and heaved until the black plastic finally shot out of its mouth, all covered in seaweed and slimy fish scales. The beast then laid down at my feet and leaned against my own rock seat, gave the tiniest yawn and settled back to sleep.

This whole time, Sandy was still jawing on about his ancestors. The legend was that this stone and the princess's magic blood gave power to his ancestors; they became a fierce and marauding tribe holding domination over all the islands in the Hebrides. Rumors of its magical abilities spread abroad and to keep their lodestone safe, they painstakingly built the huge broch without doors or windows and placed the stone inside. For thousands of years, his clan ruled the waters and the land hereabouts, keeping the crystal out of the hands of their enemies.

'So what happened?' I asked, trying not to allow the disbelief color my voice, still keeping a careful eye on the boulder by my side. 'Your clan, they're not so powerful now are they?'

He shook his head. 'It happened on a dark and stormy night. The men of the clan were out raiding on the mainland, down past the Isle of Skye, this was back in the time of King James the First, of Scotland mind, not his weak-minded descendant who inherited the English throne. The organized Witch Kin, they were based in Edinburgh right from the start, and they were jealous of our power. They cast a spell and took control of the stone.'

'They got into the tower?'

He shot me a pained look. 'It's not a tower, I told you, it's a Broch. There's a world of difference.

'And yes,' he continued, nodding his head. 'They found the secret entrance, the only way in, and they took possession of it. And ever since that day, very few know of its existence, only the high-ups in the Kin.'

'And you,' I prodded him, trying to get him to the end of the story.

'Yes, and the remnants of my clan,' he agreed. 'My great-grannie told me the stories when I was a wee lad.'

'So your family just, what? Let it go without a fight?'

'There was a terrible battle, yet neither side won,' he said. 'The McClouds were made strong by living in close contact with the Stone for fifteen hundred years, but they didn't have the sophistication of the Kin and their magic, and it was too much for them to conquer. There was an uneasy compromise made wherein the McClouds would be the caretakers of the Clach Seun, and the Kin would ensure the safety of it for all time.'

'Are you still the keepers?' I tried to keep the growing excitement out of my voice. If he knew the way into the tower... This would make it much easier for Sandy to help free my mother.

He shook his head. 'A couple of hundred years ago, there was another Sandy McCloud, my direct ancestor, he tried to lead an uprising, for the Kin had tried to forbid us from raiding other clans, said it was barbaric behavior. This was the straw that broke the camel's back, as you can well understand, for we had to show strength to other lands else they would come and over-run us. It was our tradition, and the traditions of all the Scottish clans. To make a long story short, the rebellion failed and the McClouds were sent away from their ancestral home in disgrace, and the glory of the Clan McCloud faded quickly, along with the legend of the stone. The Kin have seen to that.

'Yet for all that, the Crystal Charm Stone still recognizes our blood and welcomes us back. It does not care about the Kin's rules.'

The wind was rising, the lowering sun stretched the shadows long, and the air was growing chilled. The gory tale he'd told me was unsettling to my mind, even if half of it was made up. Crystal Charm Stone indeed. I was inclined to agree with Timothy, such a thing was no more real that King Arthur's sword. It smacked too much of nostalgia for a time forgotten and lost, the 'golden age' of man, the expulsion from the Garden of Eden.

'Well, it's a good story, Sandy,' I began.

He looked affronted and not a little hurt. 'You don't believe me?'

'Of course I do! But, it all happened so long ago,' I hastened to say. 'Events become mythologized over time, and while there's perhaps a nugget of truth buried deep inside the story, it's probably grown out of proportion over time. But there's something else about the tow... the broch.'

He stood up, his mouth set in a straight line. 'I'm sorry to have bothered you with my foolishness,' he began formally.

'Calm down,' I said, tugging on his coat and making him sit back down. Christ, I sure had a knack for pissing people off. Sandy was the only person I could almost count as a friend on this island, I couldn't afford to alienate him.

'How would you explain all the excess magic you were carrying this afternoon, then?' He was sulking. 'I'm telling you, it came from touching the Broch, where the Crystal Charm Stone still dwells.'

It came from the power of the medallion, I was sure, but his mention of things kept in the tower was my opening.

'Sandy,' I said, then took a deep breath and plunged in. 'Is it possible that a Normal person, a non-witch could be locked inside the Broch? With the Charm Stone, of course.'

'A human being with no magic capabilities?'

I nodded, but he was already shaking his head.

'No Normal could withstand the power of the *Clach Seun*,' he said with absolute confidence.

I sighed. Him and his stupid legend of a magical stone. I wanted to scream at him – the stone didn't exist, but my mother did, and if she wasn't locked inside this mysterious tower, where could she be?

'You mentioned an entrance into the Broch.' I forced myself to speak slowly, not to let my frustration overflow. 'Where is it?'

He shook his head again. 'That's a secret.'

'But do you know where it is? Sandy, this is really important,' I said, the urgency making my voice tight. 'I need to go inside, to see if my mother is being held captive there.'

'She's not,' he said flatly.

'I heard her voice,' I told him. 'It was coming from inside the broch.'

'Impossible.'

'But the story of the Crystal Charm Stone is possible? You've never even seen it!'

He looked at me sadly, and continued to shake his head.

'How do you know? Have you been there, inside it?' Excitement was taking me anew. I was sure, without a doubt, that Sandy held the key.

He stood up again. 'Dara, your mother is not being held inside the Broch. She's a Normal, isn't she? I told you, there's no way she could withstand the power of the stone, not without having years of exposure to build up her immunity,' he said, kindness softening his voice. 'And you cannot get inside the Broch. Even if you knew how to, the Kin have enough Forbidding spells loaded over the entrance that you couldn't possibly make it through.'

We walked back to the castle together, but worlds apart mentally. I had no way to tell what was on his mind, but mine was furiously working, analysing every word that had been said between us.

He strongly believed in his family's legend, that much was obvious, Sandy believed the tall tale to his very bones, this fairy-tale. I considered the story and wondered where the actual truth might lie, for as I had said, there was at least an ounce of truth in every historical legend passed down through the ages.

I'd felt euphoria as the tower had risen before me, there was no denying that, the feeling of home-coming, of security and happiness. But how much of that feeling had been because of the medallion soaking up the unfettered magic of the island, away from the spells cast by the Kin around the castle which stymied the use of this power?

How much had been because of my mother within the tower? The lightness of being I'd experienced may have come from my subconscious mind and its recognition of her proximity. Surely that was the explanation, the only sane explanation I could accept.

I had to go back, get in there, find the entrance in order to free her.

Before the castle's oak door closed behind me, I looked out and away from the walls of the garden, and up into the lowering clouds. It was almost dark out, but tomorrow would be a fresh start.

'Not long now, Mom,' I whispered. 'It won't be long now.'

15

After lunch, a hurried affair consisting of chunks of homemade bread with hard cheese and a spicy condiment called chutney, Pauline told us we were expected to go to Professor Rasmussen's classroom. Somehow Pauline knew all this, I never saw any schedules posted on a bulletin board or anything. When we got there, we all took a seat around a large lab bench.

Whereas Professor Durand was a cranky, bitchy witch, Herr Rasmussen was another kind of scary. Tall and thin with gray hair that stood all around his head like electrified dandelion fluff, his pale eyes blazed out from behind rimless spectacles, sharp like flint and just as hard; I got the feeling that those eyes saw everything, even things that were meant to be unseen. His laboratory was as spotlessly clean as the white smock he wore.

'Well, look at you all,' he said while we took our seats at the lab benches. He had an odd Nordic accent I couldn't quite place. 'Another fine set of young witches.'

He beamed around the room as he spoke; his smile softened the effect of his eyes. 'But there are seven this year, now that is an interesting occurrence.'

I slouched on my stool to stay out of his firing range after suffering Durand's attack, yet I knew there was little I could do but bear it. Yes there were seven, and it was my fault. I tensed my shoulders in preparation. I could feel him staring at me, those intense eyes honing in on me.

'You,' he said. 'Ms. De Teilhard. You are the little witch from across the ocean, that is correct?'

I looked up at him and nodded. My jaw was set in resignation. Let him torture me. He would eventually lose interest if I didn't play into his hands. Show no fear, I told myself.

'Oh yes, the daughter of Jon de Teilhard, I know him well, from various Councils we have served on,' Rasmussen continued, his manner very chatty and disarming. This didn't put me at ease, not at all but instead caused me to tense further for I had watched Hank the cat back home play with his mice, so I was well-versed in all the feints and games of a torturer. I was expecting the worst. 'And the charming Cate, she is your mother? You do not have the resemblance to her so much.'

'No,' I said, slowly. 'She is not my mother.'

I head a low titter run through the classroom. My ears were starting a slow burn as I heard the dreaded word bastard whispered.

'Ah, yes, yes, yes of course! You are the half-blood Witchling, are you not? Yes, born on the wrong side of the blanket, as they say in English, eh?'

I stared at him as he winked and smiled, as if he didn't even realize how he was insulting me, bringing up my illegitimacy in a room full of Kin, where personal blood lines mattered so much.

I nodded again, barely. 'That's right.'

He must have heard the increased muttering from the others at the half-blood remark, for his face grew severe as he turned around to address them.

'You know what they say about the half-bloods?' he asked, looking around the room at the others as if seeing them for the first time. 'They are the way of the future – yes!'

Someone gasped, I think it may have been Pauline.

His face hardened just the slightest. 'Soon, we will all be a race of diluted witch blood, and I for one believe that is not a bad thing.' He nodded emphatically.

'No more rascism! No more excuses to put another down, to think oneself better than one's fellow. The halflings will merge the races!'

I felt a warmth begin in my chest, like a thawing after a hard winter freeze as my heart melted just a little bit on hearing his words. No one, and I mean no one related to the Kin had ever spoken like this before.

His proclamation was met with stony faces all around the table. He harrumphed into his hand as if remembering who his audience was, and he raised his eyebrows at me. 'Of course, you will find not everyone is of that opinion.'

Rasmussen stood behind the podium at the top of the room, and nodded to indicate that the session had begun.

'Physical Magic,' he proclaimed in his odd Nordic accent after we'd all taken places at the lab benches. He stood at an old-fashioned blackboard with chalk in his hand. 'What is this?'

A groan went around the room.

'You, Mr. Smythe,' he said, pointing at Oliver, who had groaned the loudest. 'What is Physical Magic to you?'

'Something I'd thought we'd finished with in middle school,' Oliver said with disdain, tapping a pencil against the lab bench top.

'You probably did,' Rasmussen agreed. 'And you think you know it all by now, eh?'

Oliver glanced at Timothy and shrugged. 'Well, Pure Mind is the way of the future.'

Rasmussen snorted. 'And so you think Physical is not important, eh? Your teachers didn't bother honing your physical skills, because that's not the present flavor of the month. Well, I see we have a lot of work ahead of us.'

No one dared to groan aloud this time.

'I want to see your mediums.'

Everyone brought an object out of their pockets and purses and bags. Win's was a piece of green jade, carved in the shape of a fat dragon and small enough to fit inside an enclosed fist. Fergie's hands played with her handkerchief-sized piece of raw blue silk, while Sandy laid his on the table next to him; it looked to be a stout piece of driftwood a foot long, silvered and weathered by the ocean salt. Timothy laid a perfect crystal ball on a stand in front of him, while Oliver, the scoffer of Physical Magic, ostentatiously caressed a wand made from exotic hardwood, wrapped in gold and bejewelled all around the handle. It must have cost a bundle, that one.

Rasmussen walked around the table, nodding at each item. When he reached Pauline, his eyebrows rose a notch at the polished iron wand before her. But he stopped when he came to me, for I had brought nothing.

I waited as the silence grew. I could feel sweat starting to spread in my armpits. Stress sweat, I think it's called, the sweat that forms when the body is in fight or flight mode but is unable to take either action. It smells different from the normal, honest sweat of hard labor – it holds the odor of fear.

From what I could see on the table, the mediums were objects used presumably for Physical Magic. Of course I had nothing to show, for I'd never taken formal magic courses. I didn't even know how one got to choose what one's medium was, let alone how it was used in practicing magic.

He cleared his throat. I twisted in my seat to look up at him.

'I don't have one,' I said, stating the obvious.

His eyes were like pebbles behind the rimless lenses. 'I see.'

He walked back to the front of the room, to a set of wands hung on the wall like pool cues. After careful consideration he plucked one out, came back to me.

'You will use this,' he said, his voice not unkind. 'A plain ash wand. Until we figure out what your medium shall be.'

If he heard the snickers along the table, he did not show it. I could feel my cheeks starting a slow burn again, for I'd guessed that the ash wand was what they started little kids off with. I still had no idea what to do with it.

'I want each of you to show me a spell using your medium, any spell, so I can see your form,' Rasmussen continued. 'Timothy, you may be first.'

In a very bored manner, Timothy stared at his crystal and it began to glow, with movement inside. As a green haze settled within the ball, it turned to white until suddenly, the ball showed a picture of a village church, wreathed in snow with more falling all around it. He'd turned his medium into a snow globe, a simple feat which earned appreciative laughter from the others.

Rasmussen however was not amused. Not at all. 'That is a Mind trick. Not what I requested.'

The snow village disappeared from the crystal and Timothy's handsome face turned sullen.

'Pauline,' Rasmussen said. 'Show me what you can do using your wrought iron fencing.'

Her face grew stormy at the insult to her medium. She picked up the iron wand and held it an inch from her lips and whispered into it. She then pointed the wand to the front of the room, and the nails affixing the blackboard to the wooden struts of the wall began to pop out, flying to her wand like iron filings to a magnet which, I guessed, it was. The chalkboard fell to the floor with a crash.

'Very clever,' Rasmussen acknowledged. 'Now put it all back into place.'

It was Pauline's turn to flush red as she stared at the unmoving nails held along the length of her wand. He left her to the work, and went through each of the others in turn.

When it was my turn, I could only shake my head, the ash wand in my hand.

'I don't know how to use it,' I confessed. 'I don't know any spells.'

And Hugh had always said witches don't need spells.

He looked at me, his arms folded. 'You can at least try,' he said, one eyebrow raised.

'But to do what?' My mind was a total blank by this time. Did I want to create a snowstorm in a crystal ball, or cause the wooden manikin to dance as Oliver had? Use the wand to gather clouds outside or cause the clock's hands to stand still?

I had no reason to do any of these dumb things, even if I knew how to wield the piece of wood in my hand.

I thought of doing what I'd learned in Durant's class, opening a book or seeing what was on the pages within, but that wouldn't be acceptable. Rasmussen wanted me to use the wand to create. I stared at him helplessly. I was failing without even knowing what I was failing at.

And I could feel the ire directed at me from the others. They were quickly losing patience.

'Here,' he said as he took a piece of kindling from the woodpile and placed it before me. 'Set that alight.'

'But I told you, I don't know any spells.'

A distinct snickering was starting up in the ranks again.

'Then don't use a spell!' Rasmussen said in growing frustration to match my own. 'Spells are a tool only to concentrate the Intention. Use whatever you like, as long as it is through the wand!'

Oh. Maybe that was different. I had caused the sconce to burn last night, hadn't I? I pointed the wand at the kindling. Burn, I told it quietly. Catch alight. But nothing was happening. I quickly thought. If Intention was what was needed, could I send it out through the wand? I held my breath and tried it this way.

The only result was a whisper of smoke coming from the end of the very wand itself, not the kindling. I sat there watching it glow, as all around me the class erupted in laughter.

'Hush now, everyone!' Rasmussen faced the class with his hands on his hips and a frown firmly planted on his face. 'Physical Magic. I fear we will need to begin at the basics.'

'That's not fair!' Win stopped mid guffaw to complain. 'Why should we be punished because she doesn't know anything?'

'I didn't come to Scarp to waste my time on Physical,' Timothy agreed.

'This is a gross inconvenience,' Pauline added, turning to me with spite in her eyes.

Fergie studied the silk cloth she was nervously twisting in her hands, while I could see Sandy staring out the window as if he wished himself out on his beloved moors and hills.

'Silence!' Rasmussen roared. His beady eyes travelled all around the table at each of us. 'Half of you so-called advanced practitioners of magic were unable to cleanly accomplish your tasks. With the exception of Win, Alexander and Fergianna.'

Win sat triumphant, her arms crossed as she sneered at all the rest of us, while Fergie stared stonily at the table before her; I could only guess at how she was feeling at this moment. She'd dismissed her own magic as Hedge Witchery, had admitted she hadn't learned the more sophisticated Pure Mind at her local school, not like the others, but she probably didn't appreciate Rasmussen drawing attention to the fact.

'I have seen no evidence that you, Timothy, used your crystal ball to help weave the magic – you merely created an illusion within it. Pauline, while you used your iron wand directly as a magnet, you showed that you could not reverse the spell, therefore you were relying on the inherent properties of the medium and not your skill in working through the medium. And Oliver, this is not a joke! Laziness will show through the spell and weaken it.'

He drew a deep breath before continuing. 'You know the Competition does not focus only on Mind, although it looks like you have all forgotten this. So what I propose is, we will return to a couple of basic spells.'

Here he held up his hand to stem the growing mutterings. 'Just a couple of basics, as I said. This will enable you all to re-examine your techniques. You will thank me for this later. Practice them tonight, and show me tomorrow afternoon.'

Rasmussen flicked through a large ancient leather covered book on his desk, then a small smile came to his face, softening the thin lines of it. 'Ah, yes. This is what you shall all practice. A safety spell, just the thing. Each of you, use the one you are most familiar with, even if you think you already know it, I would advise you all to work on this one. Perfect it.'

He looked up from his book and his eyes settled on me. 'We all have need of a little safety sometimes, don't we?'

16

Herr Rasmussen allowed me to use his own book, as I had no previous spells to draw on, although he would not give me assistance in learning it.

'You will do it, if you want to,' he said with an odd sort of smile as he left me to it.

I stayed behind in the class after everyone had left, with the book laid before me. It wasn't making any sense at all, no matter how often I read the instructions for the spell. For one thing, it was hand written in an old form of the alphabet, and I had an uncomfortable feeling that what I pronounced as f's were supposed to be s's, and vice versa.

Not that it mattered how I pronounced the words, for it was all in Latin or Old French or something, and none of the words made sense. How could I create the Intention if I didn't know what the Intention was? I finally threw down the scorched wand in frustration. Nothing was working, yet it was vital that I learn how to do this spell.

But I hadn't totally given up hope yet, for there were still a couple of hours between supper and the communal gathering in the Common Room, and I meant to use that time wisely.

After another lacklustre supper in the Refectory, I cornered Fergie and Sandy, my only allies on this island.

'I need help with this spell stuff,' I told them point blank, after the others had left the dining hall.

They both nodded in agreement, knowing my situation, but then I saw them eyeing each other with suspicion. Neither had any reason to trust the other, not in the competitive atmosphere of this island. The fire in the grate was burning down now; I'd never noticed how dark it was in this large room.

'I'd be glad to teach you what I can,' Sandy said, very stiffly. 'I know you have what it takes, I've seen it for myself. But I don't think others here will have your best interests at heart.'

Fergie looked up at him, her eyes flashing fire once she grasped what he was saying. 'What do you mean by that, Sandy?'

'You're one of them, aren't you?' He was still stinging from the mockery from last night, and holding a grudge against the five. It was true, Fergie had joined in on that and she had the grace to blush.

'You know nothing about me,' she muttered.

I sighed. 'Hey you guys, peace out, would you? I've gotten to know both of you, a little,' I said. 'And believe it or not, neither of you is like those four Kin witches, okay? And you both know I have no intention of competing with you, I'm just here because, well, I have to go through the motions for Johanna.'

I stared at Sandy first, then Fergie, till they both gave reluctant nods.

'Here's the book.' I lifted the heavy tome out of my bag and placed it on the table with a thud, then flicked through it till I found the right page. Yes, I suppose I could have used Mind magic to open it, but I needed to save my energy.

'My first problem is, I don't even know how to pronounce the spell, let alone understand what the words mean.' I looked at Fergie. 'Can you help me with this?'

She studied the words, then shrugged. 'We didn't do languages where I came from, only Latin,' she said. 'The rest of it is all Greek to me.'

'No languages?' Sandy looked shocked. 'What sort of education did you have?'

I could see her about to give him a nasty retort, so I hurriedly cut in.

'What do you think, Sandy? Do you recognize it?'

He studied the page, then nodded. 'It's Old German, looks like,' he said. 'Probably from the seventeenth century. I can give you the jist of it, enough so we know the basics of the spell, and we may be able to figure it out from there.'

'Why don't I just teach you what I do?' Fergie said, impatient with the book work. 'It'll take forever to figure that one out. I can show you in five minutes, it's the easiest thing in the world.'

'For you, it is, and for me,' Sandy turned on her. 'But how is a cloth spell going to help Dara? Or a driftwood enchanting? She needs to find her own way with the ash wand or Rasmussen won't accept it.'

'Oh, right.' She looked up at me, then back at the wand in my hand, then shrugged. 'Well, if you ask me, I think you're screwed.'

'No way, Fergie,' I replied. 'I'm going to do this, and we're not leaving till we do. So put your thinking cap on and let's get to work.'

Sandy translated the words from the spell, with Fergie adding commentary as to the Intent of the spell.

'So, let me get this straight, what we have so far,' I said at last, putting a hand up to rub the crick out of my neck. 'To perform a safety spell, I need to say these words while holding the intent in my head?'

'That's right,' said Fergie. 'And directing the power through the wand.'

'Except you don't necessarily have to say the words out loud,' Sandy noted. 'At least I don't. I can think the words and it works out fine.'

'So saying, or thinking, the words, focuses the Intention?'
They both nodded.

'And don't forget to also hold the object of your protection spell in the forefront of your mind at the same time,' Fergie added. 'So it helps to have it right in front of you.'

'I don't understand, where does the wand come in?' I sat back on the bench, frustrated. 'How am I supposed to keep my mind on three things at once?'

They had no answer for me. For their part, they were finding it difficult to understand why I was floundering and couldn't grasp these basic concepts they'd learned as children.

'And what is a safety spell, anyway? That's so... nebulous! Why can't I do something more concrete, like, like filling water in a bowl, or turning my pen into a butterfly?' I was close to having a meltdown right on the spot.

I looked up to see them both looking at me like I'd gone crazy.

Fergie screwed up her face. 'Why would you want to do either of those things?'

'It's not the season for butterflies,' Sandy added.

'So why would I want to put a safety spell on something? And how would I know?'

'That's easy,' Fergie said.

'You want to keep things safe, you know, from bullies.' Sandy nodded to emphasize his point. 'Like your lunch money.'

'Or your favorite doll, so no one rips it away from you and tears the head off.'

'That's why this is one of the first spells they teach to kids,' Sandy said, confidence building in his voice. 'Sort of like magical martial arts.'

'Why don't we act like we're the bullies and we want to take her pen?'

'Yes, that's a good idea,' Sandy answered after a beat. 'You got that Dara?'

'Why would you want to take my pen?'

'Because we're bullies, and want to antagonize you,' Sandy said.

'And make life as miserable for you as possible.'

I looked at my new friends, an inkling of understanding coming to light. 'Like Witch Kin kids,' I said. 'Like my half-sister Sasha and her friends.'

'Probably,' Fergie said.

'Okay, let's do this,' I said. I grasped that wand so hard I could feel the grain of the wood beneath my fingers, and I aimed it at the pen.

'Remember, say the words, point the wand and focus your intention on not letting anyone else near that pen,' Sandy urged.

I squinted at the pen with the wand held straight, and repeated the words.

'*Lassen Keiner....*'

'*Berurhen*,' Sandy prompted.

'*Berurhen dies.*' I hoped I was getting the pronunciation right.

I felt something give, something small, but whether it was magic happening or just a blood vessel popping in my head I couldn't tell. The pen still sat there; it wasn't glowing or anything.

'Try it, Sandy,' Fergie urged. She hovered over the pen, excited.

He reached out a tentative hand and patted the air around the pen, about an inch away. 'I think you did it,' he said as the pen rolled out of his reach, rolling over the uneven surface of the Refectory table. 'Yes, you did!'

He cut off my whoop of excitement and pride.

'Now you've got to do it using the wand,' he objected.

'I did, I had the wand in my hand the whole time.'

He shook his head. 'Pointing it is not the same as using your medium.' Sandy crossed his arms and looked up at me.

I threw down the wand in frustration. 'What difference does it make?'

'You've got to be able to use your medium,' he stated, his tone matter-of-fact and brooking no argument.

'But why? I can do just as well with just my mind. I don't need the wand.'

'I think,' Fergie began, and she bit her lip and looked at Sandy. 'I think she doesn't understand why we use the mediums. Maybe no one has ever explained it to her.'

'Oh,' Sandy said, then gave a small smile as he turned to me. 'Sorry about that, such a basic concept, I didn't even think about it.'

I waited, not giving a smile in return. This had better be good.

'The mediums, you see,' he started. 'The mediums are used to store energy.'

'Like a battery,' Fergie suggested.

'Yes! Just like a self-charging battery in a car,' he said. 'The more you use it, the more energy gets stored in it. So right now...'

He pointed at my wand. 'There's no energy in it, is there?'

I shook my head. No, there was no power in it, it was no more than a simple, polished piece of wood with a charred end.

'Rasmussen would have deactivated it before putting it away, ready for someone new,' he said. 'So it's a blank slate, just waiting for you to rewrite it over with your magic prints.'

'Like a computer program?'

'Similar. And the more energy, power, magic that you direct through your medium, the more it will charge, which means you have to use less magic each time you use it.'

'Till eventually, it becomes almost a part of you,' Fergie added. 'You'll use it without even thinking.'

'Try to feel an affinity with it,' Sandy urged. 'Get your mind into the wand, otherwise it won't take.'

I looked at the wood in my hands with disgust. It was a useless, dead stick as far as I was concerned, good for nothing better than kindling. But I tried. I tried to send my mind into it, feel the woodenness of it, trace the old paths of the sap veins from when it was alive and growing, yet nothing happened.

'Try the spell again, now.'

With not much hope but plenty of determination, I closed my eyes, concentrated, attempted to send my energy through the wand as I spoke the words, yet nothing was flowing this time. I let the stick clatter onto the table again.

'It's no good,' I said. 'I'm a failure. I can't even use a stupid, first-grader wand.'

'Maybe... maybe it's broken?' Sandy sounded doubtful, for all of us knew Rasmussen would never replace a broken wand onto his wall. 'I mean, the scorching, earlier. Maybe that's what did it.'

I shrugged. It didn't matter now anyway.

'Oh,' Fergie said. 'Wait now.'

We turned to look at her, surprised by the hope in her voice.

'Maybe, just maybe, you already have a medium, and that's why this isn't working.' Her eyes were shining as they looked up at me expectantly.

I shook my head, hating to quench the hope she'd ignited in all three of us. 'I don't. I've never used a medium before.'

She grabbed my arm and shook it. 'The coin! That metal thing you have! That had a load of magic stored in it. Although...'

The medallion. I stared at Fergie, hope firing anew. It wasn't my magic, and Mom, well, she was a Normal with not an ounce of magic in her, but maybe. Just maybe.

'Although what?' Sandy demanded.

'The magic is tainted,' Fergie admitted with an apologetic look at me. 'I don't know how that will work.'

'Why don't you get it, and we'll give it a try?' Sandy asked, ready to ignore any doubts as to the coin's viability.

I nodded. 'Yeah, okay. I'll get it.' I looked back at both of them. 'But I can't get hold of it tonight.'

It was dark out already, I couldn't go traipsing through the moors and over the hills to rescue the coin. I didn't want to tell Sandy I'd hidden it by his precious Broch; I had a feeling he wouldn't look too kindly on that action.

'Tomorrow,' I promised. I would go back to the Broch to-morrow, retrieve the coin, and hopefully talk with my mother again.

··········

I headed to bed early that night, for I had a lot to think about and I couldn't stand to listen to the constant sniping over tea and scones in the Common Room. Too much had happened already in such a short time.

There were so many things I had to figure out and wrap my head around. The facts I knew, and those I strongly suspected to be true all flew around inside my head like a flock of starlings; whirling and individually screaming for attention so that I couldn't concentrate on one thread without another quickly grabbing my focus.

My mother was locked inside a stone tower on an island I just happened to be sent to – what were the odds of that?

Very unlikely, I knew; there must be some meaning behind it all. Was it the Kin in action? It had to be, for they were the ones who suggested I come here, leaving me not much choice in the matter. Lose my magic completely, or come to Scarp; it was a no-brainer to any half-witch wanting to better herself.

My mind went back to the morning hike around the hills. Happening upon the broch had felt like a home-coming to me, it drew me through the gorse like a moth to the flame. How could this be explained except by the fact that I'd sensed my mother deep within its impenetrable walls?

Yet something niggled me still, and I had to admit it to myself, and that was the question of how I could have heard Mom's voice so clearly through the solid rock. There was no logical explanation for that; the answer could only lie in the very magic that infused the whole island, for surely this would help sound travel better especially when there was a close emotional connection between us? Perhaps the power of the coin had enabled the solidity of the stone to melt to allow the soundwaves to pass through, after all.

Sandy had claimed that the power of the legendary Crystal Charm Stone within the Broch had more to do with it all, but I still couldn't quite believe in that story. In fact, I wasn't satisfied with any of these answers, but I brushed over it to deal with a much more important issue, which was the need to rescue her.

He knew the secret way into the Broch, although he'd denied it. Tomorrow, I would find her again, and he would help me. Somehow, I would make him help.

As I was drifting off with this comfortable thought in my mind, I felt a niggling, almost a physical movement of something stirring in my brain, like a worm reawakened from hibernation in a spring shower.

I sat bolt upright. I knew that feeling.

'No,' I whispered. 'No, you're not real.'

A laugh echoed in my head. Willem.

'Get out. Get out of my head.'

Now, Dara, is that anyway to greet me? Aren't you happy I found you?

'You're not real,' I whispered into the blanket I was clutching to my face. 'You're nothing but an auditory illusion.'

Is that what they are telling you, your precious Kin? I've been watching, you know. I've seen your struggle with the wand. What is this nonsense? You can aim higher than this, Dara.

'Stop it stop it stop it, you're not really here.' I was chanting like a prayer.

Oh, I'm real enough. You do know there is an easier way to reach your dreams? You don't need this torture, all this uncertainty. You don't need to suffer this pain. Come with me, I'll show you how real magic works.

'I don't want you here,' I whispered again. 'Go away.'

The Kin have always been false to you, Dara. Remember that. I bid you adieu for now, dearest. Till tomorrow....

He was gone. Despite the cold air in the room, I was sweating. I stilled my breathing, willing my heart to match the slower pace when a slight movement alerted me to Fergie's presence in the bed across from me. I looked over to see her wide gray eyes reflected in the moonlight of our uncurtained window.

'Alright, then?' she asked uncertainly.

'Yeah,' I said as I turned over on my side, away from her. 'Just a bad dream.'

I hoped and prayed it was a bad dream, but I knew the difference. In my heart, I knew that Willem was here on the island, and inside my head, and I knew I hadn't healed at all.

17

Using magic could really take the good out of you and yet even with all my exhaustion and jet lag, I couldn't sleep. The more I dwelled on it, the more certain I became that the shepherd had in fact been Willem, despite Sandy's disclaimer, even if none of it made logical sense. After all, Sandy told me the first evening that he'd been on the island a couple of months; he'd volunteered for sheep duty having had experience on his family's croft near Ness, at the northern end of Lewis and Harris. Sandy knew the shepherd.

Unless... unless Willem had cast a Disillusion spell on himself, thereby posing as the hermit. But likewise, that didn't add up because if I could see through it, then the wee Scotsman could too, for Sandy had more witch blood running in his veins than I did.

It was a dilemma I had to solve, and I got my chance early the next morning after breakfast, for we had some time before our next session. The sun now shone weakly in the crisp morning air and I took a thermos of strong tea from the

Refectory. I might need fortifications, after all, and I definitely needed caffeine to keep me alert.

There were two things I had to accomplish that morning, yet I didn't want to make myself late for Durand's session again; I had to retrieve the medallion and talk with my mother again, but first I had to find that shepherd in order to prove to myself that it wasn't Willem, that the sorcerer hadn't somehow followed me to Scarp. I needed to put my mind at rest before I did anything else.

I avoided Fergie and Sandy, and I was pretty sure no one saw me as I slipped out the side door, making my way along the base of the castle walls, staying out of sight of the windows until I could break cover and dash for the shelter of a cottage ruin, one with just the stone walls standing. These would hide me till I turned the corner at the bottom of the hill.

Once clear of the castle, I breathed deeply of the moist clear air, tinged with heather and rotting vegetation. It was a good, honest smell, and the sun even warmed me as I followed the path upwards. I wasn't sure of what exactly I was looking for, but I kept an eye out for a shepherd's hut or some such habitation. Sandy had said he lived somewhere up in the hills. It couldn't be too far away, surely.

After a half an hour of wandering along rabbit trails in the gorse, I'd had no luck; there were no signs of people or civilization on this face of the mountain. It was as good a time as any to have a spot of tea. I settled near a sparkly brook which gushed out of the rock and let the sun's low rays warm my face. I was just after finishing the last of my tea, my face tipped up to catch the dregs from the cup when out of the corner of my eye I saw what I'd been looking for.

The hut was just down the hill to my right, and I might have noticed it before this if I'd not been looking for a rectangular wooden structure. The doorway caught my eye first, a few planks of weathered, unpainted wood the same colour as the rock walls surrounding them, but with a roof made from turf with grass and ancient sticks of heather growing from it, there was even a blueberry bush. The small circular building was almost indistinguishable from the moors and rocks surrounding it.

Even as I stared at it, the door opened slowly, and out stepped the very person I was looking for. He stooped to pass through the portal even though he was much the same height as myself. And like me, he had a slight build. As he carefully shut the rough door behind him, I saw his small white fingers on the hasp, digits so pale and soft no self-respecting shepherd would lay claim to them. I knew that hand, and the memory of it caressing my cheek sent shivers down my spine.

He looked up at me on my perch and let his hood fall away.

'Dara,' Willem said in his clipped Dutch accent and he smiled, baring his teeth. He had the gall to pretend to be pleasantly surprised. 'You found me.'

'You.'

It really was him. My mind buzzed with questions – how did he get here? Why was he here? What were his intentions? They could not be good.

'I see you are admiring my new abode,' he said, looking fondly over the hobbit house as if this was a chance meeting on a street corner. 'My bothy, I believe the Scots call it. A wee bit more comfortable than the steam boat, if not as warm as my bunk next to the boiler room. Would you care to see inside? Perhaps have a warm drink, I remember you are partial to hot chocolate.'

The bastard. That was the drink he'd given to Brin to send him into a grief spin. He had to remind me of my part in that affair?

'What did you do to the shepherd?'

He looked back at me with a quizzical air.

'How did you fool Sandy?' I pressed on. 'You used some kind of spell on him, didn't you?'

Willem shook his head. 'Oh, Dara, there's so much you don't know,' he said, then he looked away to the hills across the water as if pondering a new idea.

There was no doubt in my mind now that he had followed me here. Word of my whereabouts had spread quickly through the Kin world, after all; Fergie had heard the news on the ferry, just hours after the Inquiry had finished. His steamship must have taken him directly to Scotland, and he no doubt had connections all over the supernatural world.

Besides that, there were all sorts of ways he could have tracked me down here to Scarp – the most likely being a tracking spell, a kind of magical GPS app on the coin. He'd had plenty of opportunity to apply one while he held it last month, before Brin wrested it from him on the harbor front, and with it, he would know where I was at any moment of time, anywhere in the world.

And I'd led him right to this island, the holy island of the Kin.

'Willem,' I said as I forced down the bile in my throat. 'What are you doing here?'

'What do you think, my dearest?'

Still the same slippery sorcerer, refusing to answer a question out right, meeting queries with questions of his own.

"I think,' I said carefully. 'I think you're planning mayhem against the Kin.' It was a good guess, after all, considering who I was speaking to. He'd forced me to help him bring down the veil between Alt and real time, leaving my magic prints and smell all over the whole rotten deal, setting off the Inquiry which was the reason I was here on this island in the first place.

He inclined his head to one side. 'That's an appealing idea,' he said. 'Sounds quite delicious. Did you have anything specific in mind for us to do?

'We make such a good team, you and I,' he continued smoothly. 'And perhaps we have unfinished business?'

'I have no business with you,' I said, gritting my teeth. Anger shot through me, hot and sudden and with no bounds and I found myself unaccountably protective of Scarp. I wanted him off this island and now before he could start the havoc he undoubtedly had in mind, for Willem did nothing without a reason and would not have come all this way without it benefitting himself. 'Get out of here, get off this island, you have no right to be here.'

He ignored me as if I was no more than a kitten spitting in fury.

'My offer still stands, you know. What we discussed as we said our farewells at the harbor.' He looked back at me with a calculating air.

He started it right then as we were facing off eye to eye, when my mind was full of emotion and my defences down; his gaze began to hypnotize as he sent out the first tendrils of icy fingers lightly touching my mind, seeking out the place he knew was inside of me. He had burned it into me, that tainted dark corner deep inside, and he was sure of his welcome there. While the thinking part of me blanched in disgust at his touch, still there was that tiny spot of addiction, still raw from last month that yearned for the heroin of his touch, that rose to meet his power and hungered for more.

'As I said before,' he continued in a soft voice I could barely hear over the cries of gulls and wind in the bushes. 'We're the same, you and I. We're liars and cheats and shunned by the Kin. Fortunately, you fooled them and they didn't bind your power. What a clever woman you are turning out to be.'

He held me caught in his gaze, and that small despised corner of me grew, melting, spreading throughout my mind. 'Come to me, Dara,' he said. 'Come, let me show you my world.'

I felt my feet move towards him.

'NO!' I screamed the word somehow, whether in my mind or perhaps out loud, and I had the satisfaction of seeing him flinch. 'No, I am not like you, I will not have any part of what you're doing, Willem. I've been given a last chance to straighten out my life. I'm ordering you to leave this island right now, and if you don't, I'll... I'll throw you off a cliff myself!'

And I meant it in my very bones. He was not going to screw up my life again. I leaned closer to him and hissed at him. 'So help me God I will tell the Kin you're here if you don't go now.'

But he merely laughed at me, a cold sound on that lonely hillside. His brown robe flapped a little in the wind.

'What about the coin, Dara? Your precious medallion with the dirty magic on it? You'll have to tell them about that,' he said, a grin on his face. 'You can't bluff me, you know.'

I stopped in my tracks, my fists tightly clenched. Yes, that coin Fergie had helped me smuggle on to the island. I dropped my hands and let go of my breath, deflating like a balloon. In order to tell the Kin about his presence on the island, I'd have to acknowledge that he followed me here, for without that bit of metal he could have had no idea where I was.

This was deja vu all over again, for hadn't I been in a similar situation just last month with this same player?

Then it hit me, the solution to my dilemma, the way to get myself off the hook. The coin was unimportant now, for I'd found my mother and she was here on the island. The weight of the past few months lifted off me suddenly with this realization. I didn't need the coin to use as a medium for I had doubts that it would be any good to me, anyway. I could tell Johanna everything, and she would certainly help me heal from his touch.

Hah! I'd been given a second chance, and I could make the right choice this time.

'You know what, Willem?' I said as I gathered my bag and thermos and prepared to make my way back down the hillside. I straightened my back and turned to his small figure. 'You can do your worst, for you have no power over me. You are about to get your ass whupped so bad you won't see it coming.'

I laughed out loud with victory. But then so did he, and his laughter followed me down the hill and he called out after me.

'Perhaps you shouldn't take action before you know the whole story, my sweet, or you might find yourself in a very precarious situation,' he said. 'But always remember, my offer is open.'

The sorcerer's voice held no fear, as if he knew something I did not, and that greatly unsettled me. More than that, it chilled me to my core and the thoughts raced round and round in my head as I hurried back down to the castle. What part of the puzzle was I missing? What could Willem possibly know that I didn't?

I would confess to Johanna about Willem. Either she would know he was part of my illusions, or she would hunt him down and take care of the problem herself, of that I had no doubt. I would tell all.

Except the part about finding my mother here on Scarp. I couldn't let on to Johanna that I knew about that.

18

The atmosphere inside the castle had darkened considerably even in the short time I'd been outside, and it wasn't just the clouds covering the sun. There was a tension everywhere, I could almost taste it in the air.

I found myself shivering as I walked up the grand staircase to her study. Was I going crazy? I shook my head. No, Willem existed, I'd just spoken with him. There was no way I could have imagined all the details; the sight of his creepy little white hands, even his use of the word 'bothy' – I'd never heard the term before, I couldn't have made it up, could I?

I drew a deep breath as I summoned up the nerve to knock on Johanna's door. This would be nerve-wracking, for I was juggling with the facts.

'Do not tell her that I know about the broch,' I whispered to myself as I closed my eyes tight. 'For then she'll know I know about Mom, and God alone knows what will happen to us then.'

'Enter.'

Her eyebrows rose in surprise when she saw me on the threshold. She wore reading glasses connected around her neck by a golden chain.

'Dara. Shouldn't you be in class with Professor Durand? How can I help you?'

I took another deep breath and walked in. Where to begin?

'Sit down,' she commanded, then looked at me across the wide expanse of her desk. 'I'm glad you came here actually. I need to discuss something with you.'

Of course. Durand would have complained to her about the previous day, when he'd accused me of drinking from that forbidden well.

'The loose magic,' I began.

She nodded encouragingly.

'It comes from this coin that...' I had to cut myself off, for I'd almost told her it had been my mother's. 'It... it somehow soaked up magic from the island,' I continued, gaining courage. 'That's where the loose magic must have come from. I didn't drink from the magical Well like Professor Durand said.'

She nodded thoughtfully. 'That's an odd thing, but yes, this would explain it. May I see this coin?'

'Well, no,' I said, thinking fast. Don't mention the broch. 'I hid it out by... on the moors.'

'Why?'

'Because it scared me!' I was glad to be able to speak the truth finally. 'It was glowing, and full of magic, and Fergie said it was tainted...'

'And you didn't want to be caught with it.' She had a small smile on her face now, but that could have signified anything. It could have been the warmth of an elder remembering her own foolish days of youth, or it could have been the satisfaction of a cat finally cornering a mouse. 'You'll find that magic can be an unstable element; an innocent seeming object might have a fatal flaw in its design which attracts magic to pool in it. It can be a very dangerous thing in the wrong hands. May I ask, what is the history of this coin? How it came to be in your possession?'

'I found it in an old store, a bargain basement magic shop, and I... knew right away it held magic.' I didn't mention that I'd been attracted to it in the first place of the hint of my mother it had carried.

'Ah, the curiosity of the young.' She was silent for a moment.

'Fergie thought it might be my medium?'

'No,' she replied quickly and emphatically. 'I doubt that. Don't be fooled by your attraction to it. In fact, you did well to leave it outside so it can't cause disruptions within you. You're still healing, and an object like this will not be good for this process.'

I took another deep breath and steeled myself for the next bit.

'About that. I've seen Willem.'

'De Vriejz? Here, on the island?' This made her sit up, but her expression was incredulous.

I nodded. 'Out there.' I pointed at the window to the hills beyond. 'Just then. I came right over to tell you.'

'And where was he, precisely?'

I explained to Johanna about having seen him before by the barn, and of how I'd run across him up on the hillside by the bothy.

'Did you touch him?'

'No, God no! Why would I want to do that?'

'We could lift any smells of him off you, if you had,' she said. 'And would know for certain that this happened, that it wasn't all just hallucinations from the damage in your mind.'

'It really happened. He was as real as you and me, and not five feet away from me.'

She tilted her head sympathetically. 'It may indeed have felt that way,' she began.

'Seriously,' I insisted, for I knew where she was going with that tone of voice. I was sitting on the edge of my seat now. I had to make her believe me. 'I'm not making this up! You need to go out and force him to leave the island. He hates the Kin, he's planning something against you all.'

Johanna shook her head. 'I'm not saying you made it all up,' she said in the kind of voice reserved for calming feral cats and lunatics, all soothing and non-scary, non-threatening. 'But that's the nature of hallucinations, the reason people are deceived by them. These illusions seem so real. I know it can be frightening, you might think you've lost control of your mind. But that's not the case.'

She wasn't listening to me.

'He's out there, Johanna,' I blazed. 'You need to catch him before he does whatever it is he's going to do. You can't trust him.'

Johanna held up her hand palm facing me in a distinct order for me to shut my mouth.

'Dara, Willem can't be on the island,' she said slowly. 'It's impossible. He could never get past the barriers on the strait.'

I remembered the first day when Fergie and I arrived. Moving over the water, the air had been thick with magic, pressing down on me, and I understood then that the ferryman had brought us through the magical gate erected by the Kin, one intended to stop any unwelcome visitors.

'To ease your mind, I propose to do a cleansing spell,' she continued. 'With your permission. I will need to enter your mind, and this will help a lot towards the healing.'

'You can get rid of him from my mind?' I whispered.

She nodded.

'Please,' I said. 'Please do this.'

I sat tight with my eyes shut, and I felt her moving around the desk towards me. I didn't open my eyes to see if she used a medium, and I didn't hear her chanting a spell; perhaps a witch of her calibre had no use for these tools. I could feel a feather-light touch though in my mind though, just a whispering trill as she skimmed along the surface. I waited for her to go deeper, like Willem had done, deep into the depths of my mind to that little corner of me that he had claimed for himself.

'There,' she said, and I then felt the absence of her cool touch inside my head.

'That's it?' I opened my eyes, puzzled. 'That's all you're doing?'

'It's quite a simple procedure, and I think you're healing nicely,' she told me, her blue eyes shining at her own success. 'I found no trace of him inside you. And that tells me that I made the right decision in bringing you here.'

I probed inside my head, and although he was absent right then, I could still feel the rawness of Willem's scar. How could she have missed it? She hadn't gone deep enough inside my psyche to see it, that's how. She perhaps didn't realize the depths of his damage. But how to broach this with her?

'If... if it turns out that I'm not totally healed, at some point I mean,' I said, hesitating as I chose the words. 'Could you do this again?'

'Oh, there'll be no need for that, Dara. If my touch hasn't given you the final healing you need, then, Great Goddess, I don't think there's any hope for you!'

She was laughing at the idea of her own infallibility; Johanna was, after all, the Grand Master of the Kin, Keeper of Scarp. If she failed, then, I was indeed a hopeless case, and had no business being here on the island.

'Do you feel better now?' She was asking me this in all seriousness.

I nodded, but my stomach felt like it had sunk into my boots. 'Yeah, I mean yes. Thank you.' I had to lie, for there was no way I would allow myself to be removed from the island, not now I had found my mother. A prisoner of the Kin, and perhaps of Johanna herself.

'About that coin,' she called after me as I turned to go. 'Best leave it where it is for now. We'll retrieve it once the summer comes.'

....

A nice little show, my dear, and I think she fell for it! Willem was amused. *Oh, you are too precious. A woman after my own heart.*

'Go away.' I gritted my teeth as I made my slow way down the grand staircase. 'I am nothing like you.'

The Kin are false. The tone of his whispers had changed. *You know this, they have no love for you. You are merely Johanna's pawn in this deadly game.*

'Stop it!' I halted my feet on the last step, the better to concentrate on getting this sorcerer out of my head. My fingers were massaging my temples as if that would help take the pain away. 'Just go! You have no business here. They may do wrong, but at least they're better than you! I didn't lie for you, but for my own sake. Just get out of my head!'

A stifled gasp, a swish of fabric against stone. I looked up to see Pauline huddled against the corridor leading to the old part of the castle; her face was aghast. She turned and ran down the hallway, her heavy feet thudding gracelessly on the flagstones.

'Now see what you've done,' I muttered. 'She'll know something's not right and she'll let everyone know. If you've screwed up my chances here, I'll kill you Willem.'

I left the coin where it was for now and worked extra hard after that in our sessions, trying to absorb as much knowledge as I could because I had a feeling I would need tools at my disposal during the times ahead. Despite what Sandy said, I knew my mother was being held in that tower, for we'd spoken, hadn't we? I had to assume she was safe enough there until I could find the secret entrance; once I found the way in, I also knew I had to somehow discover how to get past the barriers the Kin had erected. Because if my mother was being held in the tower by magical means, well, it would take magic to get her out.

And I was nowhere near ready for that. I couldn't even work through a medium yet.

Willem haunted me throughout the next few days; I could always feel him right there in the back of my mind, ready to pass commentary. I blocked him of course, but it seemed like he had wormed himself in me so deeply I couldn't totally remove his presence. I was constantly aware of that sneering laugh echoing in the silence like a ghostly sound track.

The times I wasn't working on my spells and magic and trying to force life into that lifeless wand, I was in the library searching through ancient books, looking for a way to clean Willem out of my head. I was open to any suggestions, short of a lobotomy; though sometimes even that sounded good if it would just get rid of the echo of that laugh. I found nothing though. Absolutely nothing that could help.

I suffered through Durand's sessions, forcing myself to keep on top of everything he demanded. It was a challenge because unlike Rasmussen, Durand felt that we should already be completely familiar with the basics of Mind and that his job was to lead us further into the depths of this study. I had a lot of catch-up to do; fortunately I'd always been a quick study. And I had to admit, despite the level of complexity at which I was expected to perform, Pure Mind magic was a much more forgiving study than Physical Magic. Durand only wanted to see the end results, not the process, so I was allowed much more creative freedom in how I got there.

Unfortunately, this meant he could claim any future failure on my part was not his fault.

I usually kept my head down and the nose to the grindstone in his sessions; not just because I was making up for lost years of study, but also because the class tended to get chatty under his direction.

I might have thrown in my lot with the Kin against Willem, but that didn't mean I wanted anything else to do with them. Just listening to the conversations between them was bad enough – these witches took arrogance to a whole other level.

But they also insisted on drawing me into them; or at least making me the subject of their jeering and tricks.

And the more I tried to ignore them, the more attention they wanted to pay to me. Pauline in particular seemed intrigued by me after hearing me talking on the staircase. She knew something was up, and it burned her to have that curiosity unsatisfied.

Durand didn't even try to stop the nonsense. When I finally was able to force water to flow up the gradient, using only Mind, sure as shooting someone would be sending a stream of it right into my eye, much to the amusement of the class.

Sandy and Fergie, of course, didn't participate in this ill treatment of me. Sandy was quite open about his disdain toward the Kin, and if they gave me too hard a time was willing to speak out and tell them off.

Fergie, not so much, but in a strange way I couldn't blame her for she was dealing with her own demons. She would give me grimaces and eye-rolls behind their backs, but we were both well aware that if I hadn't been there, she might have been the butt of their bullying. Her background was almost as much removed from the typical Kin upbringing as my own.

But all the time, I was becoming more and more resentful of the Kin and all they represented. And Johanna, for being unable to tell her that Willem had not left my head and she hadn't cured anything.

The other four Kin continued to ramp up their efforts to bully and dishearten me. I don't know why they felt the need to make me their scapegoat, surely I was already the lowest of the low, but perhaps picking on me shored up their own insecurities somehow. If anything, they were displaying the teamwork that Johanna had advised, just not for the Competition. They were a little more discrete when Sandy and Fergie were around, but I couldn't hide behind my friends all the time.

Things came to a head one day in the Common Room. I had poked my nose in hoping to find Fergie, when I overheard Win going about Normals and half-bloods and how their only purpose was to serve the Kin. She was boasting to Oliver, who had been complaining that his family was not being given the proper respect these days on his family estate.

'In my grand-parents' homeland, at least the Normals know their place. They respect that we are their overlords, and they give us proper obeisance,' she said. 'You English have been too lax, allowed too much of this democracy nonsense. You should have nipped it in the bud when it began.'

I couldn't stand it. I'd seen too much of how the Normals stuck in the Alt back home were treated; they were kept behind the veil in misery with no chance of breaking through, at the mercy of the supernaturals who fed on them, and all because of the Kin who kept the veil solidly in place.

'You mean they're your slaves, Win?' I broke into their conversation from the doorway.

Her lip curled up. 'They know what is good for them,' she said. 'Normals need guidance, they are not our equals.'

'That's true,' Pauline spoke up in rare agreement with Win. 'Normals can't possibly hope to compete without cheating.'

'Yes,' Timothy drawled as he lazily turned in his chair to look at me. 'What's this we hear? You've brought help with you in some way, eh?'

'She was talking with someone,' Pauline added spitefully. 'And that person wasn't here.'

All four of them were staring at me now.

'We don't allow cheaters,' Oliver whispered in a low menacing voice. 'Cheaters get what is coming to them in the end.'

'And there's all sorts of accidents that could happen,' Win said.

'If one were caught cheating,' Timothy added as his smooth face grew calculating and sinister.

I fled, without even closing the door behind me. Dear God. They had to be worried that I was somehow planning to win the Competition; they thought that I brought someone in to help me. The level of their paranoia astounded me. If they only knew the truth what really was at stake for me.

19

It had been building for days and I couldn't keep it in any longer.

'I hate them all.'

We were sitting in the library, Sandy, Fergie and I, pretending to ponder the abstract problem of how one could theoretically take over the island's power source. Not that I really thought we had any chance in the Competition, the three of us.

Perhaps the others thought so too, for Sandy was sitting staring out the window with a slight smile on his face, while Fergie was frantically flipping through the pages of the book in front of her, a look of utter incomprehension on her face. And I, well, I was fuming about the bastard Kin.

'Seriously,' I continued, slamming my own book shut. 'Now they're starting whispers that I'm cheating.'

'What?' Fergie pushed her book away too as if happy for the excuse to do so, and sat back in her chair. 'How're you supposed to be doing that?'

'Pauline overheard me talking... to myself the other day, and now she's telling everyone I've got a secret source of help. As if I could be any competition to them, even with outside assistance. If it wasn't all so ridiculous, I'd laugh.'

Sandy looked up, that odd smile still on his face. 'Is there a rule against having help?'

'I'm sure there is,' Fergie said, her face screwing up in a puzzled frown. 'Anyway, it's just supposed to be a theoretical problem. Not like anyone can help us with the figuring part.'

'Speaking of help, how's your work with the wand going?' Sandy asked.

I shook my head. 'I dunno, I just can't seem to grasp this whole physical magic business. I mean, I understand what you say about having a medium, but I just can't see the point.'

'Maybe the ash is wrong for you, you say you can't get into the wood. How about that medallion of yours?' Fergie suggested. 'Even if it seemed... tainted, maybe it's the right thing for you.'

Mom's coin. Johanna had said to leave it alone, but Johanna wasn't infallible, as she'd shown when she thought she healed me. Perhaps I should go retrieve it, and see if I could learn anything more about the tower. I'd been so wrapped up in this work for the past few days, I realized guiltily, that I'd quite left my mother to fend for herself. She must be wondering what happened to me.

'That's a good idea, Fergie,' I said as I stood and stretched. I took my coat from the back of my chair. 'I'll give it a try.'

'Where are you going?' Sandy asked in a sharp voice.

He had told me to stay away from his broch, but he didn't need to know where I was headed.

'Just up to my room,' I replied. 'I'll be with you shortly.'

·····•·····

The broch rose up suddenly past a corner of the hillside, the lichen splattered stone glowing golden in the sun. A magnificent day for a walk and my body welcomed the exercise.

When I reached the base of the tower, I paused to look up at its heights in awe. This structure had been built thousands of years ago, according to Sandy, each stone hand carved and placed to create this perfect surface using the most primitive tools. Or perhaps they'd used magic. There was enough of it around this island, it might as well be harnessed for something practical.

The path I'd previously made by smashing through the brambles and gorse had already disappeared, the bushes having sprung back, and it took me quite a few minutes to push through to the tower again. But once there, I immediately felt that oh-so-good feeling of returning home; my stomach unknotted itself, my shoulders relaxed and I just wanted to embrace the stone wall again and soak up all its beauty.

Remembering the loose magic which had clung to me the last time, I tried not to touch it, but leaned in close to feel the joy and comfort it emitted.

Listening closely, all I could hear was the hush of the low wind against the tower and through the brambles. A bird called out, then another answered, but after that there was only natural silence. There was no echo of Mom's voice, not this time. Did the elders remove her from the tower?

My name was being called though, and I lifted my head in apprehension. The voice was faint, coming from a distance. I shook my head to clear it of the trance the tower had brought upon me. The voice had a familiar cadence, that foreign lilt. The voice of Willem.

I looked all around me in the bushes and among the hillocks but couldn't see him anywhere until my search took me further away, down by the shoreline. At the place where the waves lapped the island, there he waited, the sun lighting his upright figure a couple of hundred feet away. It could have been a particularly tall boulder or a trick of the low cast winter sunlight, but that hooded figure was unmistakable to me.

Willem stood unmoving, yet I could feel his eyes on me even from that distance. I resolutely turned my back to him and blocked him from my mind, for I wanted nothing to do with the Dutchman.

Instead, I bent down to search for the small rocks I'd piled at the tower's base which marked the coin's hiding place. I wouldn't put it past him to have stolen my treasure.

There. The rocks were just as I left them, and I gave a small sigh of relief. A moment later and I held it in my hand, brushing the dirt off its shining surface.

The medallion still glowed luminescent with the power it had absorbed, like a battery recharging here at the base of this tower of magic. Perhaps it would turn out to be my medium. How fitting. I held it aloft, and listened, but still my mother's voice didn't come through.

Willem's did though, wheedling and calling me to join him on the rocky shore.

'Why don't you come up here if you want to talk with me?' I yelled at him through the distance. 'Or better yet, why don't you just leave this island, stop following me! I don't want anything to do with you!'

'Dara,' he cajoled. 'You don't need to be like that. We have unfinished business, you and I. Come down, spare me a minute of your time.'

'No,' I replied firmly. 'I've seen enough of you to last a lifetime. I can't trust you.' I turned my back to his distant figure and tried to block my mind from him, but it didn't work. Something inside of me didn't allow it, perhaps it was that little corner of me that he'd burned himself into last month, perhaps it was the weakness inside of me that wanted someone else to take charge and offer me the easy path to my dreams. His voice remained inside my head like a virus.

'Can't trust me? But I left your oh-so-important medallion where you carelessly hid it at the base of the broch, didn't I? Let me show you my good intentions towards you.'

When I said nothing, he continued.

'How are your lessons in magic going?' He paused to let me think about that. 'Have you begun to learn anything yet? Anything worthwhile?'

I kept my back to him and began to hum under my breath to block his voice. The Happy Birthday song of all things, it was all I could think of, and I felt a little ridiculous. How could he know I'd learned little here yet save the enforced lessons to stop Durand sneering at me; that I was failing to pick up the basics of Physical Magic? Willem was phishing, that was all, casting his net wide in his attempt to get me down in his physical presence so he could hoodwink me and use my natural magic for his own ends yet again.

'I can teach you so much, and not just the pretentious Kin magic,' he was shouting now, getting upset with me, his voice carrying clearly on the wind from the sea. 'Don't you see? My offer still stands, Dara. You and me, we can own the world!'

175

Still I managed to withstand him. Perhaps I should have walked away right then, but I didn't, and that was my downfall. I was loathe to leave the comforting presence of the broch and the warmth of its solidity.

'You want to enter their precious tower, don't you?' Damn Willem. 'You think your mother is being kept inside, I know.'

With that I stood up straight again, gave myself a mental check, but he wasn't inside me, there were no icy tentacles needling their way deep inside my head. How did he know about Mom? I'd told him nothing last month, not mentioned her at all.

I waited for him to continue.

'She's not in there, Dara.' His voice was quiet now.

I searched every nuance of his tone, looking for falsehood, but there was none there. Willem, damn him, he was speaking the truth as he knew it.

'And I know where she is.'

I took a hesitant step toward the path trampled in the gorse, then another slow step into the brambles. The thorns caught at the cotton of my winter hoodie but I brushed them aside, careless of the hooks and pulled threads.

'I've met her in my travels, in the Northern Kingdom.'

There was not an ounce of lie in his voice, and I knew Willem well enough by now to know this, bastard as he was, evil failed sorcerer, man without a conscience, he was all these things. He lied when it suited him, he lied to rich women in order to convince them to give him their gold and jewels, he lied to those he thought beneath him because their lives didn't matter to him.

But he'd never yet lied to me, not outright, and he wasn't lying now. Strangely enough for all that he was such a selfish shithead, Willem respected me, and his offer of partnership had felt genuine, unwanted though it was.

I made my way slowly to the shoreline where he waited, all the while cursing myself for getting involved with him again, even in the slightest bit, but the carrot he dangled in front of my face was too tempting.

At last I stood in front of him, eye to eye. He let the hood fall from his shaved skull, and the harsh morning light showed every line on his face, every hurdle he'd suffered from the hands of the established Sorcerer's Guild and the Witch Kin. I reached into the back pocket of my jeans and withdrew my phone. Flicking the camera app, I held it up in front of him and clicked, capturing the sorcerer forever as proof that I was not crazy.

'Tell me.'

Willem shook his head, the sunlight catching every bristle on his shorn blond head. 'What can I say? It was far from here I saw her. In the Northern Kingdoms.' He gestured loosely in the north-east direction.

'And?'

'And what? I didn't know she was your mother, and I didn't know you were looking for her.' He shrugged. 'Marian was just another guest of the Ice King. It happens when people screw up with magic sometimes.'

I could only stare at him, totally speechless for a moment, hardly able to take in what he was saying. When I could muster my thoughts, I began. 'But I heard her, right there up by the broch,' I whispered. 'She was there inside it, she had to be.'

I'd come so close to finding my mother, I couldn't bear for her to be gone from my grasp so easily. I could feel a tear of frustration and anger forming in the corner of my eye, but I wouldn't let it escape in Willem's presence. Yes, he respected me as an equal, but any signs of weakness and he would consider me fair game.

'So how did...?' I began to ask him how he knew now that the person he'd seen was my mother, but he interrupted me.

'I will show you,' he said quickly. 'You trust me?'

'How can you do that?'

'You have the medallion,' he replied. 'You say it has a connection to her?'

I nodded.

'Okay. You already connected with her once,' he said. 'I know where she is geographically, so we should be able to make contact.'

'Is such a thing possible?' I breathed, yet I knew it was so. I had already connected with her, when I thought she was inside the broch. The medallion must have been the key.

But why here on Scarp, and not before? I would worry about that another time.

He snapped his fingers. 'Pass it over to me.'

I did so reluctantly.

'Ah yes,' he sighed as he beheld it in his palm. 'It has soaked up the magic here, eh?'

'Is it the magic of Scarp?'

'Sort of.' He shot a sly look at me, and nodded. 'Now. I need you to connect with my mind.'

I held back, naturally. It was bad enough having him in my own head without returning the favor.

'Come, don't be shy,' he said, impatience coloring his voice. 'You know how it is done. It's the only way I can show you Marian.'

I shut my eyes and sent my own mind out towards his. I didn't bother being hesitant or feather-weight with my touch, not like Johanna had done; I plowed into him hard enough to make him wince.

20

He murmured. 'Such strength, in one so young.'

The process wasn't painful. Willem must have been using my coin as a medium, drawing on the power it held, for when I opened my metaphysical eye in his head, I saw my mother, as he'd said. All around her was ice, and she appeared to be performing some mundane task, pouring wine into a goblet. Those denim blue eyes stared off into the distance. She didn't appear to have been mistreated.

I could have been watching a movie of myself, we looked so much the same; when I felt Willem's spark of desire for her I quickly withdrew before I physically threw up.

I sat myself down on a boulder. This was exhausting, however did he do this?

'This is the work of the Kin, you know that.'

'How?'

He shrugged. 'I don't know, but something nasty happened to get her there in the Court of the Ice King. I can still smell the taint off this metal, even infused with Scarp as it is.'

'How do I know this is real, what you just showed me?' Even as I asked, I knew the question wasn't necessary.

Willem laughed. 'Ever heard of honor amongst thieves, Dara?' he asked, then his voice took on a musing tone. 'You look so much alike, the two of you. When I saw you in your home town, I knew immediately who you were.'

'Why does she stay there? How can she get back home?'

'That's the problem with his Kingdom. You can't get here from there.'

'When did you realize?' More to the point, how did he know I'd been looking for my mother, thought her locked up in the tower? All these and so many more questions were bubbling up inside my head, but I didn't get a chance to ask them, not right then.

'That's all I know about your mother, okay?' His voice was impatient. 'After, when all this is done with, we will have plenty of time and we will go there together, you and I, and free her. But that can't happen unless...'

'Unless what?' My heart was sinking into my boots. Willem had an agenda, of course he did.

'You're still dragging that coin around with you,' he threw over his shoulder.

'That's how you followed me here, wasn't it?' I was bitter. The one thing I couldn't let go of, and it was the one thing he'd used to track me here to the island of Scarp, like a magical GPS system.

'At least I know you won't tell the Kin about me. We have an agreement, eh, Dara?'

'Too late,' I said quietly. 'I've already alerted them to your presence.'

'Oh? Really? And why are they not here, capturing me in their nets of golden spells, taking and removing me and punishing me?'

I was silent.

'Because they don't believe you!' He cawed with laughter. 'And that's a good thing, a very good thing for you Dara. Do you know, if they truly had faith in you, what would be the consequences?'

He had his hands on his hips and triumph in his voice, and took evident delight in spelling out the possibilities of what would happen if Johanna had been able to see past her nose and believe me.

Willem licked his finger and slashed the air. 'Number one. They would remove the coin from you. Wipe all the magic memory from it, and you would have lost the contact with your mother. For you know, the coin is what allowed you to speak with her,' he added. 'Look at it – is it glowing?'

I reluctantly took it out of my pocket. Yes, he was right, the medallion was still pulsing as if lit from within.

'That's from being so close to the broch,' he told me in a normal conversational voice. 'It has soaked up magic from the Source of this island, the Crystal Charm Stone. Metal does this.'

What? The Crystal Charm Stone existed? Before I could wrap my head around his words, he was off again.

'Where was I?' he mused. 'Ah yes. Number Two.'

He made a huge gesture in the air again. He was enjoying himself, the little drama queen.

'If the Kin actually believed you about the coin, and my presence on the island,' he continued, then had the audacity to wink at me. 'That would save you so much trouble, would it not? You would not be forced to make decisions for yourself, and grow. It's the easy way out. I know you, eh, Dara? So much easier to let someone else handle the situation, than to put on your big girl panties and take the reins in your own hands.'

He snickered, then mimicked my voice. 'Daddy! Hugh! Come save me!'

Willem, as a person, had no redeeming qualities. He deserved everything the Kin would throw at him when I gave them further evidence of his presence here on Scarp. They would believe the photograph. And I would show them. Just... not yet. I needed to get more information about my mother's whereabouts before I turned him in.

'And Number Three?' I steeled myself. I had to keep him talking, he would let something slip soon enough, he was so pleased with himself he couldn't help but taunt me.

Here he smiled at me, a gentle and almost loving smile.

'Then I will be put away,' he said with a tinge of sadness coloring his voice. His pale eyes grew weary all of a sudden, and he bowed his head. 'And deservedly so, in the eyes of the Kin. The Movement, of course, will carry on without me as a major player, and it will succeed regardless. I won't live to see the glory, but, well, that's the game we're playing. You give your all for a cause, and it may swallow you up. But still the cause lives on.'

'What's this cause, this movement you're talking about?' I hardly dared to ask.

'The cause of freedom, Dara,' he replied softly. 'Remember the poor lost souls in Alt, back in the New World?'

He meant, of course, my home in Newfoundland. Yes, I remembered the humans, the Normals who were stuck in the endless time loop of Alt behind the veil the Kin had brought down to keep the supernaturals out of the Normal world.

'All over the world, much the same situation exists,' he continued. 'Whether behind the Veil or within the human world. The Kin do nothing to alleviate matters.'

He stared off into the distance for a moment, as if in contemplation, then shook himself.

'And Number Four, of course, let us not forget the last precious outcome which will happen after you run to tell the Kin and show this photo,' he said. All altruism had left his face now, leaving only his mighty sneer and his staccato Dutch accent hammering out each word. 'Dara will never find her Mummy, not with Willem locked away or worse. For ever will the poor woman stay in the freezing wastes of the Ice King's land, until the moment her sad heart cannot take the absolute hopelessness of it anymore, and it will flutter, like a wounded bird, flutter until it gives up the ghost. And her body will be tossed away, unloved, unmourned... because her daughter chose to ease her conscience rather than save her...'

'Damn you, Willem!'

'Oh yes?'

'Damn you,' I repeated, with less anger and conviction now and the tears threatening to fall. I sat heavily on the nearest boulder, hugging myself to keep his words away and hating the sorcerer even more than I'd ever done before, but he'd heard the acquiescence in my voice.

I had so many questions still that only he could answer.

'Later, later,' he said briskly. 'It will all become clear. When you win the Competition, fair and square.'

···•·•····

I left him shortly after that, clutching the glowing medallion in my hand, thinking hard and furiously as I hurried back to the castle. I had so many questions still, yet I needed time to process the answers I'd been given.

What scared me was the ease with which Willem did everything; following me to the magically fortressed island, slipping beneath the regard of the very strong witches here, remaining out of sight of everyone except me, and the way he assumed I would go along with his plans.

And even scarier was how easy it was to slip in alongside him, to trust him, and let him do the thinking. His words made perfect sense on the surface, but there was unease in the very pit of my belly. I really needed to discuss this whole thing out loud, to hear myself talk, bounce it off someone else.

Willem said my mother's situation was the work of the Kin, which brought it back to Cate, and possibly Johanna and... my father. Mom couldn't even know that, for she had told me to contact Dad.

The bloody Kin with their entitled ways. Their arrogance. Rotten to the core, all of them. If I could pay them back for all the suffering they'd caused me over my lifetime, I would, so help me...

I slowed my pace as I reached the castle grounds. But I could. It was as simple as joining Willem, lending him my assistance with whatever it was he needed. Then he would help me free my mother, of that I had no doubt.

For as he said, there was honor amongst thieves.

Up in our shared room, I threw myself on the bed, too many thoughts in my head.

But... what did Willem mean about me winning the Competition? I allowed myself a few minutes of a dream where I waltzed in and snatched victory from under their stuck-up noses, the despised half-blood beating them all out. Wouldn't that shut them all up pretty quickly?

And he had said without help from him, so Pauline couldn't say I was cheating. I had no idea what he meant, but a little bit of vengeance would feel good right now. Against the Kin.

My phone interrupted my revengeful thoughts. Hugh.

My finger hovered over the answer button, then flicked it to the left, rejecting the call. I had no desire to speak with any of them, yes, even him.

....

Rasmussen's eyes glinted behind his rimless spectacles as he stopped me before I could take my seat in his class.

'How has the wand been working for you?' he asked in a low voice.

I took a breath to answer, then just shook my head. 'Not really,' I mumbled.

'Hmm. I've been thinking about this; I don't understand why you're having such difficulties, a witch with your power. There must be something we can use, some other material that would work for you. Do you not feel an affinity for anything – rock, fabric, metal?'

This puzzle was bothering him a lot, I could tell by the way his shaggy eyebrows were drawn together.

'Maybe I'm just not meant to have a medium?' I ventured, but he immediately shook his head to negate the suggestion.

'Nein! Everyone, every witch worth their salt must be able to use physical magic. I will think more on this matter.'

He took his place at his lab bench, leaving me free to slip in beside Sandy.

While we waited for Rasmussen to begin, I used a hair elastic to tie my hair in a ponytail. It was always best to be prepared for Physical Magic, and a loose hair into the mix could throw a whole spell off. I left it hanging over my shoulder, absently toying with it and twirling it through my fingers.

'Where were you?' He kept his voice to a whisper. He seemed fascinated by the ends of my ponytail.

'Just out for a walk,' I told him. No way I was going to share the news about Willem. No frigging way.

'You were at the Broch,' he hissed, and pointed to my hair. 'You've got... Wipe it off, quick, before anyone notices.'

I looked down at my hair, and sure enough, little bits of blue energy were fizzing away. Damn! My hair must have brushed against the stone. I quickly stroked the magic out of my hair and surreptitiously shook it off my hands under the table top.

'I told you not to go out there,' he scolded me, still speaking so he wouldn't be overheard. Fergie had noticed something going on, and sent a questioning glance our way.

'Shh,' I hushed him, and opened my eyes at him to take the hint to shut up. 'Later. We'll talk about it later.'

Rasmussen set us to work on yet another grade-school level spell, using our mediums, of course.

'I think today...' he said as he rubbed his clean-shaven chin and looked out over the class. 'I think today we will work on the Peaceful Bubble spells.'

His words were met by the usual chorus of groans from the Kin, and they even had the nerve to complain to him directly.

'What is this, kindergarten?' Timothy muttered.

'There's no way on the flat earth that this is necessary for the Competitions,' Oliver challenged the professor. 'This is not useful to us at all.'

'I have better things to do with my time.' Win looked around for support. The atmosphere was growing rebellious.

'Hush now,' Rasmussen directed. 'I want to see perfect form. You first Oliver, since you're complaining the loudest.'

Oliver stood up and with his deluxe wand drew a circle around his head while he chanted the words.

'*Hoc est bulla,*' he intoned in a bored manner, and something like a huge soap bubble formed out of nothing to encompass his whole body.

It really was quite beautiful, all iridescent in the sunlight streaming through the mullioned windows of the round tower room, throwing off rainbows of colors and sparkles into the air all around him. I could see why they'd teach this to young children, it was just the sort of thing to capture a child's imagination.

'Hmm, very good,' the professor murmured. 'Now Timothy, you may try to burst his bubble.'

He raised his voice so that Oliver could hear through the buffered glimmer. 'Pay attention now Oliver, you are going to be attacked.'

Now this was more like it. The two quickly got into the game of duelling with their magic and their mediums; Timothy held the crystal ball up, directing the sunlight from the nearest window through it and angling the whole so that it shone directly on the iridescence.

Oliver countered the rays with barely perceptible movements of his wand, warding off the beams so they refracted through the bubble and back into Timothy's eyes. The pair feinted and fell back as if in a dance; they were enjoying this active game of war, like little boys in the playground.

'Okay, okay,' Rasmussen was laughing. 'You've shown us what you can do. Now, I want everyone to create your own bubble.'

Damn. I reluctantly took the ash wand in hand, carefully avoiding the splintery bits. Fergie mock grimaced at me, then shrugged. What were the words?

'*Hoc est bulla*,' I said with no expectation, and I wasn't disappointed.

Sandy shook his head. 'You have to at least try.'

I huffed and placed the dead wood on the bench top with a finality, then hunched myself down, my hands in my hoodie pocket.

'I'm sick of trying,' I said. I couldn't bring myself to hold that wand in my hand one more time. I fiddled with the medallion in my pocket as I watched the others in their practice.

A knock came at the door, Rasmussen excused himself to answer it, where he spoke for a moment. Then with the strict injunction that he didn't want to see any blood on his return, he left the room.

In his absence, the others were no longer having fun with it, the classroom had become a literal battle ground with each of them trying to outdo the other in flash and sparkle with the added hope of wounding another. Win had created a lovely silky looking bubble around herself, while Pauline was attempting to prod her way into it with a steady stream of iron sparks. The look on her face could have cut diamonds.

Timothy was now ensconced in his own bubble, his crystal ball safe in its special purse hanging off his belt as he evaded the thrusts and parries of Oliver's wand. I could see the sweat beading on him through his shimmer.

Even Fergie and Sandy had joined into the spirit of the thing, Sandy in his rough bubble which looked more like the sea outside the castle, droplets of water spraying each time Fergie sent shocks of power by means of her silk which she flicked around like a wet towel.

What was I doing here? I had no place amongst these wielders of magic, Kin all of them; yes, even my friends. I didn't belong. I was a failure.

Screw this. I was leaving to find my own peaceful bubble elsewhere.

'Hoc est bulla my ass,' I said, flicking the coin in my pocket.

And it happened. Suddenly my world was full of color, as if I was plunged into the center of a stained glass window, the brilliant deep reds and blues and purples and greens filling my eyes. As if through a haze I could see the action in the room slowing as I was noticed. Timothy watched me with his jaw to the floor, not even noticing as Oliver sliced through his bubble. Sandy and Fergie immediately stopped their games, Sandy's bubble disappearing in a spray of salty mist.

Pauline turned and stared, outraged, then lifted her iron wand and aimed it at me. I could see the iron sparks like bullets heading toward me, and could only watch as they shattered my new bubble, glass shards flying off in an explosion of sharp splinters, a rainbow of destruction.

21

The class was deathly silent, save for the sound of the last tinkles of broken glass falling all around. I coughed, the movement loosening fine shards from my face and from my hair.

'You did it,' Fergie observed breathlessly. Her eyes shone in joy for my accomplishment. 'You've finally mastered the medium of the wand.'

Everyone in the room looked at the ash wand which still lay on the bench top where I'd tossed it in despair.

'No she didn't,' Win said quickly. 'She used Mind.'

'She had to have,' Oliver agreed, flicking his long blond locks out of his face. ''That is so cheating!'

They were advancing towards me, all of them, except Sandy and Fergie who looked on in dismay.

'If she cheats at a minor thing like this, there's no telling what she'll do for the Competition.' This came from Timothy, his eyes narrowed.

'I knew she would cheat! I told you I heard her talking with someone,' Pauline said, her voice rising. 'Someone who wasn't there. She's got outside help!'

'That's the only way a half-blood like her could do this.'

'Let's bring her to Johanna.' Pauline was almost on me, menacing over me where I sat. 'And show her the error of her decision.'

I pushed her away and fled the room. A cowardly action, perhaps, but I felt I had no choice, for yes, the Kin were half right, I hadn't used the ash wand. But I hadn't been cheating; I had found my medium. It was the coin, the one tainted with magic gone wrong. My flight was that of one whose world had just turned upside down, and I needed space to wrap my head around what this meant for me and my future as a witch.

··········

Johanna and Rasmussen didn't send for me, so I could only assume the others didn't tell her about my perceived cheating. That didn't make me feel any better, for I suspected that Pauline, Win, Oliver and Timothy might be planning to take matters into their own hands. I didn't go down for supper, not that I was afraid to show my face, but I just didn't want to give them the opportunity to wreak their revenge or play their tricks on me. My half-sister Sasha and her friends had taught me well growing up; besides, I had no appetite.

After giving them all a couple of hours to calm down, I ventured out and came upon Sandy in the Common Room. He appeared to be idling away the hours after supper, leafing through a magazine about the British Royal Family of all things.

Good, sane Sandy. Peculiar in his belief about the Crystal Charm Stone, perhaps, but everyone had quirks if you dug deep enough.

'Hey, how're you feeling now?' He seemed glad enough to toss the magazine aside.

I scratched my head. Tiny shards of glass fell to the sofa.

'That was quite the show,' he continued. 'How did you do it? I thought you weren't having any luck with the wand.'

'It wasn't the wand,' I began.

He was silent for a moment before he spoke. 'Did you use Mind?' he asked me point blank.

I shook my head, still playing with the coin in my pocket. 'No.'

I looked up at him. 'Can I talk with you?' I asked him. 'I mean, really talk. I can't share this with anyone. I need to bounce it off you, to figure out what I need to do.'

He must have seen how pale my face was, and patted the sofa cushion next to him. 'Sit. We're all alone, no one will hear us. Let it out.'

I let myself slump next to him, then angled myself so that we were facing each other. Where to begin?

'The shepherd,' I said carefully. 'How well do you know him?'

Sandy's face was blank for a moment. 'What shepherd?'

'The one we saw the other day, you remember, the one who ran away. The hermit.'

'Ah, of course, the shepherd,' he said, his face still void of expression. 'Don't know him well. Why?'

'You've been here, what, a couple of months?'

He nodded, a single dip of his head.

'So you know him a bit, at least,' I continued.

'Yes,' he replied, then took a deep breath. 'Dara, where is this leading?'

'I have reason to think the shepherd may have been harmed.'

'What?!' His face was incredulous. 'But he... I mean, I saw him today, and he seemed fine.'

I shook my head. Willem could have magicked him into thinking he saw the hermit. I didn't trust anything.

'I think,' I continued, carefully marshalling my thoughts, wondering how much I could tell him. 'I think the island has somehow been invaded by an unfriendly sorcerer. And I think it might be my fault.'

'What does it have to do with the shepherd?' His voice was getting quieter.

'There's someone on the island, and he's posing as the hermit,' I told him. 'This is a sorcerer, a failed sorcerer, who has followed me here to the island. I think he's planning something really diabolical.'

Sandy drew away from me a fraction of an inch.

'He's like that,' I assured him. 'Pretty evil when it comes to the Kin. He'll do anything to embarrass them or hurt them if he can.'

He took a deep breath and rubbed at the stubble on his cheeks.

'No, no,' he said, shaking his head, and then his hand dropped and he began tracing out a line in the weave of his kilt. He looked up at me again. 'You say you know this... this person?'

I nodded glumly.

He began to shake his head again, but stopped midway, as if settling on a decision. He looked me straight in the eye as he spoke. 'I find this all a bit fantastic. You know, first you think your mother is locked up in the Broch, and now this? Dara, d'ye have some kind of persecution complex? This is no' really normal behavior.'

Sandy put his arm around my shoulder. I could feel his breath softly on my cheek as he spoke.

'I spoke with Hamish, the shepherd,' his voice gentle in my ear. 'He's fine, and hasn't noticed anything amiss with the island. I don't know who you saw, or think you saw, Dara, but I really do believe things aren't as you fear.'

'You spoke with him?' I turned and searched Sandy's face for the reassurance I needed. 'You spoke with the shepherd, and everything's okay with him?'

Thank God. I wasn't responsible for someone's death. That was a relief.

Sandy got up and took the kettle from the hob, and set about with the ritual of making a pot of tea.

Cake was waiting on the sideboard next to him, as if everything was normal, as though the fraught tensions and everything that had passed in the classroom had never been. Nobody else was present, though, just me and the wee Scotsman, and after pouring tea he gave us each two large helpings of the frosted lemon loaf.

'If they wanted their fair share, they'd be here to take it,' he said with a grin. 'If you don't want it, I'll eat yours too.'

'No chance,' I said, realizing that I was starving by now. I set to eating it, not even bothering with a fork seeing as how it was just Sandy to see my bad manners. The sweet, sweet lemony frosting melted with the soft freshness of the cake and for a moment I was in heaven, forgetting all about my woes for that short space of time. He'd made the tea just right too, not too weak and yet not so strong it was bitter. I sighed and leaned back into the sofa, slowly licking each finger after every crumb and drop had disappeared from my plate.

The sweet respite didn't last long, for now that my hunger had been sated, my mind returned to worrying about my situation. So the shepherd was unhurt, that was a load off my mind, but it was a small one. I was still wrestling with the knowledge of the medallion's power in my hands, and what that meant for me, my future. And my entanglement with Willem.

'So it wasn't the wand.' He might have been reading my mind. 'You really have them worried now.'

I looked up at Sandy.

'And they're not going to let this go. You've shown yourself to be serious competition,' he added. 'How did you do it?'

I shook my head, and slowly reached into my pocket. 'It was this. I guess Fergie was right in the first place, and this is my medium.'

The coin shone bright, reflecting the firelight, expanding it so I could see its glow reflected on Sandy's face. He gave a low whistle, but didn't attempt to touch it.

'It was my mother's,' I whispered, entranced by the light of the metal. 'But... she's Normal, so I don't know quite where it all came from.'

'A mystery, then,' he said, and he too sat in quiet contemplation.

Then he nodded to himself, as if making a decision. 'We can do this, you know.'

'Do what?'

'We can win the Competition.' His voice was low, less than a whisper, then he laughed.

The abrupt change in conversation threw me off for a moment. 'Where's this coming from?'

'Johanna said we should work in teams,' he said, ignoring my question. 'You and me, Dara, we could do it between us.'

'Sandy, remember who you're talking to before you ask me to join up,' I objected. 'I don't know anything about spells and things. I don't even know where the power of the island comes from, let alone how to divert it. I'd be useless to you. Try Fergie, she's a much better bet.'

'She's just a Hedge Witch,' he said dismissing her. 'She'd be no good to us.'

He turned to look at me, his pale eyes glittering from the reflected light off my coin. 'And the power of Scarp, well, the Crystal Charm Stone is at the heart of it.'

Jesus, not this again. He must have seen the disbelief in my eyes. Instead of taking offense, he leaned forward.

'Think about it, I mean really consider the matter,' he said, keeping his voice low. 'They all think it's merely the intersection of the ley lines that positions Scarp as the powerhouse it is in the magic world. But there's lots of similar places around the world that have these seams of magic flowing through them. Yes, the ley lines play a large part in the island's power, but that's not the whole story.'

He took a deep breath and settled back into the sofa. 'The Charm Stone is real. I've seen it. It concentrates the power of the island, don't you see? It is strategically placed right at the intersection, it acts as a magnifier.'

Sandy was so fervent, how could I not take his words seriously? And if what he said was true, then perhaps he knew also the way to divert the energy of it, theoretically. And he was offering to bring me aboard, to win the Competition, when he really had no need to.

I could be a winner, and beat out those bully Kin. That would show them.

'You said the stone is within the broch,' I replied slowly. 'The tower with no doors or windows.'

'Yes,' he said. 'That's correct.'

'And you know how to get to it?'

'My great-grannie told me where the entrance to the broch is. Although she'd never been on the island, her gran had passed all the legends down. And it was just like they said it would be.'

He smiled in triumph, as if he could see the possibilities taking root in my own mind.

Still I hedged. If something sounded too good to be true, well, it probably was. 'I thought there were too many barrier spells up for anyone to pass through.'

He nodded. 'There are barrier spells,' he agreed. 'But any spell can be undone, especially when we have that on our side.' Sandy was looking at my coin in my hand, still glowing in the light of the fire.

I followed his eyes. 'I don't understand, how could this help? You know I'm next to useless in something of this nature, Sandy, I don't know how to remove spells of that strength,' I said. 'And I would have to know what I was doing, in order for the coin to be useful.'

He gave a secretive smile. 'It's okay, I have it figured out,' he answered, then looked up at me again. 'So, are you with me?'

Hell, yes. If there was even a chance that we could do this thing, well, there was no way I could say no.

'Alright,' he said, quickly getting to his feet. 'Come on then.'

He grabbed my hand and hauled me up to standing.

'You're about to see something that's been hidden for thousands of years and most people don't even believe in its existence. But you, Dara, you will be one of the few who will have ever seen the Crystal Charm Stone. Your life is about to change.'

22

He started at a fast pace, pulling me along behind him as we made our way through the corridor. Despite his urgency, he was cautious, checking around each corner to make sure we weren't spotted before running to the next. We entered into the oldest depths of the castle, to a part I was sure I'd never seen before.

'Where are we?' There were no lights burning in this section. The only light came from a narrow arrow slit of a window high above our heads, where a sliver of silvery moonlight crept in. The darkness was spooking me out. 'Can't you at least light a sconce?'

He put his finger to his lips as we came to a small rough-hewn plank door. He paused.

'Where are we going?' I hissed in his ear as he struggled to open the portal.

His only answer was a slight smile. When he pushed the door, it gave a groan and reluctantly opened. Inside, I could see nothing except ancient worn steps going down into the bowels of the castle. It was pitch black down there, yet a warm breeze drifted up. The air was balmy, it smelled green and rich and alive like sunshine and mangoes and colors.

Suddenly, there was a soft blue light in front of me. Sandy had lit, or caused to light, the end of his medium. The silvery driftwood glowed in his hand.

'Come on, down the stairs,' he said. 'Quickly.'

When we reach the last step of the circular stone staircase, we turned a corner and I could see, past the glow of his medium, light sparking in the distance, glimmering off the dampness of the stone walls. So we were in a tunnel, a long straight corridor with an arched stone roof, high enough that we didn't have to bend over to walk its length. I'd gone no more than ten feet when I realized which direction we were headed.

Doing a quick orientation in my head, picturing an imaginary map, figuring out the turns and twists I'd followed so far. If I was right, we were in a tunnel headed in a north westerly direction; in other words, under the mountain and towards the broch.

'This is it, isn't it?' I stopped for a moment. 'This is the secret entrance to the broch!'

My friend kept on going without me, his light held high. He appeared to be struggling as if forcing himself against a strong wind, and despite trying to pick up my pace to catch up with him, I found myself going slower too, it was like beating a path through the first big snow fall or wading through hip-deep water, and that's when I realized there was a heavy force field all around us.

There was strong magic in the air, and it was getting thicker the further we travelled down into the tunnel. I could almost

201

taste the phosphorescence in the air all around me; the balmy, tropical essence had thinned and what met my nose now was a sulfurous tinge with bitter lemon. It stung my eyes a little, and as I blinked away the tears, that's when we reached the last turn.

We had arrived at an active web of sheer power covering the whole width of the tunnel. It wasn't like the veil between Alt and real, like at home, for here on Scarp there was no such division between supernatural and normal. This was an actual curtain of magic, a spell guarding the entrance to the broch, a delicate tracing of magic like the finest spider's web. I'd never physically seen a spell before.

And beyond that web, oh, what a sight to behold.

The tunnel widened into a cavern, a huge space stretching up further than the eye could see. And before us, set on a plinth at waist level, was the truth of Sandy's legend.

The Crystal Charm Stone did exist, and it lay before us in all its magnificent unnatural glory, sending a rainbow of glow all through the huge space, like a crystal lit from within by the pure light of the universe. The arcs of color throbbed and pulsed against the rock walls. It was beautiful, it was peaceful, it was... what I had felt through the stone walls of the Broch, like a homecoming.

'Don't!' Sandy clutched my arm just in time, preventing me from going further and getting caught in the web of the magic protecting the portal.

I stepped back, wrenching my eyes away from that beautiful stone, and examined the portcullis of spells more closely.

'How'd they do this?' I whispered to him. 'There's dozens of spells here, and they're all interwoven together like a great big magical quilt.'

Sandy looked at me oddly. 'How'd you know that?'

'I can see them,' I said. 'Just as well as you. I may not know much about magic, but spells like these are hard to miss.'

His jaw slowly dropped as he understood what I was saying. 'What, you're saying you can see the individual spells?' There was disbelief on his face.

I nodded. 'Can't you?'

He shook his head slowly. 'No, Dara, that's not normal.'

After a moment, he continued. 'Bring out your coin,' he said, excitement building in his voice. 'Bring it out and see what the effect on it is.'

I stared at him as I brought it out of my pocket. The metal began to become alive in my hand, and the closer I brought it to the web of spells, the more it moved. 'It's ... it's like it's soaking up the magic, I think.' We both watched it, fascinated.

Suddenly, I heard a scraping noise echo behind us, as if someone had stumbled on a loose pebble. Sandy whirled around and held his torch aloft, just in time to see a shadowy leg disappear into the dark of the corner far ahead of us, back the way we had come from.

'Dammit!' Sandy hissed. 'Someone followed us!'

I was loathe to tear myself away from the source of my good feelings, but Sandy had already started back down the tunnel with his lit wand. It was slow going through the magical force field and the other person had a head start on him. I could see Sandy's outline in the dark up, static loose molecules of magic clinging to him like he was drenched in sparkling water. By the time we were able to run again at any decent pace, we could hear the echoes of feet pounding up the stone staircase.

There was, of course, no one in evidence by the time we burst through the portal back into the castle.

'Do you think they saw the Crystal Charm stone?' I asked him in the barest whisper, for we had no way of knowing if anyone was close enough to overhear us, perhaps hidden in the numerous nooks and crannies of the ancient walls.

He shook his head. 'I don't know if they got close enough,' he replied, also keeping his voice low. 'But whoever it is now knows about the existence of the tunnel, and you can be damn well sure they'll be down there again soon enough. We don't have a lot of time.'

Sandy glanced over at me. 'I think we need to clean up before we go back,' he said, pointing at me. 'Or they'll really be asking questions.'

Looking down at my body, I could see the dew of magic clinging to me too, showing my every movement in the darkened corridor.

I tried to brush it off, but the action merely smeared the magicked particles like cotton candy on corduroy, making my outline even more visible.

'Leave that for now,' he hissed, his ears pricked as if he'd heard something else, then he began to hurry toward another part of the castle I was unfamiliar with. That didn't stop me from staying close on his heels.

He finally came to a halt inside the cavernous kitchens, deep within the innards of the old castle. These rooms were empty at this time of night, and the huge fire in the grate was banked yet still emitted a welcome warmth. My eyes followed the line of the high ceilings, which stretched up in blackness to a skylight. Through it, I could see the winter stars sparkling white against the night.

All around me slabs of marble and stone stood in for counter space, and huge pots and pans squatted on rough plank shelving that covered one wall. Everything was over-sized, I guess that was needed if one was cooking for a whole castle's worth of people, once upon a time, but right now I felt like Jack in the Beanstalk wandering into the giant's lair.

We brought up stools in front of the fireplace and huddled close. The wooden seat was wide enough that I could perch atop it cross-legged. There was little light save that from the coals still burning in the grate.

'We're totally alone here,' he said, then he turned to me with a look of expectation. He crossed his arms together over his chest for warmth. 'Well? What do you think of my legend now?'

We stared at each other in the dim red light of the coals. We held the secret to the island's power source. Now, the only puzzle that remained was the matter of getting to the stone.

'We could win the Competition,' I said, as if he wasn't think-ing the exact same thing. 'But what I don't understand is...'

He raised his eyebrows at me.

'Why haven't you already won?' I asked him. Sandy didn't need me; I couldn't add anything to his chances that I could see. 'You've had the advantage over everyone, because you knew the stone was there. Why didn't you just figure out the anti-spells or whatever, and win over everyone else? What's holding you back?'

He said nothing, just set his jaw and looked into the glowing coals. This was the only light source here, and his face was deeply shadowed from this light. His hair shone burnished copper.

'Don't you know how to lift the gate spell?'

He laughed, rather bitterly I thought. 'Lift the gate?' he said. 'I don't even know what the spells are which make it up. I knew they were in place, I could feel the wall of magic stopping me from accessing the stone, but it would take me a year of study to figure out which each spell is.'

Sandy looked at me with excitement. 'But you're telling me you could see the actual gates, and that they're an interweaving of many. That makes sense. And I see now why...'

He didn't finish his sentence, but my mind had already returned to the glorious sights of the evening. The Crystal Charm Stone was the single most thing of beauty I could ever imagine; it was perfection, like what you were told by the priests heaven was like. Even the gate keeping it safe was a work of art, a labor of adoration like the statues in a medieval cathedral.

'Yes, I can see the gate,' I replied picturing the dancing bands of multicolored energy all interwoven into themselves. That was strong magic and it had been created with serious intent. I'd never seen a spell show so physically before, never knew it was possible.

In fact, come to think of it, I'd never seen a spell before in my life. I sat up straighter on my stool. How could I have seen it, when Sandy, a full blood witch and trained, couldn't? I looked at the coin still in my hand, glowing, the runes squirming. This must somehow be the clue to everything, how I could connect with my mother, how I could suddenly see the colors of spells and magic. Could the coin be working in conjunction with the Charm Stone?

And why didn't other people's mediums do the same thing?

I was awestruck at the force I now held in my hand, and frissons of excitement bubbled up my spine. I could do anything. In. The. World.

Yet I was scared as hell too, for I understood so little.

He was still watching me from the corners of his eyes, a closed expression on his face, or perhaps it was just the glow from the coals which lent a sinister cast to his visage.

'Okay.' I nodded as I thought aloud. 'For the competition. We should get Fergie on board with this.'

'Fergie? Why?'

'You weren't sure about what spells would be used on the gate, right?'

He reluctantly agreed.

'So that's why you didn't just scoop up the prize before we even got started. You needed me to see the spells.'

'Maybe.'

I shot him a hard look.

'Yes, then,' he said. 'For the sake of argument.'

'Well, I can see the spells, but I have no idea what they mean,' I continued. 'And I think Fergie might have a better understanding of them.'

'She's a Hedge Witch,' he objected, a sneer in his voice. 'She's barely literate, only knows Latin and Gaelic. I don't see how she'd be a match for the spells spun by the Kin elders.'

That was the second time he'd cast this slur on her. It bothered me, hearing these words come from him; Sandy was the last person I'd suspect of prejudice. 'And you think that makes her a lesser witch? What's wrong with you? And have you got a better idea?'

The logs shifted in the large fireplace, falling away from the flames. The huge room was suddenly a lot darker, the shadows looming.

'Sorry, I didn't mean that the way it came out. But...' He failed miserably in his attempt to smooth over his faux pas.

'But what?' I shot back at him.

'She'll be no use to us in the long run, Dara. Don't you realize? It's all about the stone,' he said urgently. 'Open your mind. Think of the possibilities if we could wrest control of the Crystal Charm Stone.'

'But we only need to know *how* to do it, we're not actually going to *take* the stone,' I said, yet his eyes were like steel, cutting into me. The huge kitchen had suddenly turned icy cold on my back, and I became conscious of the sound of a clock slowly ticking somewhere in the depths behind me.

'What? Are you seriously thinking of really taking the stone? Sandy, it's just a game, we don't have to go that far to prove ourselves. Theoretical, I believe were Johanna's words.' I tried to search the shadows in his face to see if he was having me on.

'We can go further than that, though, don't you see?' His voice was a fervent whisper. 'We can take down the whole lot of them.'

'We? Them?' What was he on about?

His eyes widened just a little in response. 'We, Dara, you and me,' he quickly said. 'You know you have incredible power, don't you? That gate spell down in the tunnel, I could only sense it, feel the strength of it, that's how I knew it was there. But you actually saw it, physically. That's pretty amazing. Think what we could do, together, if we had access to the stone.'

His face was glowing with the fervency of one who believes impossible things, thinking he had found the solution for all of life's earthly woes. I was becoming scared for him, and *of* him, too.

'What? What would we do?' I was mesmerized by the force of him, fascinated by what I saw in his eyes. I also felt that

Sandy was dancing on the lip of the well of insanity. One misstep and he could be lost to us forever.

'We can return the stone to its rightful owner.'

'Sandy. What are you talking about? Why would we want to do such a thing?'

The idea of even touching that terrible power made me shrivel inside, yet I'd felt the longing, like a moth to a flame. Only a suicidal fool would dream of doing this, and for what purpose? Who was the rightful owner anyway? Sandy, as the last of his clan? Or should we go further back in time, and pass it to the Ice King?

Oh.

The Ice King. What would happen if, say, someone stole the stone from Scarp and presented it to the Ice King? Would he allow that person's mother to be free? I stared at Sandy. Yeah, he might be crazy, but sometimes genius could be mistaken for insanity by those who didn't know any better, couldn't it?

But even if I could get through the barrier, and take the stone and escape the island alive, how would I find my way to that northern kingdom? Willem had said you couldn't get there by the normal routes. There were no sea lanes or reindeer roads that could lead you there.

Unless the stone would know to find its own way home.

'We can take back the island,' he whispered. 'It's not just me, there's a whole army of us, tired of living under the iron fist of the Kin. We're all over the world, and we're just waiting for that moment of time to rise up. You, Dara, you could be part of that. You have the power to save us all.'

His eyes gleamed fervently in the light of the dying coals. And I could save my mother. We stayed that way for a long moment, the two of us looking at each other, private dreams running through our minds.

But I'd been down this road before, and even if he were right about being able to steal the Crystal Charm Stone, especially if he was right about it, I wanted no part in his schemes. This route led only to trouble and binding of magic. Right there and then, I had an ominous presentiment that this would not end well.

No way. This witch was going to keep her head down and play by the rules. Even if it meant her mother had to wait. At least that's what I thought I wanted to do.

I left him then, left him sitting alone in the chilly cavernous kitchen, for I couldn't take that brand of crazy anymore.

23

We didn't find out who had followed us into the tunnel the previous night, but I knew it had to have been one of the Fearsome Four – Oliver, Timothy, Pauline or Win. Sandy thought it had been Timothy, because the person had disappeared by the time we reached the top of the stairs, and he had the longest legs. I laid bets it was Pauline, because she was such a horrible nosy parker who already suspected me of some kind of chicanery.

We still hadn't told Fergie about the Crystal Charm Stone. I wanted to, but Sandy insisted we keep it to ourselves for now.

'The more people who know about it, the more chance that someone will ruin it for us,' he hissed when I cornered him before he went to look after the animals.

She must have known something was up, I could see the hurt on her face when Sandy and I had our frequent whispered huddles. Even now, she was watching us, her large mouth downturned at the corners, her eyes all bruised and sad, and beneath that a little angry, too.

'It's only Fergie,' I said. 'She won't tell, the others don't talk to her.'

'Absolutely not. She'd do anything to keep in with the Kin.'

'Well, someone already knows, because they followed us into the tunnel last night,' I confronted him. 'We'd better act fast or they'll take the idea. I'm sure all of those Kin know how to take down a barrier spell or two, especially as it's just theoretical. The more brain power we have on our side the better, and we need to do it sooner rather than later.'

'No, the time's just not right yet.' His forehead scrunched up as if he was worried.

'You're not seriously thinking of... doing what you talked about last night,' I said. 'Sandy, are you?'

Right there and then I made him promise that we would keep this on a theoretical level, though I didn't think the promise was worth much. And it turned out I was right.

....

Physical Magic class was not grabbing my interest that day, I was impatient for it to finish. It seemed to go forever; I fidgeted with the coin as I waited for him to finally clue up. Sandy and I had agreed to hang back after Rasmussen's session. We were going to try to pick his mind.

'I'll meet you later, Fergie,' I said to her as she lingered by my bench after all the others had left the room. I put the coin down as I stood up; Rasmussen was packing up his papers and we had to catch him before he left. 'You go on.'

'No, I don't mind.' Her expression and tone were rather surly, she obviously did mind about something, and had chosen this moment to discuss it with me. She stood in my way, blocking my path to Sandy, her arms crossed pugnaciously. 'I'll wait. I want to talk with you.'

I could feel Sandy's glare from across the room. We really needed to speak with Rasmussen; I had to get Fergie out of the way, even though the whole thing would be much easier if he would agree to let her on board. I'd work on that, but until then, I couldn't let her overhear the conversation we were going to have with the Professor.

'Maybe,' I suggested, thinking wildly. 'Maybe you could do me a favor? I need the big black book that's on the table in our room. Would you mind getting that for me?'

'What, the *Arte of Engines*? Whatever do you need that for?' The sneer on her face told me she knew this was just a ruse, for the book was an incredibly long and boring explanation of the mechanics of a steam engine that Rasmussen had suggested I make myself familiar with. I tried to read a little each evening before sleep, but all I was getting from it was a solid eight hours of shut-eye every night.

'I need to ask him about some points in it.' We had a stare-down; both of us knew I lied. 'I'll keep him occupied till you get back. Please?'

I could see the storm clouds gathering on her face and I thought she was going to refuse to go, but then she turned on her heel and stomped out of the room, yelling over her shoulder as she did so, 'Go get your own book! I can take a hint and I'll not stay where I'm not wanted!'

The idea of running after her flashed through my mind, she was my friend and I'd done her wrong. But this drama would have to be dealt with later, and I pushed her out of my mind for now. I needed to join Sandy who had cornered the professor and was in the process of drawing knowledge from him.

'Barrier spells, eh?' Rasmussen was rubbing his chin and watching Sandy with a sharp look in his eye. I held my breath. He must know why we were asking.

'Theoretically, of course.' I jumped in to the conversation as I joined them, giving Sandy a good poke in the ribs with my elbow as I did so. 'How would you theoretically take down barrier spells?'

'Ah, the theory of it all,' Rasmussen said. 'That is an interesting question, for there are many types of barrier spells which can be erected. Perhaps you want to tell me more about the spells themselves?'

I thought for a moment. We couldn't come right out and say we wanted to know how to take down the gates guarding the Crystal Charm Stone, for that would be cheating according to the rules of the Competition and I knew Rasmussen would be fully aware of this, and would refuse to help us.

'Um, like a wall of spells, or a curtain...'

'Ah. And is this curtain made up of a lot of little spells, all built on each other like building blocks?' Rasmussen was trying to help us. 'Or one large spell, comprised of many little spells within it? For either of those, you would need to look at each small spell individually, and remove them that way. It is a lot of work.'

'More like a lot of small spells, all woven together.'

'Ah, that is a different scenario then! In that case, you would need to unravel the whole at once.'

'Unravel?'

'Yes, if you can see the weaving of the spells?'

I nodded.

'Interesting. Then that must be handled very particularly. For if you do not unravel the whole all at once, say if you just pick at the warp of the spells one by one, then you are left in a situation where the weft spells are unbalanced, and that can rebound on you if you are standing close to them, which of course you must be, if you are attempting to undo the spells.'

He beamed at us. 'Does that help solve your theoretical problem?'

'Um,' I looked at Sandy with my eyebrows raised. I knew next to nothing about the weaving of spells, so he had to pick up my slack.

My friend was shaking his head. 'Not really,' he said, his voice full of doubt. 'That would take a hell of a long time to do, wouldn't it?'

Rasmussen laughed. 'It would take the weaver of the spells a long time, yes, for they would know the nature of each spell woven into the whole. For someone who did not have this prior knowledge, it might take a lifetime.'

His bright eyes glinted like flint in the sunshine behind his rimless spectacles. Sandy and I looked at each other, and he shook his head. Rasmussen hadn't been as much help as he has supposed, except to highlight the impossibility of the task. I pictured again the curtain of spells stretched across the entrance to the cavern which held the stone. The whole was a solid weaving, with a heft like a heavy curtain or drapery.

A solid curtain of fabric, but not a solid brick wall. Curtains were made to be pulled back.

'Could one...' I began, then hesitated, looking for the right words. 'Could one simply pull aside the net of spells? I mean, bypass the whole undoing of the spells, because you wouldn't necessarily have to go to all that trouble.'

I felt Sandy start at my side.

Rasmussen stared at me for a long moment. 'If one could do that, then going to the trouble of weaving the net of spells would be quite pointless, don't you think?'

I put my head to one side, and shrugged. 'It was just an idea. I guess I didn't think that one out.'

'Perhaps one should think about that idea a little more in depth,' Rasmussen said, his bright eyes boring into me. 'Theoretically, of course. If one could actually see the net of spells in a hypothetical barrier, well then, one has a distinct advantage over any who cannot see the net.'

I met his eyes with a thrill of excitement and thought quickly. 'So one could hold aside the curtain,' I said.

He nodded. 'If one could see where the anchor points were, then it should be easy enough,' he said. 'But of course, that course of action involves holding the spells in one's hands, and could lead to third degree burns.'

Rasmussen laughed again. 'It would take more than one witch to hold off that damage from occurring,' he said genially. 'But of course, it could be done. Theoretically.'

He grew quiet, and continued to bore into me with his pebbly eyes. I felt like he could see right through my intentions. 'One would need the aid of a strong medium in order to work this magic,' he said. 'If one does not have a medium that is closely aligned, it would be a very difficult task for any witch. And that is why Physical Magic is a more useful tool than Pure Mind.'

·····•·····

'We absolutely need Fergie on board,' I hissed at Sandy once we had exited the round tower room and the heavy door was safely shut.

'No.' Sandy headed down the stone steps rather than take the corridor which eventually led to the Common Room, and I hurried to keep up with him.

'But don't you see?' I persevered in a whisper. 'It would take at least two people to loosen and pull back the gate, while the other slipped in to take the stone.'

'We can't get her involved.'

'But Sandy, remember how Johanna said team work would be necessary?' He picked up his pace without answering. He was almost at the bottom of the staircase.

'We can't win the stupid competition alone!' In my need to get him on board, I forgot to keep my voice low, and he stopped immediately, staring straight ahead.

I clattered down the stairs and caught up to him, saw the look of horror on his face and immediately after that, saw the reason why. Timothy lounged against the stone wall just around the corner, a sneer on his face.

'Oh, someone has hopes of winning the Competition, do they?' His long dreadlocks glittered in the morning sun from the window. He must have put a shimmer on himself. Timothy stood up straight and crossed his arms, effectively blocking the way to entrance to the hallway.

'No,' Sandy replied shortly as he attempted to push past him. 'Give over, Timothy. What sort of game are you playing at?'

'I'm playing to win, my friend,' the other said. 'And I think you might have information you'd like to share.'

'I've got nothing for you.' Again Sandy roughly tried to push him out of the way, but Timothy had the advantage of height and an athletic torso which refused to move.

'So what?' Timothy sneered down at the short Scotsman. 'You'd work with a half-blood? Share your glory with the likes of her?' He flicked his dreadlocks and glitter floated in the sunlight, as he pushed Sandy in the shoulder.

'Stop it, I told you!' Sandy's face was suffused with rage, and his shoulders hunched like a football player ready to burst through the opposition's line. 'If you don't get out of my way I'll feckin' kill you, you bloody Sassenach!'

'Give it up already, you guys!' I attempted to come between them before someone's blood got smeared on the walls. I stood directly in front of Timothy, daring him to touch me, counting on his being the perfect English gentleman who would never raise a hand to a woman. And if he did, well, that was his own lookout, for I'd learned to fight dirty in the back streets of my hometown, where we never pulled our punches.

Timothy must have seen that in my face, because he turned and haughtily sniffed, and generally acted as if he'd lost interest in the affair.

'We're watching you,' he said, as he slid his eyes over me. 'There's to be no cheating. And that means you, half-blood.' With that he turned and left us.

··········

Sandy and I walked slowly through the castle, in the unused corridors where there were fewer corners and nooks for anyone to lurk behind and overhear us. Still, we kept our voices low.

'Who followed us down there last night?'

He shook his head. 'It couldn't have been Timothy after all,' he replied. 'That one would be stupid enough to tell us if he knew about the stone.'

I kept my disagreement to myself. 'At any rate, we're going to have to finish working out the plan of how we would theoretically hold back the curtain of spells,' I said. 'Someone saw us, and it'll just be a matter of time before they work out the puzzle.'

'No,' Sandy spoke quickly. 'It's not time yet.'

'You said that before. What are we waiting for?' Out of habit, I reached for the coin in my pocket to play with it, to occupy my hands while I thought. 'Sandy, we're not going to take the stone. That's just plain nuts. Have you wondered how we're going to lift it? You just going to sling it into your knapsack and toss it over your shoulder? It's overkill, we don't need to prove we can actually do it, just on paper.'

He set his mouth in a grim line.

'Besides,' I continued. 'We can't do it between the two of us. We need someone else on board, and Fergie is the natural choice. I don't know enough about spells and things, and she, well, even if she is just a Hedge Witch as you say, she'll be a hell of a lot more useful than me.'

He gave a sigh. 'I don't trust her. I never have.'

'Between the two of us, we can't figure out the barrier spells,' I insisted.

His eyes were shadowed. 'But you don't know the whole story.' He set his mouth grimly and refused to explain what he meant.

24

I was starving, but it wasn't yet time for lunch. The porridge had been on the thin side that morning, with no berries or cream or other fruit to help fortify us for the day.

But I now knew the route to the kitchen.

'I wouldn't.' Sandy shook his head. 'You won't be welcomed there, not when the staff are working. You could go to the Common Room to see if there's any biscuits leftover in the tin.' He didn't sound hopeful.

'The worst they can tell me is no. We could probably make a sandwich or something. Anything.'

He stopped to stare at me. 'How can you even think about eating at a time like this?'

'I'm hungry, that's how.'

He drew himself near and spoke in a low voice. 'We are about to be a part of the most exhilarating change ever to happen in the world of the Kin, and all you can think about is your belly?'

'Yeah. I mean, we need to keep our strength up, don't we?'

Sandy was probably fueling himself through adrenaline and expectation, but that wasn't working for me.

We came to the long corridor which ran front to back of the castle. 'I'm going to the kitchens,' I announced loudly, and turned down the hallway. 'You can come with me or not.'

He chose not.

I stepped into the cavernous expanse with the high ceilings and huge fireplaces and mysterious cupboards and marble counter tops. The walls had all been whitewashed a long time ago; they bore the build-up of a couple of decades of grease and smoke, black streaks rising to the ceiling from all around the fireplaces. Only one was lit, the logs giving off a welcome warmth. Yet, the room appeared to be unoccupied.

As there was no one available to ask permission, I found the bread stored in a large cabinet behind a metal grill, and hacked off a couple of chunks with a butcher's knife. It was freshly baked that day and it squished under the non-serrated edges of the knife but no matter, for I had also found butter and jam in the larder. They'd been holding out on me – I'd hardly seen the sweet red stuff since I got here. I lathered it all on a hunk of bread and fortified myself.

Something clanked in a near corridor, and I heard the sounds of footsteps drawing near. I quickly took my hunk of bread, the butter dish and jam and escaped to the Common Room, which was empty at this time of day as I'd thought it would be. A low fire burned there and I stretched out length-ways on the longest sofa.

And finally with blood sugar levels starting to rise again my mind could get back to work.

The door creaking open brought me back to earth. I paused where I was, realizing I was hidden from view in the depths of the lumpy old couch whose back was to the opening, but I was about to call out to alert the person of my presence.

'That's all we need from you, Fergie,' I heard Pauline's wheedling voice from the corridor. 'Try to get more information.'

'But I'm not speaking with her.'

'Do you want *them* to win? To exclude you?'

'Well, no, but...'

'Just do as I say,' Pauline continued.

'How do I know you guys won't cut me out of the credit?'

'I am the daughter of an elder, and I'm part of the Kin, I'm honorable.' I could just picture Pauline puffing herself up with pride as she spoke. It was far too late to announce my presence. I kept very still and hoped they would pass on again without coming in and discovering me. I didn't like the way this conversation was going – had Fergie gone over to the dark side? A pang of remorse hit me, for we had been ignoring her lately.

'Come on, now, Fergie.' Timothy cut in. 'We've known each other for ages. Would I do that to you?'

'I, oh, this doesn't feel right.'

'All's fair in love and war, eh, Ferg?' Timothy cajoled.

'I think I know how to open the barrier spells,' Pauline said in a low voice.

'You can hold off on that,' Timothy said. "Why don't we see what Fergie here can get from them?'

'You're planning to steal Sandy and Dara's work.' I heard the slight tinge of bitterness in Fergie's voice, but neither of the other two picked up on it.

'I doubt they can come up with anything that could compare with my own.'

'How do you even know what the barrier spells are made of?'

'Oh, I have a good idea.' Pauline was smug in her confidence.

'Besides, we can always get Win to blast them with Dragon Magic.'

'We'll worry about that later,' Pauline dismissed.

I heard their footsteps continuing on down the hall, and I took a deep breath. Bastards! They would stoop so low as to steal the work they thought Sandy and I had done. That was the Kin for you.

I began to haul myself upright, but right at that same moment I heard Fergie's voice.

'Ooh look, jam!'

We stopped, me half-sitting up, Fergie in mid-stride, and we stared at each other.

'Well, hello, traitor.' I was the first to speak.

'It's not what you think!'

Fergie continued her way over to the table and set about making a jam sandwich, her back held stiffly. She gave a toss of her curls and a sniff.

'Sure looks pretty bad from where I'm sitting.'

'Well, how about you and Sandy?' She flung back at me as she turned around, her sandwich dripping its sweet red juice on to the table. 'You two have pretty much deserted me, going off on your own, discovering the Crystal...'

She stopped in mid-sentence and stuffed the rest of the bread in her mouth.

I sat up fully now. 'That was you following us in the tunnel? But why? Why be so secretive about it?'

'You dare to ask me why?' she asked through a mouth full of jam. It was not a pretty sight. 'I thought we were beginning to be a group, the three of us. But then you're always going off with Sandy, and I was feeling like the third wheel.

'I knew you were on to something, and you were cutting me out,' she continued. 'That was pretty rubbish, you know.'

Fergie swallowed a big lump, then looked down at the bread in her hand and took another angry bite. She chewed a little more slowly, then swallowed again. 'I guess I was feeling left out.'

'So you know about the tunnel and what's in it...'

'That the Crystal Charm Stone exists? Yeah,' Fergie said. She wiped a bit of jam from the corner of her lip and licked her finger. 'That blew all of us away. Who'd have thought little Sandy had it right all the time?'

'All of us? You told the others? Are you working with them? Fergie!'

'Oh come on, Dara,' Fergie said, coming round to sit on the sofa beside me. 'I was hurt. I knew I didn't have a chance of winning the Competition, but after I followed you guys, well, I thought maybe if I gave this info to the rest of them, make it a level playing field so to speak, they'd...'

'Stop bullying you? Accept you as part of the gang?'

Fergie sighed and rolled her eyes. 'Fat chance of that happening, eh? Well, for what it's worth, I'm sorry. Sorry for telling them about the tunnel.'

I thought for a moment, then nodded. 'How close are the others to finding out how to win the Competition?'

She thought for a moment. 'They haven't yet agreed how to lift the barrier of spells. Pauline thinks it's this complicated whole set of spells, which she is sure she can undo given time, but Win just wants to blast it."

I winced.

'I know, right? That'd just bounce right back in her face and she'd end up heavily singed at the best if they went that route.' Fergie grinned suddenly. 'So they haven't really come to an agreement amongst themselves. Pauline wants to be in charge of course, but the others aren't having any of that. Timothy figures he knows how to divert the energy of the stone by matching his own crystal to it. I guess it's just a matter of time till they agree on a method, and bring it to Johanna. I'd say tomorrow morning.'

With a rustle of his wool kilt, Sandy stepped quickly into the Common Room and slammed the door. I could feel the anger he brought into the room with him, like a force-field of aggression.

'What the hell, Dara?' he hissed. 'You haven't told...'

'Hey, chill out,' I said, jumping to my feet as Fergie flattened herself into the back of the sofa, trying to make herself less visible. 'What's done is done. We got followed into the tunnel. Everyone else knows and they've ramped up their efforts to find a plan.'

It took him a moment to fight his rage and digest this information. His eyes narrowed as he looked at me. 'That means we've got to do it tonight.'

'Ah, no.' I was quick to disagree. His crazy plan to steal the Crystal? I had to discourage that. 'A little too soon. That's not the plan.'

'Do what tonight?' Fergie asked. 'You mean you've already got it all figured out and you're going to Johanna tonight?' Her eyes lit with glee.

'No,' I said to her, thinking fast. I wasn't about to tell her Sandy's plan, I couldn't let her get mixed up in this. Besides, she'd already shown herself to be untrustworthy. 'He means... a dry run. A dress rehearsal. We want to see if we can do it, if it actually works.'

'Can I help?' Fergie's face was shining with excitement. 'Oh, God, there must be...'

'No,' Sandy cut in. 'It's just me and Dara.'

As her face fell, I realized that if we forced her out, I wouldn't blame her for going back to the Kin and telling them what she thought we were planning. Best to keep her close, I decided.

'I will warn you,' Fergie said as she gave a quick glance around the otherwise empty room, and she leaned in closer. 'They've got something planned. There's no way they're going to let you back down into the tunnel, they're going to set traps for you and at the same time they are furiously trying to come up with a solution.'

'It can't be that bad,' I said a little nervously. 'We'll just take extra care to avoid anything they put in our way.'

Fergie looked at me with fear in her eyes. 'You don't un-derstand,' she said, shaking her head. 'They are out for blood. *Your* blood. They will never let you win the Competition, even if they have to kill you doing it.'

She was afraid for me, and she was telling the truth. The Kin wanted me out of the way. They wanted to take my future out from under me. My blood was beginning a slow boil at the arrogance of those who had everything in their lives already, unwilling to give me the ghost of a chance. This had been the story of my life with the Kin. I would never get anywhere, never reach my dreams.

No more. I looked up from where my fingers played with the coin and met Sandy's gaze. My anger must have shown on my face for he gave a small smile and a nod.

'Do me a favor?' Fergie looked nervously first at Sandy, then at me. 'Don't tell them I told you all this. Please. I have to live in Scotland, these guys are going to be in my future for the rest of my life if I want to do anything with my magic.' She bit her lip. 'I don't know what they have planned, but I would advise you to stop right here. You can't beat the Kin.'

··········

Sandy drew me aside after Fergie had slunk out of the Common Room. We'd promised not to let the others know what she had confessed to us, but we would still need her on board to figure out the barrier spells. I only hoped she would come down into the tunnel with us again.

'It's time you knew the rest of the story,' he said. 'Come with me.'

With that he turned and led me down the corridor to the outside entrance, the one leading to the barn and beyond.

I tried to speak with him, to discuss the details of how to hold back the barrier in the tunnel that led to the Crystal Charm Stone, and to figure out how to theoretically lift the stone or at least divert its energy. Once we had that down, we could go to Johanna with our results and claim the prize. My future would be assured, but he ignored all this talk, turning the conversation instead to the island's shepherd.

'What does he have to do with anything?' I asked guiltily, knowing there was a strong possibility that his hermit had come to harm at the hands of Willem, and that this was my fault for leading the sorcerer to the island.

'I think he's the key to it all,' Sandy continued, mysteriously.

And so I confessed to everything, I told him all about the illusions that were real, to all my contacts with Willem so far on Scarp, and how I thought his shepherd was probably dead.

Sandy listened in silence as we sat out by the barn, leaning against the stone walls where we were sheltered from the wind. 'What do you believe, Dara?'

I thought long and hard, and I shook my head. 'I know what I saw, and said, and heard and felt,' I said. 'But it doesn't matter. None of that matters. Let's just get this Competition over and done with, then I can show them all. Worry about the rest of it later. And I'm sorry about your shepherd.'

I felt Sandy relax a little beside me. His eyes cut off to the distance, to the hills and the sea beyond. 'I think it's time we went to prove to all of them that you're right.'

'What do you mean?'

'Where will we find Willem?'

'He's staying in your shepherd's bothy,' I said. 'I think... I really think he may have harmed your friend.'

I let that sink in. 'I mean, I think you already have met him,' I added. 'But he cast a spell so that you thought he was the shepherd.'

'Then we must definitely go to see him.' Sandy's face was hidden from me as he turned to look at the sea. I thought he might be shedding a tear or two for the hermit.

'There'll be time for that later,' I told him, trying to keep my voice kind without showing my burning impatience.

'No.' This came out quickly like an automatic reaction. 'We're going to find your sorcerer now.'

'Sandy, I'm sorry about your friend,' I said again. 'I had no idea that Willem had tracked me here to the island. I guess it's my fault if...'

'Right then.' Sandy jumped up from the table. 'Dara, you're coming with me.'

He'd already taken off, heading up the hill. His short legs could really get up some speed as he raced over the rocks and gorse like a sure-footed mountain goat in his boots. His legs were strong under the kilt, and he had been walking hills and moorlands all his life. I struggled to keep up with him.

As we made our way up the hill, Sandy began to talk. 'Do you see, now, after what Fergie said they're planning? They have no intention of letting you or me win this competition, it's all a farce. It's time to pay them back and take control away from them all. It's all politics, you know.'

'Slow down,' I gasped. He paused a moment to let me catch up, then started again but at least at a lesser pace. 'What are you talking about?'

'We can't let things continue in this way, and we have the power to stop them,' he said. He held aside a gorse bush so it didn't flick back on me.

As we continued up the hill, no longer following any human path, I realized we were heading in the direction of the shepherd's bothy.

'Wait, Sandy!' But he had sprinted up ahead of me again, his face grim.

I felt a deep regret at having told him about the sorcerer, for Willem was my only link with my mother. If Sandy found him, there would be bloodshed in retribution for Hamish's life, or worse, he would turn him into the Kin. I gulped and forced myself to run faster. Right now, he needed little to further ignite his rage. He would haul Willem down to Johanna, my role in attracting Willem to the island would be ascertained, and I would be finished. Never mind having my magic bound, there would be nothing left to help me find my mother.

Of course, Willem would not let this happen, and the sorcerer had killed for less than this.

'Wait!' I screamed after his fast disappearing back.

But to no avail. He continued on a path known only to himself and the rabbits, and he soon arrived at the bothy where I had happened upon the sorcerer before. As I topped the last hill before the shepherd's hut and turned that corner of the hillside, I saw that I was far too late to stop him entering. He didn't even bother knocking, just opened the door and strode on in, knowing to duck his head as if he'd been here many times before.

I was just in time to see the swish of Sandy's kilt disappear into the open door.

'Be careful!' Oh God, Sandy would be no match for the sorcerer in a war of spells. I had to help him. I raced after him through the door, fully expecting to see the two in a wrestling match as Sandy wreaked revenge for his friend's death.

Instead, they were both sitting quite companionably on the stone benches which served as table, seats and bed in the tiny bothy.

Willem turned to me with a benevolent smile.

25

It took a moment for my eyes to adjust to the sudden dimness inside the bothy after the harsh winter sunlight outside, unfettered as it was by shadows or clouds.

'Welcome, Dara. We have much to discuss now,' Willem said. The two men faced me, relaxed, no turmoil on their faces.

'Please, be seated,' he urged.

'What's going on?' I looked at the sorcerer, and then at Sandy. Willem was not hiding behind a disguise spell as far as I could make out. 'He's not your shepherd! Can't you see?'

'There's nothing wrong with Sandy's eyesight, Dara,' Willem said drily. 'We are well acquainted already.'

'I don't understand.'

'You still think it was you who drew me to Scarp?'

'The coin, you had some sort of magical GPS on it, you followed me here,' I accused him. 'I don't know how you managed to break through the island's defences.'

The two men looked at each other and smiled. Willem even tittered.

'You haven't changed at all, have you?' he asked with a fond smile. 'You still insist everything is all about you.'

'How else would you have known to come after me?' I asked him hotly. 'It has to be the coin and whatever you put on it.'

He shook his head, and the men shared a laughing glance. 'No, how many times do I have to tell you? Not you. You were incidental to this story.'

Sandy leaned back against the stone wall of the one roomed-hut and crossed his arms, as if settling in to hear an enjoyable story. I stared at him in disbelief. What had happened to his anger?

'All this was already in motion long before our fateful meeting, Dara my dearest,' Willem continued. 'I really have become quite fond of you, but you were never a part of this tale in the beginning. It is, as I say, all happy coincidence. Perhaps our paths were fated to intertwine?'

'Cursed, more like it.'

He laughed as if I'd meant that as a joke.

'When I met you in Canada, I was merely filling in time, waiting for the steamboat to arrive to take me across the ocean.'

'But the women, the money you took from them... And the creatures you created. You can't say all that wasn't premeditated.'

Willem had, with my reluctant assistance, ripped away the veil between Alt and real. There was no way all of that could have been a spur of the moment lark.

He nodded. 'Correct,' he agreed. 'I'd allowed myself time in my schedule to create a little havoc against Jon de Teilhard.

We go back a long way, Jon and I, and it felt good to let him know I was still alive and kicking.

'But I digress. This moment in time, this is what I've been working towards for years, what many of us have been combining our efforts towards. This is the work of the century. And it would not have been possible without my dear friend Alexander McCloud.'

Sandy smiled proudly.

'How are you involved in all of this?' I looked with dismay at my fellow student.

The Scotsman cleared his throat. 'How else do you think Willem could get past the defences of the island but with a McCloud ushering him through? *The* McCloud, I should add, there are no more of my line, thus I hold title to the island and the island knows this.

'Scarp will never deny me access, and any who enter with me. It was a simple enough thing to take a wee boat across the strait to pick up Willem, after I'd been established here all fall.'

'I don't think anyone suspected you at all,' Willem added with admiration.

I did my best to ignore the Dutchman as I zeroed in on my friend.

'But why, Sandy? Why would you choose to get mixed up with all this?' Yet even as the words were leaving my mouth, I knew the answer. Old grudges die hard, and Sandy had been fed the tales by his great-grandmother from a very young age. He probably even saw himself as a modern-day Arthur, come to free his ancestral lands from the villainous Kin. 'Do you even realize what Willem is planning?'

'And high time it is! The Kin have held us down for too long, all of us,' Sandy spit out. 'You'll find this rebellion will only rise in popularity once people find out what we have accomplished.'

'And she thought I followed her here,' Willem said as an aside to Sandy, giggling as he harped on the point. 'In the face of the greatest popular movement of all time, Dara thought it was all about *her*.'

'What is it, then? What are you hoping to do on this island far away from anywhere else?' I asked him, fervently ignoring the Dutchman's comments.

Sandy leaned forward intently. 'The Crystal Charm Stone, of course, Dara,' he said. 'That's what this is all about. Who-ever controls access to that, controls all of the world.'

I finally sat on the cold stone bench opposite them, shivers rising through my spine. 'And I suppose, you, Willem, you're the mastermind of this revolution? The Che Guevara of the movement?'

He barked with laughter. 'Me? I am merely a humble foot soldier, executing my orders for the greater good.'

At a look from Sandy, he put his head to one side and modestly reconsidered. 'Well, perhaps an officer in the war. But no more than that. There are far more powerful beings than me behind it.'

He smiled at me with his little teeth. 'You should really come with us, Dara. Join the cause. We could use good witches like you.'

He chuckled. 'The offer will dry up soon, but right now it still stands.'

I looked at the two of them, trying to hide my thoughts from my face and my mind, while still trying to feel what I knew.

I'd been here before, forced to make a choice, and this time I vowed I would not be so weak as to choose the easy-for-me route, for I knew that would only lead to trouble. It should have been an easy choice to choose the right over the wrong, but it never was. This had been in the works for years, he said, and if Willem and his team could have made it so far as to infiltrate Scarp, then there were pretty good odds they could succeed in their goal. The sorcerer was telling me the truth, and he would accept me as a partner. I would learn much at his side, but at what price?

On the other hand, the price of not going along with him? My future, my mother's future. It was a no brainer, really. Especially if I could throw it all in the face of the Kin.

'So, you have figured out Johanna's puzzle?'

I looked up sharply, then glanced to Sandy. What business was the Competition to the sorcerer?

'The theoretical question,' Willem continued as he got up and moved to the stone fireplace below the open air window which drew the smoke out of the small space. 'How could one, if one was so inclined, disrupt the flow of Scarp's power lines, and thus take over the power which the Kin have been feeding off for untold generations?'

'Did you tell him...?' I directed my whispered question to Sandy, although the space was so small Willem could not have helped but heard.

'Did Sandy tell me?' Willem stopped and turned to face me, silently laughing hard enough to make his body shake. 'Who do you think masterminded this quest?'

'I don't understand. What would *you* have to do with this?

'Johanna said that I suggested it to her, a hypothetical question with the idea to cut down on the violence which has been getting out of hand,' Sandy reminded me. 'Well, the idea was Willem's.'

'Such an irony.' I could hear the smile in the Dutchman's voice as he opened a metal canister. 'When I've known all along how to hack the system. They just wouldn't give me the access.'

'But we can get there,' Sandy said. 'And we have the power now.'

Willem turned to me then, to hand me a mug of rough clay. 'Tea?'

I took it in my hand, but openly sniffed the brew with suspicion. He laughed again.

'No, no secret spells or magic used, I promise,' he said as he handed a similar mug to Sandy. 'Just honest to goodness Breakfast Tea, a blend I am very partial to myself.'

We sat then, the three of us at this mad tea party in the run down bothy.

'Wait now,' I said, finally cluing in as to what they were talking about. 'You don't mean you're planning to actually divert the energies somehow? And you expect me to help?'

I couldn't believe what I was hearing. Sandy had danced around that, yes, but I'd thought it was just wishful thinking on his part, the underdog wanting to reclaim his heritage. This... this was bigger. Far bigger.

And they expected me to play a role.

'What are you trying to achieve with this action, Willem?' I let the full extent of my disbelief show through. 'You're going to waltz in and take the Crystal Charm Stone? Are you nuts? I've seen, I've felt the power of that thing from a distance. It would kill anyone who went near it. It's suicidal.'

'Not me, dear heart,' he said. 'I won't be in the castle or the tunnel. That's where you come in.'

'Right,' I scoffed. 'You expect me to go to a certain death. This is so not happening, dude. Why would I, what's in it for me? And what's the purpose of this nonsense?'

'The answer is quite simple, I should think,' said Willem, chiding me. 'Even you must have figured that one out immediately. You want to find your mother. She is with the Ice King, for whatever reasons she may have, and she is unable to leave. I am the only person you know who has access to his court, who can come and go at will. Ergo, you shall earn this privilege of being my partner by working with me.'

'But why? Why are you planning this?' I really couldn't see beyond the point of the tunnel, for no one would make it out alive. No way would the Kin allow this to happen. Walk off with the stone? Not likely.

'Because the Ice King needs to reclaim what is his.'

'But this will... the Kin...' I realized what the effect would be on the Witch Kin. Losing their source of power, they would revert back to being simple witches, if there was such a thing. They would lose their seat, their source of power, their domination over the whole world, not just in Scotland or in my hometown. I couldn't even begin to imagine the scope of their downfall.

My father. Cate. Those entitled witches in Scarp. I couldn't help that small smile forming on my face. I could show them all.

'How will you ever get it past them?' My voice was quiet.

'You'll see.'

26

Meanwhile, the day was drawing in. I closed my eyes as the enormity of his plans washed over me. If Willem was successful, the whole world would change. Not just mine, or my future.

And if I went along with him, which would be crazy, what would I gain? My mother's freedom.

Would I be an outlaw, if the Kin's rule of law melted down and there were no longer any laws to break? If the Kin were broken, how could they punish me?

What *could* my future look like?

Willem held no power over me, this was my decision to make. Yes, he knew where my mother was, and had access to the Ice Kingdom but he couldn't be the only one, there must be someone somewhere who would also gain me access. This was no doubt a place where it was very cold most of the year round, and presumably to the north. How large was the North Pole, or even the upper most latitudes of the globe? Not so big really, because the population in that huge area was tiny. Small enough that people being people, they knew what everyone else was up to, and would know of my Mom. Geographical boundaries, and magical borders, would not be so difficult to access once I was working with the Kin.

Because there was no way Willem could steal the Crystal Charm Stone right from under the noses of the Kin. I was wavering on the razor's edge here, all I had were my wits, and they were never my strongest point. However, the wisp of a plan was forming in my mind.

Willem had burned a hole right through my consciousness, enabling him to easily crawl back in whenever I was weakened. If I could ascertain just one thing, then I could turn the tide of events and never need the sorcerer and his magic.

The dregs in my mug had long since grown cold. I dashed them to the dirt floor beneath our feet.

'What is it you expect of me?' I broke into their conversation. 'What is it you want me to do to help your cause?'

The pair both peered at me through the gloom, as if they'd forgotten my existence, then Willem looked down at the wet ground by my feet with a disapproving air.

'We expect nothing of you, Dara, that you would not do of your own volition,' Willem said, his face severe. 'You will be you, and will carry on doing what you will do, until the moment comes when you need to act. And when that moment arrives, you will know it, and you will understand what you must do.'

This cryptic talk made no sense to me and I let him know. He laughed and spoke again, his eyes on mine all the while.

'I know you Dara,' he said, his voice soft and melodious. 'Better than you know yourself, perhaps. I have been inside you, you must remember, and I have seen you, felt you. I love that you opened up to me and allowed me the space in your mind, that little corner that is all mine.'

As he spoke, hypnotizing me, I could feel the first cold draft of him as he touched me inside, into that dark hidden crevice he had burned himself into that unforgettable night. And like a Tundra flower responding to the icy northern sun, that corner stirred and opened and I had to allow it else he would suspect my own plan.

It was the hardest thing I'd ever tried to do, allowing this invasion into the depths of my mind while keeping all I didn't want him to see away from the cold tendrils of his touch. I forced myself to breathe deeply, evenly, and to keep my heart at its steady relaxed pace; I forced myself to think thoughts of failure and despair and giving up all fight, so that was all that he would feel in me.

I could see the bright yellow flare of his surprise that I gave in so easily, then the green of his greed as he pushed in further and further, moving around in my mind, expanding that small crevice I'd thought had healed over, stretching the scar tissue to its utmost as he settled in like a cold blooded lizard into the warmth that was me.

I closed my lids, I couldn't stand to have his eyes on mine any longer. I could hear him breathing quickly in the silence of the bothy.

What is your deepest desire?

The picture of Mom flashed to my mind without me even trying.

I thought so. Come with me.

And suddenly, we were there again, in the room of the ice King's palace, a chamber of glittering ice that sparkled with prisms of color; the rainbows of hues glinted over the blue white walls, all solid ice, yet even the warm tones of yellow and red were icy. No windows allowed sunlight, if there was a sun in that cold land, and no cloth furnishings softened the harsh whiteness. A fearsome figure sat on a dais, his throne made of reindeer antlers and whale bones. Frost glittered from his long beard as he drank from a goblet of crystal and talked with his council in low tones. His crown was created from the finest bones of birds, and he was clothed fully in the thickest of furs; it was hard to tell what was clothing and what was his own furry pelt. Yet a great log burned in the stone fireplace to his left, a log of proportions I'd never seen in my lifetime, and I could hear the crackling of the wood. He made a great roar at something that displeased him.

God, I could even smell the burning of the pine sap, and the sweetness of the needles which covered the floor under his feet. I, or we, were right there in the room.

The woman was bent over a table, preparing a meal of roasted beast of some kind, and a whole fish seared to a crisp, its eye staring blankly out at the cavernous space. She was thinner than I remembered, worn with the weight of ages. She wearily brought her hand to her face to push a stray lock back, her blond highlights dulled to a mousy brown in this land without sun.

Mom. I couldn't help it, the thought leaped out of my mind.

She gave a start, and quickly glanced toward the men, but they had noticed nothing. My mother stayed perfectly still with her head cocked to one side like a sparrow on the alert for danger.

Mom, I'm here.

She let out the breath I didn't know she'd been holding, bowed her head and closed her eyes, bringing her hands before her like a prayer. And that's when I noticed the glittering band of ice surrounding her wrist, like a bracelet. *No. Get away. Don't let him see you, don't let him know you're here.*

My mother was no guest to this august being. She was enslaved.

Willem quickly withdrew us, whisking us out of this pine-scented land. But it had been enough to show me I could contact Mom through the sorcerer's mind. I kept my smile secret. I knew what I was going to do to save my mother, and that was the most important thing. I wasn't on the side of the Kin, and I wasn't on Willem's side.

I opened my eyes and stared at Willem. 'He, it, whatever he is, he has made her a slave, that's why she can't leave.'

Willem shrugged. 'Perhaps an enforced guest, hmm? At least you see the need to remove her from his clutches. He is temperamental, the Ice King; I don't envy anyone whose life is at his whim.'

'You mean, her life is in danger?'

'Let's just say his slaves don't tend to have long lifespans, and Marian has lasted far longer than most.'

'We have to act fast,' Sandy said, impatient with what he saw as non-action. 'The others know about the Crystal Charm Stone and the tunnel. They're planning something to stop us. We need to act quickly.'

'I thought you said none of them believed in it.' Willem scowled at him. 'We are not ready to act yet.'

'It's now or never. Once one of them figures out the necessary charms and spells and actions and presents it to the Kin, they'll close off the access.'

'But they won't think to take the stone themselves,' Willem observed. 'They'll only present the solution as a hypothetical exercise.'

I shook my head to clear it of the noise of their quibbling, and walked over to the small glassless window opening. My mother was being forcibly confined by this Ice King. Willem held the key to my entry there.

'You still haven't told me what you want me to do,' I said. 'Explicitly. I need to know your whole plan. And I haven't agreed to anything yet.'

'I think you have agreed, Dara, only you don't realize this, yet.' Willem was quiet for a moment as he stared at me. 'You will help Sandy hold back the net of spells. While he keeps it open, you shall take the Charm Stone in your hands and walk out of the castle with it, to meet me by the pier.'

'I'll get burned to a crisp the moment I lay a hand on the stone,' I objected. 'How is that going to help anyone, especially me?'

'That's the joy of it,' Willem replied. 'You will work with me.'

'You're coming down the tunnel with us?'

He shook his head. 'No need, my dear. Don't you see? This is the beauty of the new and improved plan now that we have you on board. With our very special connection, I can enter your mind, and we can work together, the perfect melding of power - witch and sorcerer. Only neither of us is fully one or the other, eh?'

Willem was watching me with what could pass for a fond smile. 'You know, you really are quite dear to me, Dara,' he said. 'I have grown oh so fond of you, and it makes my heart sing to see that you have chosen me.'

'I'm not choosing you, Willem,' I replied, my voice devoid of emotion. 'I don't have much choice in the matter as far as I can see.'

'That's what you say,' he noted. 'But I think I know you better than you know yourself, dear one.'

He may have been right. Then again, he didn't know everything.

Willem stood up and draped one hand on my shoulder and with the other he grasped my left hand to help me stand. He gave a big show of hugging me which I had to endure without visibly cringing at the physical touch, then he let me go on my way.

Sandy and I walked back to the castle in the twilight of the afternoon in total silence. The sun had taken an early goodnight behind a cover of dark blue and charcoal clouds, and even the shadows had melted into the dusk. Without him ahead of me, leading the way, I might not have found the twisty path on this mountain side.

I was still chilled to the bone from the whole 'Willem in my head' experience, and not a little bothered by my body and mind's reaction to him. I hated this betrayal.

What was lying ahead for me? He'd said he would be with me the whole while, if we were to pull this off. If he'd given me orders, I could at least have the satisfaction of disobeying, of doing the opposite to what he demanded, anything to stop this in its tracks. But he hadn't, so I couldn't divert the train of affairs.

27

I couldn't stomach the thought of eating after this, no matter how hungry I was. I could barely swallow my burning rage, let alone a lunch of cold mutton stew. And I had a doozy of a headache coming on.

Like a wounded animal, I needed to get away for some quiet time to deal with my thoughts. An underground burrow would be ideal, far from the noise and the lights and the ill will of the Kin, but the castle had lots of dark gloomy spots in which to curl up and nurse my hurts and try to make sense of everything that was happening.

Hugh had said I might suffer delusions because of the harm Willem had inflicted on me. Hallucinations. Was this it? Had my mind placed Willem in the shepherd's robes because some dirty, tainted corner of it still longed for his touch?

But this was no illusion. Sandy and Willem planned to steal the Crystal Charm Stone and I was going to assist them. Or at least, that's what they believed.

My plan? It was simple, yet also the most dangerous thing I'd ever contemplated; it would require a delicate balancing act and a ton of faith that I could actually carry it out. I had already proven I could contact my mother through Willem's connection inside my head. So I would appear to be working with Willem and Sandy, right up to the moment I was about to lay my hands on the stone. I knew the sorcerer well, he would almost be beside himself with excitement at that point and that's when I would demand to see my mother once more. He would argue and push against me, I knew, but I also was sure he would do it, just to get our hands on the crystal.

I would use that moment to cast the safety spell we'd learned, using the power of the crystal to strengthen my Intention, and then I would let go of the stone and walk away. By this means I could foil Willem and save my mother at the same time. It was a long shot, yes, but after having seen my mom enslaved by that horrid beast the Ice King, there was nothing more important to me at that moment in time.

The fear, the nervous excitement, the trepidation I was feeling at my bold plan, was all combining to make me feel quite sick. It was almost a physical illness, my head starting to pound like the pressure was too much and my pulse racing, throbbing through my veins. Outside, all was grayness, the silvery light of the cloud covered day. I opened the window to catch the cool breeze and let myself breathe in deeply of the salt sea and the moors, barely hearing the far sounds of waves and wind amidst all that pulsing inside my head. It grew louder and louder, ever more insistent until I could feel it banging inside my skull, reverberating through my very bones and the stone ledge I sat on.

I had to get outside, away from all of this. My head still pounding, I jumped off that ledge like the hounds of winter were chasing me and out through the nearest exit from the castle. I was getting to know this place pretty well in the week I'd been there so far.

The paths leading away from the castle were now like second nature to me, and I knew all the rabbit tracks and where they led. I aimed for the heights, the hill above the castle.

And still the pounding, throbbing followed me, louder, entirely filling my head. Was this the Armageddon Willem had promised, come so soon?

Just when I felt about to explode, it did, but it wasn't inside me after all. I felt the pulsing in my skull but the air all around me filled with a harsh whirring noise, lights flashed outside, and I could feel the earth trembling beneath my feet. I must have been out of touch from the real world for too long, the world of mechanical cars and trains and planes, for the minute I saw the large body in the air I recognized the sound for what it was.

A helicopter in from the mainland, the chop-chop of its rotors unmistakable now as it came round the hill. This was a big 'copter, the kind with two sets of rotors, front and back, like the ones used by big oil to transport their workers offshore for the three-week rotations to the ocean rigs, back home. The kind that big businesses all over the world used, the ones with lots of might and money behind them. But this wasn't painted the standard Hi-Viz yellow; it was black with tasteful gold runes running along the side.

It was the Kin's own private helicopter. It settled just out of sight, the beat slowing until all that was left was the throb of the echo reverberating in the air. I ran further up the hill, hiding behind a lonely rowan tree growing in the midst of a pile of sharp boulders, the only thing which had saved it from the ravages of hungry sheep and allowed it to mature, and I peered out to watch the huge beast settle.

The movement of the rotors had just begun to peter out, slowing by slight degrees, when the door opened. After a pause, the passenger disembarked. This 'copter was of such a great size, he had no need to duck under the blades.

His unmistakable broad shoulders in that long black wool coat of his were a welcome vision to my eyes; his familiar confident air like a balm to my senses. Yet at the same time that my heart was soaring at the sight of him, I was conscious of a weight forming in the pit of my stomach, filling me with something like dread.

For I knew, without even forming the thought, that his presence on the island was a wrench in my plan to save my mother. I would not be able to tell him what I meant to do; I couldn't even breathe a word about Willem being on Scarp, for Hugh would act in my best interests and scuttle the whole thing.

Hugh. Shit shit and triple shit. I had no choice, I had to go speak to him but what I would say, I had no idea. Unless... unless he had a way to bring me to the Ice King's court.

He couldn't see me from my perch above his head, obscured by the scraggly rowan tree as I was, although I saw him lift a hand as if to shield the low sun from his eyes as he searched the hillside. I ducked down, and closed my mind to him, just in case he was sending out feelers.

Perhaps it was time to lay my cards out on the table before him, tell him everything that had happened. How the medallion was tainted with dirty magic, and I had brought it on to the island with me. How Willem planned to use my power for his own ends. How I'd tried to tell Johanna, but she didn't believe me.

Yes, this much was clear in my head.

The Crystal Charm Stone did exist, and was hidden inside the broch with no entrance except for the deep heavily magicked tunnel from the castle. What had Sandy said about it? It was the lodestone of magic in the western world, the magical north that directed all flow of magic in the ley lines which criss-crossed the earth.

I was so torn; this was a matter of life and death for me, and for my mother. I had no choice in the matter. Now that Hugh was on the island, I needed to go to him and tell everything I knew. Tell him about Willem. Tell him how I'd found my medium finally, and tell him how we were on the brink of winning the Competition, too.

He'd be happy for me.

Yet I couldn't tell him, for Mom's sake.

....

His figure was fast disappearing past the hill out of sight, so I tore off down the heathery hillside off the beaten sheep tracks, making a beeline for his tall figure. He'd almost reached the castle gate when I yelled at him, screamed his name, trying to pitch my voice over the rising wind.

Hugh stopped and turned to watch me running through the seaside meadow, his green eyes warmly smiling at me. I stopped abruptly a few feet away from him, although I wanted to run straight into the arms he held out ready to hug me with.

'I need to speak with you,' I said, bending at the waist and holding on to the stitch in my side.

He cocked a puzzled eyebrow at me, so sure he'd been of his welcome. The wind ruffled the thick black waves of his hair.

It would have been so easy to just fall into his embrace right then and let him hold me, and unburden myself and trust he would take care of everything. It could be that easy.

I opened my mouth to say more, but he gently took me by the arm and led me into the new wing of the castle through the grand Victorian entrance. I looked up in awe again at the high ceilings all painted midnight blue with golden stars. I noticed other things too, stuff I hadn't seen on that first night, like the intricate mosaic tiles laid around the hearths of the fireplaces, the carved faces in the corner moldings. It was warm in here, warmth like I hadn't felt since I reached the island.

'Come in here,' he suggested, opening a door I hadn't been in before, and I found myself in a small sitting room, a comfortable place with pristine cream carpeting and pale blue silk sofas, with a fine Queen Anne dining table and chairs in another corner. The wood panelling lent more warmth to the atmosphere, while a fire burned in the pretty tiled grate. It was a feminine room.

'I'm sure Johanna won't mind us using her sitting room,' he said as he lightly tugged the velvet sash on the wall to the left of the fireplace.

One of the kitchen servers appeared silently at the door with a tray of tea and scones.

'We heard you was coming,' she said, smiling at Hugh as she set down the tray. She glanced at me with a sniff. 'You'll be needing another cup then.'

'If you would be so kind, Hylda,' Hugh said with his most charming smile.

She took out another matching cup, saucer and side plate from a Queen Anne sideboard, then smiled at him again before leaving the room.

'I never heard her speak before, let alone smile,' I said, looking at the door through which she'd exited. I was aware that I was stalling, still uncertain of the direction this conversation would take.

'That's because as a student, you have to earn her good will,' he said. 'Good manners will open the most surprising doors, you'll find.' He passed me the cup and saucer, then settled back on the sofa across from me, his green eyes appraising me.

'What are you doing here on Scarp?'

He smiled at me, and ignored my question. 'Scarp is agreeing with you. You're...different. You're almost glowing with health.'

Christ, trust him to see that. Yes, my short time on the island had changed me, but it wasn't the outdoor exercise or the diet lending me this look of health, I knew. My natural power had somehow expanded exponentially – I was able to see spells, and God alone knew what else I was now capable of. I would find out of course, that very night.

Sure, some things about me had changed, but if Hugh knew what I was planning to pull off in the tunnel, he would say I hadn't changed at all. Still the errant witch.

'Johanna phoned me,' he said. 'Told me you were having a few... difficulties.'

He didn't know the half of it. I nodded.

'Yeah.'

'She said she performed a cleansing spell,' he continued casually, yet I knew he was watching me carefully, sizing up my every reaction. 'How did that go?'

What could I tell him? That the Master Elder, Keeper of Scarp had failed in her healing magic, that she hadn't plumbed the depths of me to successfully wipe out the scar of Willem?

I shrugged and watched the steam rise from my cup.

'I've been thinking a lot about you,' he said quietly. 'About... us.'

I squeezed my eyes tightly shut. Not now, this was so not the time for talking about a future between us. By not telling him everything about Willem and the plans to steal the crystal, I was betraying his trust in me, and the knowledge of this hurt me to the core.

Yet, there was still a chance. If I didn't need Willem to find my mother, then perhaps...

'You said there was no way to get to the Ice King,' I said, suddenly opening my eyes and leaning forward. I ignored the splash of hot tea on my jeans.

His face grew blank as he sat back a little. 'That's correct.' His unspoken question hung in the air between us.

'But there must be some way,' I insisted. 'I mean, it's not like he lives off in a magic cloud somewhere, right? Not like he's in... I don't know, Narnia, and we can't find the right closet door to enter.'

Hugh inclined his head. 'Actually, yes, it is,' he observed. 'He is of this world, but he also isn't, if you get my meaning. That's not someone you ever want to meet. How do you know about... what's the meaning of this? Why are you asking, Dara?'

I waited a beat before I answered. 'It just came up in a conversation recently,' I said. 'I'd think like to go there someday. After all this.'

Hugh shook his head and kept shaking it as he spoke. 'I wouldn't advise it, even if it was politically possible. The Ice Kingdom's borders have been closed for years, both geographically and magically. The only way to get there is...'

'Yes?'

'It's by invitation only,' he replied, not meeting my eye. 'And that welcome comes at a high cost.'

Exactly like Willem had said. I was quickly growing frustrated; either Hugh could help me get to the Ice Kingdom and I could cancel my plans with Willem, or he couldn't.

'There are ways there,' he replied. 'But the situation is dicey, there's always politics when it comes to the Ice King, and...'

'Yes or no?'

He stopped short. 'No, then, if you insist on an easy answer.'

We sat in silence for a couple of minutes, each moment dragging on until I couldn't bear it any longer. My decision was made, and there would be no going back. This might be the last conversation Hugh and I would ever have, and I wanted him to think well of me.

'We're going to win the Competition,' I said softly.

'Dara...' he started, then shook his head. 'I think, with the pressure and everything, the strangeness, and the stress you've been under, it would make anyone start to unravel at the edges, especially someone like you who isn't accustomed to high force fields of magic. My advice to you is to leave the Competition alone. Just concentrate on getting as much out of your time here as possible.'

'You don't understand,' I said. 'We're going to win the Competition.'

'This Competition is unwinnable. It's merely an exercise for Johanna to judge the inventiveness of the seven, to see how they work alongside others. Nice to dream about, but...'

'How about if I told you there was a way?'

He smiled at me, and he meant it. 'Then I would wish you the best of luck. And I do.'

I stood up then, and he rose with me, and I gave him a good long hug, possibly the last contact we would ever have. I couldn't allow myself to kiss him, because that would be my undoing, I'd never be able to carry out my plan. For I was going to go through with it, and I could only hope I would save my mother.

28

Sandy didn't show up for the communal meal. Fergie and I ate a tense supper in the Refectory with the four others. There hadn't been much conversation at the table, for we'd made the mistake of walking in together, and ever since then Oliver paid particular silent attention to Fergie, not bothering to hide the suspicion on his face. This of course made her more flustered with the excitement she couldn't hide, so much so that she dropped her spoon a couple of times.

By the end of the meal, they were all staring at her, knowing for certain she had switched camps, and probably able to guess from the paleness of my face that something was about to happen. She had kept trying to whisper questions at me, I had to just shake my head and kick her foot under the table, which made us look even more suspicious.

On our way to the agreed meeting place, the hobbit door leading to the tunnel, I drew Fergie aside. I had to warn her of the danger she was opening herself to by aligning with us. We were hidden in one of the side nooks leading to nowhere in this ancient stone castle.

'Tonight, Fergie,' I began. 'We lied, it's not a dry run. The plan is to take the Crystal Charm Stone away from the island.' And I told her everything that Willem was planning.

'He wants you to steal the stone.' Her voice was flat in disbelief, but her face showed the horror she was feeling. 'That's impossible. How could anyone carry that power? It'd burn you to a crisp!'

'Yes,' I said. 'But I'm not going to do it. The moment I touch the Crystal Charm Stone, I'm going to use Willem's own connection to my mind to send a safety spell to Mom.'

She paused as she drew in a deep breath. 'Dara, you were barely able to do that in class. What makes you think you can do that tonight, especially when you're under pressure? Please, don't even try this.'

I leaned against the stone wall, suddenly acknowledging the insanity of what I planned. She was right. Who was I to think I could pull off this stunt? Dara Martin, half blood witch. The whole thing was madness. But even in my despair, a glimmer of hope flared through me and I latched on to it like a drowning woman grabs a rope. I may have been a reluctant student of Willem's sorceries, but he had taught me well.

'Maybe you can help. I can connect your mind at the same time, and you can do the spell!'

'Erm.... Dunno about that,' she said uncomfortably. 'Not sure exactly what you mean by connecting the minds.'

'I'll show you,' I replied, and looked into her gray eyes as I confidently sent out feelers to her.

But I touched nothing. Fergie's mind was an impenetrable fortress, a solid mass of base rock; there were no chinks into the barriers of her head. I pushed, I insinuated, I tried creeping in like a morning mist, but there was no getting in.

'You're going to have to allow me in, or it won't work,' I complained finally.

'I still dunno what you're talking about,' she said, shaking her head.

'Well, that won't work.' I leaned back against the stone wall and dropped my head. What had I been thinking? Of course there was no way I could pull it off. Best just to quit now, and not get involved in Willem's scheme. If it wasn't for Mom in the land of the Ice King...

Fergie shrugged. 'Why don't I just say the spell with you? That'll add power to yours, and it's a lot easier than this creeping about other people's heads that you're talking about.'

'That'll work? Just... saying the words with me?' There was so much I didn't understand about wielding magic, so much I still had to learn. 'How about intention?'

She almost rolled her eyes at that. 'I will have the intention of working with you to put a safety spell on your mother,' she said. 'It's as simple as that.'

I nodded. 'Okay then, problem solved. I guess.' I thought about it all a little more.

'I want you to fully appreciate what you're signing up for,' I told her slowly. 'And for God's sake please don't breathe a word of this to Sandy, don't let him read your mind.'

We looked deep into each other's eyes, and she nodded. Her uncertainties had fallen away and I could see she recognized the seriousness of the night's events.

'I got your back,' she said. 'In case Sandy tries anything. I don't trust him, I never have.'

Her gray eyes were shadowed but I could feel the steely strength behind her words and I relaxed, just a little, for the first time that evening.

'Good thinking. And as you know... you won't see a lot of the action,' I told her as we made to leave our little hidey-hole. 'But it'll be happening. The moment when I lay my hands on the stone, that's the time I'll be doing the safety spell.'

We stopped and looked at each other again. 'You're a real friend,' I said softly.

She smiled ruefully. 'Well, sometimes maybe.' She drew a breath as if to say more, but was interrupted by the sound of a heavy foot slapping the flagstone floor. We both jumped out of the nook in time to see the gray wool skirt of Pauline's frock disappearing around the corner.

'I'll get her!' Fergie hissed and made to run off, but I held her back.

'It's no good,' I said. 'We're late for Sandy and we need to get this over with, hopefully before she amasses the troupe and comes after us. Leave her.'

'How much did she overhear?'

I shrugged. 'I don't know, and not much we can do about it now. Let's just go and meet Sandy.'

....

'You didn't tell anyone, did you?' Sandy whispered furiously to Fergie as we paused outside the door into the tunnel, shining the light of his driftwood wand directly into her face. I knew he was just trying to scare her into submission, to keep her cowed so she would only do what he told her to do.

'No!' She stood up to him with her hands on her hips, but with an uncertain look in her eye and a quiver on her lip. I prayed she didn't lose heart.

He paused to cock an ear all around him before he opened the hobbit door.

'Were you followed?' I could barely hear him.

'No,' I assured him, shaking my head. Although Pauline may have been spying on Fergie and I, there'd been no sign of her or the others as we'd made our way to the tunnel entrance. Which, now I thought about it, perhaps was an odd thing. But they had no way of knowing what we were about to do.

'Alright then,' he said. He took a deep breath and pulled open the small solid door.

Once inside the portal, we could feel the heaviness of the magic in the air vibrating discordantly, but we pushed past. Sandy hesitated, his hand on the door. I could tell what he was thinking; an open door would alert any passers-by that someone was in the tunnel.

''We don't want to leave it closed,' I said in his ear. 'We're going to be leaving in a hurry.'

He nodded with reluctance and led the way down, down the circular stairs, deep into the tunnel.

Fergie poked me. 'This is a lot better going down here with company,' she said. 'Not half as spooky.'

I shushed her and followed Sandy. His torch was our only light.

A cistern dripped, far away, adding to a distant puddle one slow drop at a time. I thought I heard murmurings, maybe from the right, a whispered susurration like the wind in the tree tops. Were those footsteps stealthily making their way down the stairs behind us? I looked around, but could see nothing in the blackness.

I see you brought another adventurer with you. That wasn't in the plan. Willem's voice in my head was disapproving.

She's going to help us. Sandy won't be able to hold the curtain of spells aside by himself.

Oh, you have so much to learn. It will be a pleasure to teach you.

I shivered, a chill running up my spine, and concentrated on not thinking about what lay ahead for me, so as not to alert him with a wisp of my thoughts. I could see the barrier gate up ahead; the others could sense it, and we slowed down.

'Now what?' asked Fergie in a stage whisper that bounced off the cavernous walls of the tunnel.

'Be quiet!' I could feel the tension emanating from Sandy as he spoke.

'Now,' I breathed. 'Now I have to somehow take the net of spells and hold it back.'

'It's a net? Is it woven?' This from Fergie.

I nodded, forgetting she could barely see me in the dark.

'Is it like a cloth weave, or is it more a spider's web?'

I felt Sandy turn on her and I laid my hand on his arm to stop him.

'Now what do we do?' I spoke out loud but I was addressing Willem.

Now is the moment. Steel yourself, Dara dear, we've got company. Our cozy little coupling is now a threesome.

And Sandy was with us, in my mind, or in his mind, or maybe we were in some metaphysical place where the physical had no boundaries; it was like nothing I'd ever felt before; I found myself in uncharted territory. The strangeness of being not one or two, but three, the distinct feeling of another, as if all three of our minds were stuck in a tight closet space with no barriers between us and I could feel everything Sandy was feeling. All I knew was it was crowded in there.

'I think I hear someone coming,' I heard Fergie say at a distance. 'What do we do now?'

A rush of impatience flowed from the other two, I could feel it as if coming from myself, and no sooner had it begun than Sandy lifted his wand and Fergie's voice was abruptly silenced, her mouth moving but no sound coming out, only her eyes expressing her surprise and confusion, then bone-deep fear.

We stared at each other in horror. Neither of us had foreseen that action, and now I wasn't able to count on her assistance with the safety spell. If I had been wavering the least bit on my course before, that action decided it for me.

Fergie waved her hand at me. It was a small movement, but I realized she was telling me it didn't matter, that she would think the words and hopefully that would help.

Both of you hold out your mediums, and I will unwork the spells through you. I'm so happy you've joined us, Dara, for it makes my job so much easier for me as you have the capacity to see them.

And then he was doing it. Now that space which held all three was charged with a rush of new energy, I could feel the power flowing between us. It was exhilarating, and scary as hell for I was not the one in control. Willem chanted in our minds, I couldn't even pick out the words, just the feelings and the images which flowed with them like an endless stream of flotsam running under a bridge, and I had no explanation for them or their importance in his counter spells. It was a blend

261

of feelings and colors and moods, indescribable. How these all played a role in his workings, I couldn't know.

Meanwhile I was staring at the web of spells, allowing Willem to see through my eye. As I watched and as he worked, I could see the loosening happening; a spell popping here, another flaring then losing its brilliance like a streetlight blowing out, a third simply melted away like butter in a hot frying pan.

This was powerful magic the sorcerer had, and if I stayed with him he would show me all of it.

And then we were through.

Sandy lifted his driftwood wand to part the remaining curtain enough for me to step through as instructed. I could feel his strain, not physical at all, but mental exertion, for Willem was leaving him behind to bear the brunt of the force. We had to act quickly, for Sandy would tire soon enough and the magic still in the spells would burn him.

I heard a shout from further down the passageway, but I had to ignore it, for now was the moment. I took a deep breath and walked to the opened curtain, feeling the fizz of magic all around me as I passed through, and the Crystal Charm Stone lay before me in all its glory, glowing on its stand of roughhewn rock.

As before, the rainbow of colors danced over the stone walls inside the broch, the source of light being the crystal itself. It was the size of a small cat carrier stood on end, but shaped like a miniature mountain of crystal shards, all hard edges and prisms in its terrible beauty.

I crossed the small chamber to stand on the other side of the stone. I wanted Fergie to be able to see my actions. Our eyes met over the fluctuating prisms of color and light where she waited, silenced, beyond the barrier of spells and I nodded, ever so slightly.

'Show me my mother again.'

What? What is this? I could feel Willem tearing his attention from the crystal to my demand. *After, after. Right now we must do this. There are others in the tunnel.*

He was right, I could hear footsteps running, coming closer and a voice echoing through the distance, but I couldn't worry about that right now. I stood over the stone.

'Show me my mother.' My arms begged to reach out and touch it as Willem willed me to do, but I remained steadfast in my determination.

29

I said a final time, 'Show me my mother.'

There is no need. You trust me. The stone! Take the stone, now!

'Remind me why I'm throwing away my future to help you.' My hand hovered over the stone and I forced myself not to touch it. Not yet.

He swore an oath in his own language, then we flashed back into the Ice King's court. Still the same walls of ice and the huge log burning in the grate, and the beastlike King still seated on his throne of bones. I felt the chill in the air as I looked upon his terrible visage.

With all the power and sense of self I could muster, I gripped my coin, my medium in one hand and with the other reached toward the stone, for I would need all the help I could get now that Fergie was hampered by the silencing spell. Just a light touch, that was all I needed, and I prepared to whisper the safety spell aloud while screaming it in my head, and in Willem's mind too.

The moment my finger touched the stone, I felt a fire, a blaze running through my entire body and soul, as if all the portals in the world were opening in me. It wasn't painful, not in the least, it was pure and powerful and as if all the love and joy in the world was contained within me. It was a terrible peace, in that the sadness and anger and jealousy and all of our petty human emotions that wars had been fought over were exposed to me as nothing more than ripples on a pond; meaningless and inconsequential and nothing.

My mother felt that moment happen too, I knew as she lifted her head from her task and she saw me for that split-second of time. She smiled the secret half-smile I knew so well and hope bloomed through me. I watched the Ice King glance up as if a whisper had passed over his head.

That moment's pause in wonderment cost me; it must have lowered my barrier to Willem and my intention to say the safety spell over my mother leaked through to his mind, and he knew I was not going to pick up the stone for him.

Sandy! Something flashed between the two like quicksilver and I looked up to see Fergie caught in Sandy's tight grip with his silver knife at her throat. Sandy's face wore an expression of grim satisfaction, while Fergie still couldn't even scream her terror. He had dropped the curtain of spells.

Pick up the stone.

'No, Willem,' I said fervently. 'Don't do this. I won't take the stone until you let Fergie go.'

Oh, my sweet, traitorous Dara. What is she to you, compared to your mother? Compared to your future? Sandy won't hesitate, you know this. We will both have failed, but you will have her blood on your conscience.

Yes, he was right. Willem wouldn't, because he didn't have a conscience.

Sandy's arm tensed as if he was preparing to cut her throat.

'Stop, Sandy,' I called. 'Okay, I'll pick up the crystal.'

I braced myself for that terrible flow of energy again. Could I, a simple Normal half-witch bear it? The journey out of the tunnel was a long one, surely I would burn out every nerve ending in my body. Or die trying.

I will help you carry the load of power. Willem's voice in my ears was hungry.

'Why is this crystal so important to you? I can't believe you're just doing this as a favor to someone else.' I temporized, though I could feel his impatience like a rapid drumbeat in my head.

Stop the small talk. Just do it. Allow me to help or it will kill you.

He was right. My arms picked up the physical load, it wasn't light, being pure crystal, yet not as heavy as I'd expected. Willem was right there with me to help as the force of the stone washed through me like a lightning bolt. I had to keep my eyes narrowed to stop the prismatic colors from burning my retinas. Together we shared the awe inspiring power of the crystal's flow.

Together, Willem and I, we carried the weight to the curtain of spells, where I hesitated.

You will find no barriers to your way now, Dara. The crystal will allow you to pass through physically unharmed.

I had no choice but to trust his words, and I stepped forward. He spoke the truth; I passed through that gate as effortlessly as if it were a waterfall, a mere rainbow mist. I could feel each of the myriad spells pass through me, the kaleidoscope of color and smells and emotion that I had no way to understand, and I made it to the other side unscathed. I stumbled past Sandy who still had one arm around Fergie's neck. I could see the sweat trickling into his eyes and the awe on his face as he watched my passage.

The tunnel stretched on into darkness, the only light was that which emanated from my joyful burden.

To the jetty.

How did I manage to get through the tunnel and up the circular stone steps into the castle proper? To this day, I have no idea, the whole trip was a blur. I was like someone stoned on the strongest narcotic; all I was conscious of was the irrefutable joy of life everlasting and all the terror that it entails.

Willem led me to the dark hallway exit where I'd lit the sconce, that very first night which seemed so long ago now, and out the side door into the cool clear night air. I passed the brightly lit windows of the dining room in the Victorian wing. Johanna, Rasmussen, Durand and even Hugh, all sat at the polished table, candelabra lit around, dining in fine style without a clue as to what was passing under their very noses. I felt Willem's glee at the high end heist he was pulling off. Finally, his life's work was nearing completion.

But I think they didn't stay in ignorance for too long, for the other Kin finally found us and realized the extent of my perfidy. The ensuing fireworks and drama that lit the night sky could not be ignored even by the most self-satisfied of witches.

Caught up in this surreal journey, I barely noticed the resistance in my way as the others came upon us and tried their pathetic attempts to stop me. Timothy sent the arching rainbows of his own crystal out to meet mine; they danced and played and as soon as I directed my glance to them, they bounced harmlessly off the stone walls of the garden like a psychedelic light show. Beautiful yes, but to absolutely no effect.

Poor Pauline unleashed a magic portcullis of iron as we left the walled garden, but I stepped through it easily, as if it were no more than a sprinkler tickling the hairs of my body, and Sandy, with Fergie still thrust before him, slipped thorough in my wake.

If anything, their shots of power merely increased my own as the Crystal Charm Stone hungrily sucked up all the loose magic in the air then pumped it through me. I laughed as I saw Oliver approach, and a mere flick of my eyes sent him reeling against the stone walls.

Surprisingly enough, Win was the only one who gave me a run for my money, as she called upon her powerful Dragon magic. We were just at the top of the cobbled road leading to the pier, I paused to watch the cloud of green gas as it rose from the path, rising and expanding until it morphed into a huge iridescent dragon twenty feet tall. It towered over me, sending me the foulest puffs of its breath, right from the sulphurous depths of Hell itself.

With a fearsome roar it attacked me, and I could smell my singed hair even as its fetid fire blew over me, bouncing harmlessly off the stone in my arms and wrapped itself around me, engulfing me. But made fearless by the power surging through me from the charm stone I stood in the path of its fire and stared up into its eyes, and I moved forward directly into the path of it, daring the beast to try to destroy me.

I was unstoppable. I found I had no need to speak a spell, or even form a conscious intention in my mind. My every thought was translated instantly into action; the rush of power from the stone to the dragon was invisible, but I felt it, I felt each atom of the wind that grew and rose, lifting the green scaled beast like it was a new hatched butterfly, buffeted on the fates of the gale.

And galing it was, out here, for the wind had risen to hurricane force, and lashed us with sharp nails of rain in our faces as if the island itself had risen in protest at my actions. Sandy walked behind me still forcing Fergie ahead of him, but the others, I could no longer see them.

I couldn't keep it up of course, this immense intake and outpouring of energies, even with Willem in my head to buffer the extreme force of the flow. The cobblestoned path leading to the pier was wet and slippery, and I found my feet stumbling and sliding as I made my way down the slope. The crystal was slick in my arms from the wet, and I was quickly losing my strength. The crystal shifted in my grasp.

'Over to the boat now, you and Sandy come with me!'

I paused and looked up. There was Willem waiting near the prow of a small boat, ready to board but waiting for me to give him his precious cargo, his brown robe flapping in the harsh winds. His hood had fallen; by the light of the crystal I could see the voracious need in his pale eyes as he urged me forward.

Was this what I wanted in my life? To become an outlaw with him, sailing the seas of magic like pirates, always on the run, always looking for more, never satisfied with our ill-gotten gains?

'No!' I shouted into the storm, yet my feet kept walking forward. I was now on the ancient pier, slippery with rain and sea moss. On either side of it were the endless boulders, now lashed by waves from the disturbed ocean.

He stepped forward and looked at me, a mere ten feet away now, and I could see him shake his head, just ever so slightly. 'Do not betray me now,' he said quietly, yet I could hear him above the howling wind. 'All is lost for you, you can't go back.'

Sandy pushed past me and waited for me at the boat, his knife still at Fergie's throat. 'Get aboard!' he snarled at me. 'And hurry up about it, they're coming!'

My feet would not stop in their path, yet I was screaming inside against every movement like a runner at the end of the marathon, every bone in my body ached and cried out for me to stop, but my feet could not understand the command.

I kept barrelling on, and could not stop the momentum even to stop myself from crashing toward the small boat and Willem. I plowed into him like a hurricane wind, causing us both to lose balance and fall over the edge of the pier on to the rocks below.

I may have passed out for a moment, or perhaps it was the sudden absence of the crystal's power flowing into me that caused the momentary dislocation of my mind, but when I looked up I could see it glowing still, not five feet from me. And there was a shadow reaching to it, coming from the side.

Willem. He almost had it in his grasp.

'Better even than I could have hoped, my dear,' he snarled, all pretense of a partnership between us dropped. 'Sandy, drop that wench and help me with this!'

I desperately tried to get up to reach the crystal before him, but my ankle was paining terribly and I could only manage a crawl over the slippery rocks, when all of a sudden each and every one of the boulders around us was roiling like ocean waves, as if we'd been plunged into the sea itself. I watched as the one he was on opened first one crepey eyelid, then another. Willem realized what was happening and he scrambled off the beast's back just as the giant maw opened, with its rows of flint like teeth. They gnashed where the sorcerer had been only moments before.

I guess Willem, too was feeling the effects of his extended proximity to the charm stone, even if it had been by proxy, and he was slow to react. He looked from the crystal to the waiting boat, and then back to the rock beast's terrible bite, but then his decision was made for him.

The beast's large paw swept out and playfully came down on the crystal, drawing it in, and it looked with glee at the sorcerer as if daring him to snatch it away. It leaned its fearsome head upon the stone and began to croon with pleasure.

This was not a game Willem would win and he knew it. He fled to the small boat with Sandy at its helm, and they were quickly swallowed up by the fog and wind and sheets of rain.

....

And Willem was gone. I gingerly felt through my head, lightly brushing past the bruises deep inside but there was no trace of the sorcerer, as if he'd never been, not even a fingerprint burned into the dust of my mind. I lay back on the beach, the hard pebbles under my back, but I was so sore and bruised and ill-used I couldn't think of moving.

'Gerroff the beach!' Fergie had quickly recovered from her ordeal at the sight of me down amongst the rock beasts.

All around me they still thronged, except for the biggest one which had taken the Crystal Charm Stone. It was leaning against me, I recognized the red and black markings in the pinkish granite as the one who had stolen my chocolate bar, that first day across the stretch of water from Scarp. I could feel the thrum of a purr deep within the beast.

'Oh, you stink!' I said as I roughly tried to push it away, but there was no moving that mass; at least it wasn't trying to lick me with affection. Instead, I pushed off the beast to help me stand, and made my wobbly way back to the pier where Fergie waited. She refused to jump down to help me up, unwilling to risk danger a second time that night.

'Not a chance,' she said when I suggested she come help give me a leg up. 'They're bloody rock beasts.' She did hold out her hand for me to grasp though and used her considerable strength to pull me up.

As she did so, she drew in a sharp breath. 'Feck me, Dara, you're glowing!'

I looked down at my body, and it was true, I was shimmering all over, as if I'd been dunked into an ocean of phosphorescence. Fergie wiped her hand on her pants and we watched as the glittering particles melted into the air.

'How does it feel?' she whispered.

Our eyes met, and I saw the greenish glow of me reflected into her eyes. 'It feels good,' I said, wonderment dawning. It must have been the proximity of the crystal, from carrying it in my hands for that length of time. 'Like a tingle all over, like I've just eaten the best butter pastry in the world with a double espresso. Like I have energy for days and could run a marathon...'

I winced there, because I'd shifted my weight to my twisted ankle. 'Except for that.'

'I think you'll find that will heal in very short order.' It was Johanna's voice.

I quickly lifted my head while trying to keep my balance, and I saw that the small concrete pier was now crowded with the island's inhabitants.

'Well played, Dara,' Johanna said drily. She stood over me, the other four and Durand and Rasmussen and Hugh all stood silently behind her. Perhaps it was the effect of the crystal on me that made me more sensitive, for I could see plain as day that the dryness of her tone was covering up the emotions that were running through her at that moment. I watched as the series of feelings and thoughts played over her face – puzzlement and consternation at what I had done, then a flash of anger and outrage that I had dared to get mixed up in such a heresy, then wonderment that it was even possible, and finally she settled into smugness. She had been right, after all, that day in Inverness. She had known my potential, and against the loud protests of the other elders, she had insisted on my acceptance to Scarp.

Being right softened her anger towards me, even caused her to look upon me with indulgence.

'But I did say there were to be no injuries incurred,' she continued in a severe voice. 'You failed there. And I didn't mean for you to actually steal the Crystal Charm Stone.'

We all looked down at the moving boulders beneath our feet.

'You are expected to retrieve it, the sooner the better.'

30

I sat on the edge of the pier, staring hopelessly at my rock beast. A single torch reflected the light in those black eyes as it watched me back, and I realized its petrification spell had no effect on me. I could swear there was a look of playfulness about the creature, as if it was waiting for me to give chase and lead me on a fine romp through the beaches and waters surrounding the island.

How the heck did one retrieve the lodestone of the Kin from the grasp of such a beast? I could feel the eyes of everyone on my back, the pressure from them as they stood at a safe distance, watching and waiting for me to make good my screw up. Hylda and her consort had driven a vehicle down to the beach, a sort of golf cart on treads like a snowmobile, in order to safely lug the stone back to its seat in the tunnel.

'Pss, pss,' I tried to coax it closer like you would a feral cat. 'Come on, that's a good little pebble. Come on over. How about if I give you a name? I'm going to call you Haggis.'

But he, or she or it, wasn't taken in by my charms and remained out of reach, its jaws open in a grin, ready to playfully snap at me if I came too close. It was a hopeless stand-off. I was suddenly ready to cry; all the good feeling powerfulness had dissipated, leaving me washed out and hung out to dry, and every bone and muscle in my body ached.

I felt the warmth of another person behind me, then Hugh sat down beside me on the pier, his leather jacket gleaming in the single light.

'Here,' he said. 'I brought you something to refuel with. You need to keep up your strength after all that.'

Cookies, or biscuits as they called them in Scotland. Ginger snaps full of sugar and spice. I cracked the first in half and shoved it in my mouth, and the beast's eyes widened at the sound. Ah! Of course. The beast's weakness was sugar.

'C'mon,' I purred as I held out the other half. 'Want a cookie? Does my wee beastie want a sweet, sweet bickie?' I held my breath, and realized I was sweating with tension. This had to work, there was no way I had the strength to wrestle with the beast.

It hesitated, and then it lifted its snout, sniffing the air, then it reluctantly moved an inch in my direction, still holding the crystal firmly in its grasp. I slipped off the jetty and crouched down at a distance away from it, wincing a bit as I settled on my bad ankle, and held the sweet out enticingly.

'How am I going to get the crystal back?' I asked Hugh in a soft voice.

'You're on your own there,' he said unhelpfully. 'No one else can dare to touch it.'

'I'm going to need more than one cookie to distract it long enough.'

275

He reached over and handed me the rest of the package.

I could see the indecision in the beast's eyes; it knew the cookies were attainable, but in order to gain them, it would have to leave the crystal behind. It gave a howl as loud as a foghorn, trying to scare me into dropping the package, but I held firm and forced myself not to show fear.

Finally, its greed won out, and it shuffled slowly toward me and nosed the cookie in my hand, sniffing hard. Drool of some kind was dripping from its mouth, through the rows of sharp teeth. It gave a low growl.

The stink of its breath was terrific. 'You're not to bite me, or you won't get the biscuit,' I told it severely.

It took the gingersnap from my hand – oh so delicately for such a terrible creature, and I surreptitiously wiped the slime from its tongue onto my jeans as I laid the rest of the package some further distance away. It had the taste of the cookie now, it had no choice but to follow the scent to scarf the whole lot down, leaving me free to snatch up the stone glowing behind it.

Oh, holding the crystal again was revitalizing. I could sit with it in my arms forever, feeling the music of the spheres thrumming through my entire body.

But it wasn't to be. I forced myself to jump up and lay it in the cart waiting on the pier, and Hylda and her companion immediately started the engine and began the slow drive towards the castle.

That was the last I saw of the crystal for a long, long time, but the effects of its proximity to me that night were to stay with me forever.

·····•·•·····

Hugh rushed me back to the castle with no apparent concern for my well-being. I felt bruised all over, wrung out like an old washcloth, and could hardly walk on my ankle, but still he pushed me forward.

'Your night is not over yet,' he told me crisply. 'It was Willem, wasn't it?'

I nodded.

'In your mind?'

'And Sandy's. He used both of us.'

'Where is he now?'

I searched inside me. I felt nothing, for the first time in ages. Not a whisper. I shook my head.

'I don't know. He's not in me anymore.'

'I mean, where is he physically? Can you find him for me?'

'He took off on the boat, him and Sandy.'

'Yes, I know you let them get away,' Hugh said. 'We need you to find him for us.'

We were nearing the grand Victorian entrance to the castle. I stopped and planted my feet firmly on the ground; well, except for my throbbing ankle, but the accusation stung even worse. 'You know, if you'd listened to me in the first place, none of this would have happened.'

He hadn't believed me when I'd warned him. Hugh Sabiston, the great wonder of the Kin, he could have stopped this mayhem if he had only taken me seriously. I lifted my chin at him, looking up at all six feet three of him, and for the first time ever the nine inches of difference did not cause me to feel less than him. And I could have sworn there was a new respect for me in his eyes.

'I'm sorry,' he said, and I knew it was genuine. 'But this is urgent.'

Hugh opened his arms, and I didn't fall into them as I might once have done. No, that would be too easy for him, he hadn't yet paid the price of my forgiveness. I stood my ground, my hands on my hips, waiting for a verbal acknowledgment.

He nodded again, then spoke. 'You were right.'

I let out my breath, I hadn't realized I was holding it. 'Yes.'

The bevelled glass of the door shone prisms all over his face, catching the raindrops still on his hair.

'How were you able to hold the stone and carry it all that way?' His voice was hushed. 'Willem was working through you? In your mind? That's how you were able to do... this.'

'He sure was,' I said. I shot another glance up to his green eyes. The gold flecks shone with the flickering light.

'You'll be changed forever now, you realize.'

'In a good way?'

He shook his head. 'I just don't know. Nothing like this has ever happened before, not since the first McCloud took the stone with his bride, from the Ice King.'

Then he was all business again. 'I need you to send your search throughout the entire island. Now. We need to stop him.'

I leaned against the cold stone wall of the castle and closed my eyes, sending feelers out for the essence of the sorcerer, looking for anything, the slightest hint of him, then shook my head again.

'Come with me,' Hugh said as he took my arm and picked up the pace. A lot. I found us almost at a run, a painful hobble in my case, through the castle into the old part to a set of steps I'd never seen before. The narrow steep stairs spiraled up into darkness.

'Up here,' he said. 'To the old Keep.'

We entered the room at the top, if it could be called a room, merely a stone enclosure with four openings to the cold air and wind of the sea.

'You must search for Willem,' he commanded me. 'Get out there and find him.' Hugh was waiting at the empty window space looking out over the hills, toward the broch.

I teetered by the low lip, the wind catching me and I put my arms out to steady me in order to stop the swaying. The ground was a long way away. I couldn't do this. I had to.

'I want you with me,' I said. 'Like before. Stay by my side.'

'No.' His voice was terse. 'He'll know if I'm there. You have to do this by yourself. You've done it before, without me.'

I almost smiled to myself. Yes, I had, and in Alt, too. I could do this. It was just a matter of flying, of letting go of the body. I took a deep breath and sent my mind outside.

Soaring into the air.

The moon was shining, and as the island came rushing up at me, I could pick out every bush and every sheep glowing beneath me. Willem's brown cloak would be invisible in the shadows, even if he wasn't armed with an invisibility spell.

I didn't know what I was looking for, so I had to wing it. A sparkle of loose magic perhaps, a whiff of the Dutchman's garlic breath? This wasn't working.

I needed a stronger link with him, and had to allow a deeper part of my mind to take over the search, the part that had Willem indelibly burned on it, and risk letting him inside my-self yet again. Finding the sorcerer's mind was almost second nature to me now; it scared and sickened me how easily we fit together. Yet I had to do it for it was my last hope. I prayed that I would not be causing more damage to my psyche by doing this.

Willem, I breathed. I called him forth, and felt a small stirring deep within, but the movement was quickly quenched.

Willem, I need you.

There was no answer from him, but there! A loose trail, a light dusting off to the left, over the water, towards the mainland.

Willem!

Yes, there he was, barely perceptible against the dark of the cliffs in the moonlight. He wasn't at the ancient concrete slip where the ferryman had picked us up that first day, but further north on the opposite shore. I saw a small boat's outline on the sand and a flurry of brown robe. I hovered over now, flying freely over the beach, and called out to him again. And I saw the last glimmer of the crystal's power on him, the power he had absorbed through being in my mind while I carried the stone.

He looked up, and I swore that was a smile on his face, a tender look as he recognized my touch on his mind.

'You learn quickly, my dear one,' he whispered into the rising wind. He laughed. 'But we must say our farewells. I must hurry, so this is adieu, until we meet again. And when we do, I may forgive you for tonight's betrayal. Follow the coin, it will lead you to me.'

He touched his hand lightly to his lips then gently threw his kiss to me.

Lights from a vehicle flashed on behind him, a motor started, and he disappeared into a white van waiting at the beach side.

All contact with him was now gone.

I drew back into myself and found Hugh closely staring into my eyes.

Catching a breath, for this had been hard work, I gasped and pointed north. 'He had a boat. North shore. A van was waiting for him and Sandy, and now they're gone.'

Hugh nodded quickly, then turned with the lantern still in hand. He left me to find my own way down along the spiralling stairs in the dark, still dazed from my experience, keeping the stones to my back as my feet looked for purchase.

....

I stood outside in the walled garden, Sandy's favorite place, and watched as the helicopter arrived to bring the horde of elders needed to rebuild an unhackable barrier to the tunnel and the Crystal Charm Stone. I felt a presence at my side and smelled the perfume of a cigarette burning on the sun warmed air.

'You doing all right?' I asked Fergie.

'Yeah, I guess.' She was silent for a moment. I waited for the recriminations, but they didn't come.

'Sorry about all that,' I mumbled.

'Christ,' she said finally. 'I knew the very first day you had a lot of power, but I never suspected you could ever pull that off.'

'It wasn't just me doing it.'

'I know,' she said. 'I could feel him too, when they silenced me. Were you, I mean they, were you planning to do away with the stone? To steal it?'

She couldn't know the extent of what had happened, and I didn't have the energy to explain it to her. I simply nodded and changed the subject

'This Ice King, I'd never heard of him before coming to Scarp.'

'Your parents never told you stories of him to ensure you toed the line?' she joked, then realized her faux-pas. 'But of course, not with your history. Well, the Ice King and his line have ruled the northern reaches for millennia. It's rumored to be a strange and wondrously harsh land and mysterious reign, a country like no other.'

Fergie grew silent as if lost in thought, and then she added, 'A terrible place.'

31

Once everything had settled back into place, Hugh and I went walking in the hills of Scarp. Spring had already arrived on the island, the balmier days growing longer, the wind no longer cutting like a knife. Birds sang in the low bushes, celebrating the new warm smells of regrowth.

As we walked, my eyes would occasionally stray to the coastline, searching down along the beaches, but I could see no sign of Haggis, my erstwhile pet rock beast. Ah well, he was a wild creature, and needed to be with his own kind. Besides, he was really smelly when he got up close, the kind of stink that stayed on your clothes when he rubbed up against you, like a wet dog would but Haggis brought the odor of rotting fish and seaweed, so I can't say I missed him all that much.

The fruitless search for Willem on the mainland had been aborted. The sorcerer was long gone, as I'd expected. He would have had his escape route planned out to the split second, leaving nothing to chance and making sure of his own safety above all. Sandy had no doubt accompanied him, his new partner in crime.

We sat outside on the hillside, soaking in the sun. Back home, Aunt Edna said everything was still buried under six feet of snow, with cold winds and ice underfoot and the gruel of endless shoveling, but here in the Outer Hebrides in the northwest of Scotland, there were palm trees growing in sheltered suburban gardens and spring-like weather in the midst of deepest February, all compliments of the Gulf Stream straight from the warmth of Mexico. I could grow to love this place, I thought as I closed my eyes and breathed in the salt air.

Hugh had been uncharacteristically quiet since asking me to accompany him on this walk outside the castle gates, but that was okay, because I was steeling myself for a confession. It was long past time I told him about the whole affair, especially with Willem's most recent disappearance.

He said nothing as I poured out the whole story of the coin's involvement in my affairs and my mother, since meeting the sorcerer last December. As I talked, I couldn't avoid the conclusion that we could have saved a lot of heartbreak if he'd listened to me the first time and allowed me to tell him all.

He evidently thought the same. 'But why? Why couldn't you tell me, or at least your father? He's been scouring the globe both in and out of Alt for word of your mother, and has been for the past ten years.'

I had no answer for that, for I'd had no idea; Dad had never confided in me about his search. My father had withdrawn from me when Mom disappeared and we rarely spoke, and I had first thought he had done it, then I'd assumed his wife was behind it all.

'Mom is up in the land of the Ice King.'

Hugh drew in a sharp breath. 'Dear God,' he said. 'Willem had seen her there? Can you trust his word?'

I nodded.

'I saw her too, remember.' The breeze was turning direction, and I shivered as the waves fought the north wind on the sandy beach far below, whitecaps forming and foaming as they lost the battle.

His hand found mine, lending me his warmth.

'Well,' he said, but nothing further.

'Can we go up there?'

'Not that easy,' he said slowly. 'Especially not now, not with the political situation as it is.'

'I understand,' I told him, but my mind was thinking elsewise. Willem was probably headed up north as we spoke, and he'd said the coin would help me find him. Just because Hugh and the Kin wouldn't go to the Ice Kingdom for political reasons, that didn't mean I couldn't. I'd find a way, it wasn't so distant from where we sat here in the north of Scotland. Just over the northern horizon, beyond the swelling waves. If I could get there from here.

'This coin,' Hugh said as if reading my thoughts. 'Can I see it? Do you still have it?'

My right hand reached into the pocket of my hoodie and my fingers caressed the raised surface of it. I could have given the coin over to him right there and then, told him to keep it. Hugh and his Kin magic would have found a way to figure out where the magic had originally come from, and the part it played in my mother ending up with the Ice King. They would de-spell, detox and post-mortem it, and I'd never see it again, never feel that shiver as I looked upon it and remembered all it had brought to me.

But it was my one link to my mother, my only way of reaching her in that far off land.

I turned to look up at him, and he inclined his face so close it was mere inches away from mine, his green eyes showed no barriers between us. Gone was the patina of professionalism, the burden of his work, the ice which overlaid Hugh Sabiston, Officer of the Kin. In his place was the man I first met on the harbor of old St. John's that fine fall day, the real Hugh Sabiston, the carefree half-blood witch.

I brushed a stray lock of tousled dark hair from his fine cheekbone and he drew in a quick breath, then caught my hand and brought it to his mouth, brushing it with the merest touch of his lips while me, I melted inside.

When we kissed, that inevitable touch, it was a promise binding us for years down the road, for the future time when I had found my feet and grown into the witch I was destined to be. Not yet, no, there was still too much for me to do, to learn, to become, before we could link our fortunes together.

'We'll go there, to the Ice Kingdom,' he murmured as he held me. I could feel the vibration of his voice rumble through me. 'Together. When all this is over, when you're working beside me and we...'

I nestled my head under his, fitting my body against his length. It felt right and natural, and this what I'd yearned for all those months, and his kiss told the promise of more.

Yet I couldn't begin this future with a lie between us, that could never provide a firm basis for us. They had called me an errant witch, and I had been, but no more.

On the other hand, I had no intention of giving up my coin to the Kin. Hugh would want to do the politically correct thing and hand it over for inspection, but I couldn't allow that. And it was best to set the ground rules right from the get go.

I drew the coin out of my pocket.

'I'll show it to you,' I said, slowly while I considered. 'But first I need a promise which you may not want to give.'

I looked up at him, but his head was bent down, his eyes on the coin, hungry, fascinated, searching. My hand firmly grasped his chin, drawing his face up to mine.

'Mom doesn't have the time to wait for me to become a fully-fledged witch,' I continued. 'Or for me to work through my apprenticeship with PANEC. I don't care about the state of politics between nations, and I don't care if I upset the delicate balance of negotiations. You have to help me get to the Ice Kingdom to free my mother.'

He looked at me for a long, cool moment as he deliberately weighed the pros and cons of my demands, and not just the immediate concerns but the long-lasting, far-reaching effects of what I proposed, both for the Kin he worked for, and for himself and me personally.

Finally, he gave a short nod. 'I understand,' he said. 'And we will get you there. Somehow. But you have to finish your year here at Scarp. The Kin won't allow you to not get your full education, especially now you've shown what you're capable of.'

He looked away and sighed. 'I fear that you are becoming an infuriating, enchanting and alluring witch. We will go to the Ice Kingdom, you and me. Soon. I promise.'

My hand slowly closed back over the coin till it disappeared within my grasp. Hugh's way wouldn't be, couldn't be soon enough. Not for me, not for Mom. A secretive smile touched my lips as I drew him into my arms, and I could only hope he would understand when the time came.

And it would come, not long now. I would be travelling to the Ice Kingdom to rescue my mother.

I was also an obstinate witch, but he would learn that. Very soon.

The end.

....

*Dara's story continues in **AN OBSTINATE WITCH**, Book 4 of The Witch Kin Chronicles! Available for purchase direct from the author at Liz Graham's shop or from all fine retailers.*

Aailable in Ebook, Paperback, large print version, and Audio. For the latest updates on new releases and specials, sign up to join Liz (E M) Graham's newsletter at LizGraham.ca!

The Ice King's wintry grasp. A witch cursed. A deadly Chronicle.

Contact with the Crystal Charm Stone caused deep changes in Dara Martin, leaving her with a power so great, it scares even the elders. This only happened once before in the centuries of the Kin's rule, but the witch Meg's fate is a secret buried deep in the past. Dara has no idea what her future might hold.

Whisked away from Scarp to study under the Venerable Nacthan in Edinburgh, she's forbidden to practice until the elders can understand her new magic. Yet she knows she now has the resources to rescue her mother from the Ice King's grasp, if only she knew how to get there from here.

A chance meeting leads her into the depths of the Edinburgh Vaults to Auld Meg, who'd been cursed to stone by the Kin to write the most dangerous chronicle of all. If Dara can break the spell and free the crone, she'll be able to bridge realities to the Ice Kingdom.

There'll be hell to pay with the Kin. But only if she makes it back alive.

ACKNOWLEDGEMENTS

Thank you to everyone who helped with this book, especially Alexa Opal Hamilton, my new gem - you made this book and taught me so much along the way. And of course my Gremlins with their incredible eyes. Thanks also to the Feral Feline Rescue and Rehabilitation folks in Lethbridge, Newfoundland who solved my catless issues during the Great Isolation. Twice. I love my feral rescues Daisy and Silas, and I know that given time and regular treats, they will someday love me too.

And mostly thank you to my readers – you have the magic in you.

ABOUT THE AUTHOR

Liz (E M) Graham has always been a voracious reader, and her taste in books covers almost every genre imaginable. This is probably why her writing also spans genres, from romance to mystery to paranormal. All of her works share the same wicked sense of humour and love of mystery.